HOTEL STORIES

mike tyler

3A, AA: 30

HAWAII

11

THE ART CANNOT BE DAMAGED

STORIES HOTEL

drawings by Francine Tyler

A lot had happened. A lot had happened in a life that was now winding down.

PAST LIVES

G.O. Best wanted to fuck Queen Neferttiti.

Walking in the museum in Berlin he had seen her. She had unbelievable breasts (this is a joke because Queen Neferttiti is only a bust), but he had acted like she did. He felt like she was totally there in a full-figuredness that was just totally, way-out, full-figured. I mean her whole thing was there. To him. He had her, like, really, not "in his arms" which has about as much meaning as anything that has that much meaning, in other words something that has been used so much that it shouldn't be used so much. "In his arms," what the fuck does that mean? But he had her, like as if he was fucking her. This by the way will be my only use of "as if." As if he was fucking her. Which of course he wasn't. Because she was a mannequin from some alphabet century way way way away anyway. Which says somethinc about G.O. Best.

It says this:

G.O. Best's son hated him. Hate is too weak a word. By the way what I meant up there about "alphabet" as in "alphabet century" was just basically what I said, in my own way. It's pretty obvious. She was dead (Neferttiti), and he wanted her. In New York City where I'm from there's "alphabet city" which is the avenues that have alphabet soupy names like, for example, re:, ibid., whatever, "Avenue A." It was "no man's land," a kindof white people don't go there thing. Avenue A is now like Columbus Avenue (you don't have to know what I'm talking about to know what I'm talking about). Also, the Egyptians invented the alphabet, and Columbus discovered America (Avenue A).

G.O. Best's son hated him. Hate is too weak a word. Hate is a flash in the pan (what is a "flash in the pan?"). It comes and goes. Sometimes it comes, and uh, sometimes it goes. I mean you don't hate all the time. Sometimes you do. Some people do. German skinheads I'm sure hate all the time. Even when they're hanging out with mother? Especially then. But the thing is, the thing is um, the thing is that hate, "hate" the word, for it to have meaning (you know can I just interrupt and say that the idea of "hate" as a word, considering what it is as a thing, I mean how strong it is, well it really shouldn't be just a word), there must be times when it isn't there. You're fine. You're chillin'. And then you hate.

But that wasn't what was going on with G.O. Best's son. G.O. Best's son's name (ohmygod, apostrophe mania!) was Nucleus. I'm not being symbolic. It's not my fault if G.O. Best named his son somethinc stoopid. I suppose that could be the reason (and a good one too) why his son hated him. The name. But it wasn't. Nucleus' hate was total, and although I would like to add all-consuming, and complete, etc., there's no point 'cause "total" pretty much sums it up. Ya know. It was total. Total. Night and day, from the minute he got up, from the second he got up, from the millisecond he got up, you get the idea, he was consumed, all-consumed. 1 billion zillion burgers of hate sold. So it wasn't hate. Huh? As I said hate comes and goes, and his feel-

12

ing was so total that it was more, how can I put it, it was more something else, er, um, resentment. How 'bout resentment. G.O. Best's son, Nucleus, resented his father.

G.O. Best's son, Nucleus, resented his father. His father was an internationally known thingamajeebie. I've used this trick before and like all my tricks I will use it again, but I won't explain exactly what his father did because it's not important. What is important is he was an internationally known thingamajeebie. He did the internationally known thingamajeebie thing and therefore was internationally known. There is something I will explain about him and that is that he owned restaurants. Oh yeah he was a Holocaust outlaster but I won't figure that into the story at all (NOT!). I'm writing this in Germany. Can you believe what happened here? It happened here.

Nucleus one day decided to kill his father.

The way that Dr. Best, oops that's giving somethinc away, the way that G.O. Best came to own restaurants was this way. He was complaining about the food. He was complaining about the food that he had to eat (no like what?, he was complaining about the food that he had to dress up in Victorian lingerie) and somebody he worked with told him to stop complaining and buy a restaurant if you're so damn unhappy about the food you're eating.

"Stop complaining and buy a restaurant if you're so damn unhappy about the food you're eating," somebody he worked with told G.O. Best.

G.O. Best who could do things like this, did things like this. He took over a restaurant. He didn't buy one. He rented an abandoned space of one and once he did that he realized he'd have to pay the rent. That meant he'd have to open the thing. Run a restaurant. He'd actually have to go into a kitchen. He'd never been in a kitchen before. Even in all his own homes. (Not all his own homes that he owned currently, he wasn't really that rich to own more than one, then, what I meant was all his own homes throughout his life. But also, when he was little he and his parents separated you know to escape, and um, well to describe the places he lived then as his "own" homes isn't really right either. The point is he'd never been in a kitchen).

He went into his first kitchen and he could stand the heat. Ha, ha, ha, ha. He cleaned it, the kitchen, himself. He hired a kitchen cleaning machine, something that blew, that doused, that incarcerated the whole place in steam. Boom. He cleaned that dirty kitchen. Steam, all that steam, steamed, uh, seemed, like smoke. Steam gets in your eyes. This steam/smoke in grey/white clouds bellowed/blossomed from his restaurant's windows to the street. Somebody called the fire department. The fire department came. They fined him. That was his beginning. G.O. Best's beginning as an owner of restaurants. As a restaurateur. The author, the auteur, the restaurateur, the entrepreneur, er, the successful person. What is the successful person. The successful person is the person that can open a restaurant and on the first day get fined by the fire department. And there still is a second day. And on the third day after opening a restaurant something else goes wrong (but not getting fined by the fire department) and there still is a fourth day. And on the ninth day maybe get fined by the fire department again. And there still is a tenth day.

Nucleus was a little boy when his father opened his first restaurant. Nucleus came over once after school to see what was going on. This was what was going on: His father had things out on a giant thing. Lotsa things out on a big giant thing. He had a big bowl. A big, big, bowl. He had a whipper, a beater, a whisk. He had forks and knifes. He had asparagus. He had a spatula. He had salt and pepper. He had chives. He had a big block of cheese. He had onions. He had a grater. Besides the "forks and knives" knives, he had sharp knives. Long, sharp knives. With big handles. He had wooden spoons. With big handles. The big thing the things were on was a wooden thing. A big wooden thing. He had zucchini. He had cookbooks. Big, thick cookbooks. Little folded scraps of notes and recipes too. There was other stuff. He was occupied. Nucleus' father was occupied. He had decided that his restaurant would make omelettes.

"You know what I've decided," he told Kaya, his wife, "I'm going to make omelettes in the restaurant."

"That's good," Kaya said, 'cause she had told him that if he opened a restaurant he'd have to make some food to serve in it.

He'd remembered these really good omelettes he'd had in Baltimore. What was really good 'bout them, what was really, really good 'bout them, 'specially for what he needed now, was this. They made the omelettes out in the open so you could see them, see how they were made. That was really good if you wanted to learn how to make omelettes. He'd take the train from New

15

York once a week for two months avoidin' the "cardboard sandwiches of cardboard ham in a cardboard box for $85." and kept himself hungry for the omelettes. The omelette became his amulet. (I couldn't resist). I s'ppose he looked funny, yeah I s'ppose he did, Dr. Best, G.O. Best, sittin', starin', writin' down, tastin' at that Baltimore restaurant. But so what? If you're gonna do anythinc you gotta look funny. You gotta.

"I bet you looked funny," Kaya said.

"Yeah. I don't know. I didn't notice. I didn't think about that."

Kaya was an artist. She made large colorful work with silk-screen, large paper cut-outs, collage. She came from a rich, bourgeois (I am only using "bourgeois" because it's so much fun to use) family from somewhere thingamajeeby in Europe. She had servants as a kid. Later, when they lived, and her studio was, on top of one of the restaurants that her husband owned, she would have her food brought up from downstairs by the kitchen "staff." She would tell her husband, who could never bring himself to do something like that, that these people actually enjoyed this. They liked bringing her her food. Kaya and her husband had what was termed an "open" relationship. What that actually means is open to question. Other people termed it that. I doubt they ever sat down explicitly and gave it a name (although how would I know?). Because they were economically responsible for many people's lives, and the kindof people, ya know restaurant people, who are somewhat bohemian (if I'm gonna use "bourgeois" I might as well throw this term in as well) generally as a profession, they were in the lighted center of much gossip. Although of course what was really going on was pretty much in the dark. Like everything that is really going on usually is. What happens between couples is just like what happens in the refrigerator. When the door is closed does the light go out? All the talk in the world can never crassly whisper away a look in the dim night at the person breathing next to you.

Once upon a time Nucleus and his father wanted to fuck the same girl. Nucleus was no longer a little boy, although there was lotsa talk about him "growing up." He was 31. His mother had been dead for one year. The thingamajeeby thing that G.O. Best, o.k. Dr. Best did, had to do with what his wife had suffered from. In the time that she was dying he did everything he could. I wish I could find a better expression for "everything he could." He did everything in his power. I wish I could find a better expression for "everything in his power." Dr. Best and his wife, Kaya, in the time that she was dying, had sat down with their son Nucleus (yes they did, they actually all sat down) and had a discussion. It was Nucleus' 30th birthday.

"Your mother and I have one wish, one wish," Dr. Best said. I really don't know if that's what he said because it doesn't sound like anything anybody would say, really, but the gist of it I'm pretty sure is right. "We must get along better, and you must get a job."

At 30 you already have past lives. In some ways 30 is the age of past lives, when you suddenly realize (is there any way to realize in any other way) that you have them, er, past lives. Not of course the past lives like a Princess of Egypt or somethinc (how come in those kinda past lives you're never a slave or a victim of the plague) but just the acknowledgment that in other parts of your life you seemed to be different than you are now. Saying this simply it seems pretty simple, but it's really kinda weird. Nucleus was stuck. Stuck, stuck, stuck. He was. Stuck. The stickiness that he was stuck in had to do not just with the existence of his past lives but with what having past lives meant. It was, yes forgive me, a philosophical problem. Having your parents lecture you at 30 is hard 'nuff, but sittin' in front of their full-frontal authority with your own material nakedness naked for all to see (you're stuck and everyone knows it) and your only defense, the impossible to express or to get anyone to believe or more improbably understand, that you have a philosophical problem and that's why you seem to be so, um, stuck, is really a nightmare of Poe-like proportion.

"This is a nightmare of Poe-like proportion," the ex-Literature major (one of his past lives) Nucleus said to his parents angering them just a lil' bit more.

But this discussion with his parents soon became its own past life and a year later his mother died, he and his father wanted to fuck the same girl, and Nucleus decided he was going to kill his father.

In Berlin, G.O. Best had just fallen in love. It was with Queen Neferttiti. The bust in the museum. A lot had happened. A lot had happened in a life that was now winding down. Or, in a typical manner for him, other lives were winding down, and those other lives made him think the same thing was going on with him. He did not have his son's "philosophical problem." Past lives didn't bother him, parallel lives did. His wife was dead. He had heard a lot in his Americanness, his Americanness that hid him away, taking the biggest chomp of his years, but an elephant unable to sit on the candle of his flickering memories of a European childhood, about "anger." Anger was an American word, part of the English language. Simple. Direct. Meant what it said. He had this other language. This language that he first heard. This language didn't have "anger" but words that had more, that were more, that, that were social, that included the act and the actor, that were . . . prophecies.

Was he angry at his wife? For what. For kicking the bucket, kissing the mouth of the unknown, being unfaithful to him, being unfaithful to him by being unfaithful to life. Dying. Why was he talking like this. Talking like a European intellectual novel. In America when he talked like this, to the act-ing, performing types, that worked in his restaurants, their heads became empty aquariums he was dropping exotic lipstick colored fishes with gills like plumes into, and the possibility would come about that he might get laid. That's how he saw it. Sometimes he saw it in a different way. An old fart boring the television generation with radio. Or was he the television generation? Maybe nobody even watched television anymore. He hated fat women. He would go uptown to a certain institution to see different famous types, writers and such, talk their stuff, and there would be all these fat women about. Eueye!

His life was not winding down. His life would never wind down. He always knew what to do. He, afterall, had survived. Sitting in a restaurant in Berlin, Germany near the Egyptian museum where he had just fallen in love, and wanted so much to fuck, the bust of Queen Neferttiti, a restaurant, wooden-bright, modern, computerized, green-planted and airy (never eat in restaurants, if you can, with people that work in restaurants, there's way too much that you didn't know before, that you all of a sudden know, that you really didn't need to know, or, want to know, about restaurants), an Italian restaurant, where for some reason, I guess because it was an Italian restaurant, everybody, the waiters and waitresses, spoke to you in Italian, even though it was in Germany, G.O. Best, a Jew, could look out at the land that wanted to destroy him, and think basically that the coffee he was sipping wasn't really very good.

I could start this next paragraph by saying G.O. Best didn't hate Germans or Germany, but it wouldn't be exactly right. There were times, in a certain layer in his mind, which he decided was not a very deep layer, when he wanted to take a big lock cutter, ya know a cutter that could really cut big locks, and squeeze the heads of Germans walking past him on the street, until their brains and blood became a kindof putty, a misshapen, disfigured, puke clay. So no, he didn't hate Germans or Germany. At this time he hated his son more. Hate is too weak a word. G.O. Best resented his son.

G.O. Best resented his son.

Nucleus and his mom were close.

Once upon a time Nucleus and his father wanted to fuck the same girl. She had silicon breasts. She was a daughter of a colleague of Dr. Best's from

20

abroad ("abroad"?, one loves to write things of this sort doesn't one). Dr. Best had consulted with her father about his wife, Kaya, at the time Kaya was dying. Dr. Best, a successful restaurateur, and retired international thingamajeeby, now had many homes. He owned stuff. Apartments. Restaurants. Apartments on top of restaurants. Slope, "the most successful lazy person in the history of the world,"[*] lived in one of these apartments because Slope's wife Franklin worked for Dr. Best as one of his best managers. Some of the stuff G.O. Best owned, the apartments, were sometimes empty, and sometimes he could offer them to people, you know to people to stay, to stay for a while, you know maybe to daughters of colleagues from abroad. That's how the girl that both Nucleus and his father wanted to fuck came to live on top of Dr. Best's steakhouse, SOCKS.

Verne, who worked with Slope's wife Franklin running the steakhouse SOCKS for Dr. Best, and who was unbelievably shy, hated the girl that both Nucleus and his father wanted to fuck, immediately. This doesn't really say much 'cause Verne hated everybody immediately. Her boyfriend, Victor, who was a good man, she hated immediately, until she loved him immediately. Her hatreds were somehow pathological and somewhat endearing, a hard combination, because they contained both no relationship to reality whatsoever, and an almost blow-by-blow analysis, a close-reading if you will (I will), of why this or that person deserved to be hated.

"And . . . her breasts are fake!" She told Franklin one afternoon in between

---

[*] Jesse James Joyce (J.J.J.), a young kid English painter of cartoons on walls

taking phone reservations for M.W.T.E.A.S.B.N.Y.R.H.G. (men wanting to eat at SOCKS before NY Rangers hockey games).

"She wears falsies?" Franklin, who had a combination of her own, a paradox, a good-girl Connecticut type who sometimes did wild things but only in a good-girl Connecticut way (when she ustabe cocained out she had produced an unbelievable amount of strange knitting, like 2 inch-wide scarves, 65 feet long, that she still kept to this day and showed off to friends).

"No. Silicone! SILICONE!!" Verne shouted over the Led Zeppelin CD the Mexican kitchen guys were playin'.

Dr. Best invited his colleague's daughter for dinner at SOCKS and that night they had had a cuddle. The SOCKS staff knew this because she had come down to the restaurant the next afternoon and told them.

"They're fucking?"

"No. They're not fucking. Yet." Verne kept Franklin up-to-date on the news of her boss.

Nucleus, who was being evicted from his apartment on top of SOCKS, next to the apartment now occupied by the girl both he and his father wanted to fuck (o.k. be wasn't being evicted, his father was kicking him out of his free space, because he wanted him to get a job, and because Nucleus was interfering in the restaurant below and annoying the staff, who, although, as

G.O. Best would be the first, only somewhat jokingly, to proclaim weren't very good, were still hard to find), first saw the girl both he and his father wanted to fuck on the stairs of the SOCKS building and wanted to fuck her. He invited her to the SOCKS "employee outing."

"I don't have to go, I'm already out." The pudgy, long-haired, gay, best waiter at SOCKS said on hearing about the outing.

On the way back from the SOCKS employee picnic, the pudgy, long-haired, gay, best waiter at SOCKS inebriated from the beauty of his new boyfriend who had come along for the day and from constant attention to that high watermark of American tradition, the keg (a plastic tub sloshing with warm Bud and a hose), took over the strange ship of the boozed, voyage of the damned-if-we-care, rickety yellow-school bus Verne had rented, and declared himself "Queen of the Keg," forcing the remaining tepid brew down his subject's gullets (what is a gullet?). In this drunken atmosphere of drunkenness, heavy with the drunken atmosphere of drunkenness, Nucleus got his tongue in the mouth of the girl both he and his father wanted to fuck. Even in their drunken state some of the employees of SOCKS might have told Nucleus that he was sticking his tongue into the mouth of his father's girl, but nobody liked Nucleus, he was always interfering, so nobody cared. Dr. Best, who of course didn't go to the outing, 'cause that's not the kindof thing he did, heard about his son sticking his tongue down the mouth of the girl both he and his son wanted to fuck, the next day, and immediately called SOCKS and made Franklin, Slope's wife, his most-trusted manager, cry.

Nucleus one day decided to kill his father. He was downstairs. He was downstairs from the apartment he was getting free, getting free 'cause his father owned it, and his father was letting him live in it, letting him live in it for the moment, for the moment, actually his father was kicking him out. He was downstairs and downstairs was a restaurant. Downstairs was a restaurant owned by his father. The whole building was owned by his father. The restaurant in the two bottom floors, and the basement, was called SOCKS. It was a steakhouse. On the walls in special glass cases were famous socks of famous people. Nucleus was downstairs a lot. Nucleus was downstairs a lot giving his input into the running of the restaurant. He was downstairs now doing some measuring for a giant, clear-plastic, palm tree, that changed colors with a varied flow of strangely mixed ink propelled continuously through its body. He had an idea that he wanted to install this just inside the entrance of SOCKS. So he was downstairs now doing some measuring.

Franklin, the Manager of SOCKS, who did things, things that needed to be done, could have been annoyed by people doing things that didn't need to be done. And guess what she was. But language, a social entity, creates emotions, because only certain emotions are allowed to be created. Nucleus was the boss's son. The boss's son, even if he was not considered very much by his father, and even he was up to doing something as looney as say, wanting to install a giant, clear-plastic, palm tree, that changed colors with a varied flow of strangely mixed ink propelled continuously through its body, just inside the entrance of SOCKS, was still the boss's son. You could not go up to him crouching in the doorway of your restaurant ostentatiously brandishing a floppy yellowed tape measure and muttering to himself to remember certain measurements and dump a bowl full of syrupy vinaigrette on his head.

Carrying a full-bowl of syrupy vinaigrette from the kitchen, Franklin, had to really really really work really hard not to dump the bowl on the head of the boss's son who was doing something stupid, as usual, in her restaurant. Verne, who worked for Franklin in the running of SOCKS, watched with a delighted, childish look of delight and childish expectancy, as she saw this event almost take place, knowing exactly what was going on in Franklin's mind and hoping that Franklin would actually do it.

"Do it. Do it. Do it!" Verne thought/whispered to herself.

Franklin who could do things like this, did things like this. She was able to stop herself from doing things that would stop herself from doing things. She sat the bowl with a soft thud on a nearby table.

"Nucleus, you know your father was looking for you earlier."

"What, he was at the restaurant?"

"No. On the phone. He called on the phone." This was the next day after the SOCKS employee picnic, where Nucleus had got his tongue into the mouth of the girl both he and his father wanted to fuck, and the afternoon of the

25

morning where G.O. Best, the owner of SOCKS, and Nucleus' father, had called Franklin and made her cry.

"Well why didn't he call me. I have a phone. God, I hate that." God, he hated that. He hated that, in his view, "the help," the restaurant people, were communicating messages to him. They could take messages for him, but they shouldn't communicate messages to him. He was wondering if that difference made any sense, but it did to him. His mother would have agreed.

He thought about how he would do it. This was the moment he thought about how he would do it. There were different ways he could do it. He could do it this way. He could do it that way. One way, the obvious way, was the restaurant way. There were lotsa things in the restaurant that he could do it with. He could do it with the cleavers. He even liked that word, cleavers. He also liked the idea of "doing it with the Cleavers" if you get what he meant, meaning if you watched TV as a kid. Even the giant pans could do it. I mean him holding a giant pan and whacking really hard on a skull could do it. There was a whole meat thing too. He should really think hard on the whole meat thing. SOCKS, a steakhouse, had a whole meat thing going (duh?). A whole put the noir film detective after being shot-up full of unnamed shot-up stuff into the meat freezer kindof thing. In other words SOCKS had a meat freezer. And there had to be somethinc there. Some way there to do it.

Franklin looked at Nucleus, at the way he was looking, and Verne looked at Franklin looking at the way Nucleus was looking and then looked at

26

Nucleus, and the best waiter at SOCKS, just beginning his day at work, the restaurant wasn't open yet, looked at Verne looking at Franklin looking at Nucleus and also looked at Nucleus at the way Nucleus was looking. There was somethinc wrong. There was somethinc wrong in the way Nucleus was looking. Nucleus wasn't really looking, he wasn't looking at anythinc, he was thinkin', he was thinkin' about how he would do it. This was the moment he was thinkin' about how he would do it. This was the moment he was thinkin' about how he would kill his father. It was the way he was looking, not what he was looking at, that made him look so wrong. Then he changed, then he looked at somethinc.

The something Nucleus looked at was his father about to come into the restaurant with the girl both he and his father wanted to fuck. She was laughing in that obvious sortof laughing way and holding onto his arm in that obvious sortof laughing and holding onto his arm sortof way. Resentment, hatred, and a dumb terror shocked Nucleus' senses. Like a surge of being, a philosophical overload, a second of pure sensation . . . okay, okay, what was happening was that he just got really really angry and jealous. And what he was thinking about connected to what he was feeling and to the things around him and it all pushed forward with the momentum of the punctuation mark "period" to.

.

It was hard to say who saw the baseball bat first. It's not really that hard to say, everybody saw the baseball bat first. Nucleus saw it. Franklin saw it.

Verne saw it. The best waiter at SOCKS saw it. They all knew it was there. It was a combination of knowing it was there and seeing it, that made them all saw it. There was a baseball bat hanging on the wall signed by a semi-famous hockey player in the year the NY Rangers finally won the champi-onship (don't ask me why a hockey player was signing a baseball bat, obviously he should have been signing a hockey stick). It was hanging inside the entrance of SOCKS right above where Nucleus was kneeling. Nucleus sprang up (he did! he did! he did! he sprang up) pushed the bat out of its holding pins and grabbed it and lifted it up.

When you work in a restaurant you know everything. That is your job. To know. Everything. There are many people that know everything, some reli-gious people for example (I know this is an easy target, but then if this is such an easy target, h'com this kindof religiosity has never gone away). Working in a restaurant, and you're good!, you do, actually, know, every-thing. You have a wide-angle lens of a face, and I say face 'cause I mean face, you are looking with everything, seeing with your cheeks even (yes, and your asscheeks too). You smell, you taste, and whatever those other senses are, I've forgotten them for the moment, you know, you're just very aware, okay. You must be.

With the bat raised up and his father walking through the door Nucleus was a problem. A restaurant is exactly that, una casa de problemas ("a house of problems"). You are solving problems, always. You are always solving problems. With Nucleus becoming a problem the three restaurant workers in the restaurant, Franklin, Verne, and SOCKS's best waiter sprung (they did! they did! they did! they sprung) into problem-solving action. But what a problem!! (The double exclamation point is odious!!) The most basic important central essential point, um, thing, to this problem, was that just saving Dr. Best's life was not enuff, if Dr. Best were to even notice that his son wanted to kill him, well, their relationship would be kindof, you know, it doesn't really need to be said, pretty messed up, forever. And ever. They had to stop Nucleus from killing his father and they had to stop Dr. Best from even realizing that his son was trying to kill him. All this they had to do without even thinking about all this they had to do.

All this they had to do without even thinking about all this they had to do. They started. Franklin blocked. She moved into the doorframe cutting off her boss and his girlfriend from entering and from seeing into SOCKS. Verne disarmed. Running at Nucleus with a sheer tremendous tallness she made him clumsily half-drop half-throw the bat into the air so as to prepare himself, draping his arms upright in front of his face and neck, for collision (with her). SOCK's best waiter caught the bat in the air like a football player scoring a touchdown and then dropped it loudly and deftly fastly ran between the about to be colliding Verne with the shocked frightened Nucleus and caught her in a bear hug. This enabled Nucleus to sneeze (seize) his moment, and embarasssedly shaking, waking, up, from this strange, um, thing, he was 'bout to do, he hurried out 'nother door and up the stairs of the SOCKS building to his apartment, that his father was throwing him out of.

"What was that noise?" Dr. Best said entering his steakhouse SOCKS with a daughter of an old foreign colleague who he wanted to fuck and the restaurant's manager, Franklin, who was saying something to him that he couldn't really understand and seemed to be almost blockin' his way.

"Oh, this bat just fell off the wall," Verne and SOCK's best waiter both sortof huffing and puffing said simultaneously, kindof.

"Let's make sure that doesn't happen when guests are here, yes."

"Sure G.O.," Franklin said.

G.O Best had sat down, in Berlin, on a wall. When you are traveling there is always a moment when you sit down. I call this the museum moment. There is something about walking in a museum that makes you very tired. There is something about traveling that is like walking in a museum and that makes you very tired. Sometimes when you are traveling you are walking in a museum and that makes you very tired. Traveling can make you tired. This is making me tired. This is making me tired all this talk about things making people tired. I am tired. G.O. Best was tired. G.O. Best was tired so he sat down, in Berlin, on a wall. The wall was just outside the museum in Berlin where he had fallen in love with Queen Neferttiti.

He was thinking about her, a lil' bit, sorta, (but who is her?), sortof, somebody, a her, her in general, her. Her. He was thinking about her. In the same way somebody could be thinking about him. Him. Hmmmmmmmmmm? Sitting next to him, jus' a lil' bit further, on the wall, were two girls, smoking pot.

Dr. Best smelled it.

Down the drowning lane, the footpath awash with castoff from the overrunning sewers, a figure of an old man, that is bent over and walking with a cane, not making any attempt to shield himself against the onrushing torrent from the heavens and yet not seeming to be getting wet or being pushed back or hampered in any way by the extreme winds, made his course through the puddles and melting, soggy earth, towards the shapeless blotch forming in contrast to the almost solid pattern of total chaos of the howling storm in the sky, his house.

At the door it did not even occur to him that he had not seen this carved sliver of tough tree with the brightly dull brass knocker in fifty years. He just knew that he had to open the door and go inside and he knew it would not be locked. The door, wet and warped and the hinges in need of oil, still opened cleanly, easily slipping from its frame, without much effort from the old man, and he looked through before stepping in and over its arch, a golden, sizzling light cascading to all the corners and blanketing the walls with a thick fabric of vibrating warmth from the roaring fireplace, engulfing his view. There, he saw, sitting in a simple chair, but ornate in the power of its symbol, the figure of an old man, himself, telling a story. It was called The Return of the Storyteller *and it began this way:*

*Down the drowning lane, the footpath awash with castoff from the
overrunning sewers, a figure of an old man, that is bent over and
walking with a cane, not*

Dr. Best was thinking about his wife. He was strangely high, although he
wouldn't have used that word, or even really know that thing. He had felt
strange and he had got up from the wall and made his way ("you've got to
make your own way, son") to a restaurant near the museum, a wooden-
bright, modern, computerized, green-planted and airy Italian restaurant.
His life was not winding down. His life would never wind down. But at this
instant he felt like he was winding down. His head was clearing but not
clearing to clarity; clearing to a bushy, overgrown field of purple hay. The
coffee he was sipping wasn't really very good. He thought about his wife in
a light blue long dress silky-like that had clung, bunched up, in folds, like
rare gentle ocean waves, around her calves, a curtain pulling up to expose
her ankles. He had emotion then, and although it sounds like the response
of some alien being, "he had emotion then," it is the response of a humane
bean, every humane bean, when they both feel and are awake to the fact
they are feeling. He missed her. It was simple, and stupid, and real. The self-
consciousness about the "stupid" realness did not make it less real, but in
essence might describe the essence of reality: awareness of its falseness.
Reality without its falseness, without its heightened thingy of its strange-
ness, aliveness without its sense of being alive, aliveness which just is, is
death. No one can kill another person when you are awake to what aliveness
is. You kill only because you are afraid. You kill only because you are afraid
you are alive.

G.O. Best was killing his son. Slowly and surely, just the same as if (okay, so I've used "as if" again) he had his hands around his throat. He was killing his son in the same way and for the same reasons as Hamlet's ghost of a father or Phillip II in Verdi/Schiller's Don Carlos were killing their sons (I decided here for some literary allusion, I think that's the right term, if you don't know the references don't worry it's not that important). He had a theory, which everybody sortof has, or sortof tries to have, when they confront this thing that is really sortof impossible even to sortof possibly confront, you know the thing, well the thing, the Holocaust. He had this theory, this thing, that maybe had a lot to do with, well probably did have a lot to do with, his own personality (but what was his own personality shaped by?), that when idiocy spins to horrific action, some-where in that mix there is "the fear of being wrong." The fear of being wrong provides the climate, the hothouse of nauseating ignorance, where disgusting plants root and grow. They are always in some ways, masters of language, the idiots, they make things simple, and difficult to argue with. Language is always a battle-ground where the stupider you are, the braver you are, because you don't try to work things out, but try only to make things work out, in language. We begin in life and move to language, and when the two separate, life becomes a concept, a reality unaware of its falseness, and death becomes easier to execute because it all makes sense, not screams.

Best thought:

I want to give my son something. I want to give him a present. In doing that what am I doing? Am I helping him or hurting him. Am I buying him. Am I just assuaging my own guilt. It is always this way with my son. I am always afraid to be wrong. I do feel something for him. I do. I feel it in the way that I know it's real because I think about the feeling of it because I question the feeling of it because I wonder if it's real. I've never been sure. I've always been sure. This is a feeling. This is a real feeling. In the end or in the beginning does it matter beyond that. I want to give my son something. I want to give him a present. I am afraid. I am always afraid. And I want him to do something. I want him to make me less afraid. I want him to succeed so that I don't have to worry about my gifts. I want to give him something but I want him to deserve it or earn it or not even need it or not even want it. Or that's what I say. What do I mean? What is bothering me. Why don't I just give him something if I want to give him something. Why not!!

Nucleus Best got a funny postcard from Germany. It was from his father who was in Berlin and it had on it a picture of a bust of the ancient Egyptian Queen Neferttiti and his father had said something about falling in love with her. His father also said that he could stay in the apartment on top of SOCKS, his father's steakhouse, as long as he needed to or wanted to. The night he got the postcard, Nucleus fucked the girl he had been wanting to fuck and who had been wanting to fuck him, a daughter of a colleague of his father's who was living next door.

They rolled these amazin' joints. They were like ice-cream cones.

TWO GIRLS
WHO SMOKE A LOT OF POT

They were the fucking connoisseurs of the munchies.

I gotta tell ya and I gotta tell ya this way. I um, they, ohmygod, it was, um, ah, ahum, it was, oh, they were, where was I. They, oh yeah, these girls. It's the kinda thing that could only happen in a hotel. It was a hotel story. What do I mean? What do I mean. What do I mean. He, he, eh, ha, ah, hee, hee, ahhahha, ha, ha. Ha, ha, ha. Ha, ha, ha. Ha, ha, ha. Well I don't know things just happen you   know they just happen that's all they just do. I mean things. In a hotel it's different. I met these girls in a hotel. O.k. This is it. They. I was. They were the fucking connoisseurs of the munchies. That's all.

I mean we'd go to this gas station. I don't even know what they call it in Amsterdam. It's like it's a gas. It's a gas man!!!. Hee, hee. You know all over the world they have them. Like kebob, the kebob stuff, they have that every-where. FUCK MCDONALDS. McDonalds is not the most popular food in the world. No way. Kebob. Kebob is everywhere. What is a kebob? Don't even fucking ask. You're kiddin' right? Actually, convenience stores, that's a stupid word isn't it. Convenient. Eahhdghblch!. It's horrible, right. Convenient. Everything is so convenient. Convenience. Convenience this, asshole. 7-fucking-11. Fuck you. What. I'm sorry. Oops. What was I saying?

We'd go to this gas station. You know with the surveillance cameras and the bright glass and o.k. the glass isn't bright it's just the inside is bright. It's so bright. Everything is bright. And um, ya know what I think, um, I'm pretty sure, about this, yeah, definitely, I think this, I think they took the video tapes of these girls, from the surveillance cameras, and they would play them later, the guys that worked in the store, 'cause these, I um, yeah. Anyway, they would stand there, these girls, these two girls, two girls who smoke a lot of pot, and um, they would stare, I didn't know, I really didn't know, I come from the States MAN!, America, we have everything right, these are our stores and everything, **slurpyburpies** whatever   and they knew everything, hee, hee, hee, everything, the right things to get, munchie food, good, good munchie food.

I don't know where they came from. Somewhere in Europe. They'd come and buy pot in Amsterdam and go back home and sell it. That simple. They, I don't know what I want to say about this, 'cause it's kinda telling, not showing, but I feel, o.k., is this o.k., this story's o.k., everything's o.k. right, everything's alright, right? O.k. yeah sorry. You know once I smoked this pot, I can only call it Richard Nixon pot. Yeah *tricky dicky* pot. That's all I can call it. God I got so paranoid. I can't even tell you. Whoa! What was I saying. Oh yeah, about them. The girls. They um. They were like. Mystical things. I mean I don't even believe in mystical shit. They weren't mystical. They were miss, missth, mythss, mythssthical. Mythical. They were like myths. I means myths, Greeks, whatever. Fraternities. What am   I saying?

I   never   understood   Greek   myths.   I   never   understood   Greek myths.   I   ,   um   ,   never   understood   Greek   myths.   I   didn't understand what was going on. Why. Why things happened. It's like a Preston Sturges Movie. A P.S.M. You know he writes , herumargh (cough, cough) he writes. The way he writes his movies. He starts and keeps going. He doesn't go back. If something weird happens in Act 1 he can never go back and fix it. He must explain it by having something weird happen in Act 2. And so on. Greek myths. I, un.   Um. WHy did THe two-HEadeD satyr suddenly sproUT a NOSeflute and then become a ButtERflY and then introduce fire to the world. I don't get it.

But these girls were like myths. And their myth was like this. Their myth was they could smoke more pot than anyone. Anyone. Anyone ever in the whole history of the world ever before them or after them ever anywhere. But by anyone and anywhere I mean actually something more specific. I mean this. I mean MEN. They could smoke more pot than men could smoke. And this means something. This means what meaning means. In some ways meaning is mean. Concept! Concept! Concept alert. Can you pass the chips?

I remember when I saw him, I knew he'd be in trouble. But ya know, it's funny, I didn't want to say it or even think it. But I knew it. It's weird. Hee, ho. Ho, ho, hee. (cough, cough). I ah it's funny 'bout yerself. You um don't want to admit things. But not that you don't want to admit things because you're scared or there's somethinc deep. But almost you don't want to admit things, because then things can happen. I didn't like this guy. Let's face it. I didn't. I thought he was an asshole. And.   Maybe he was. The thing is. I

39

knew. He'd be in trouble. And by not admitting it to myself that I knew this, I'd let him get in trouble.   In a way.   He   had   tattoos.

Nothing against tattoos but in this case there is something against tattoos. He had 'em. I mean look let's get this straight he wasn't a major asshole. He was kinda dippy that's all, sorta pathetic show-offy, not major asshole show-offy. Trying to be something he's not. But so what. That's what we're all trying to be. The thing that he was trying to be was the silly thing. That was the thing. It wasn't the problem that he was pretending. It was what he was pretending that was the problem. He was a surfer guy, 'cept he did-n't surf, 'cept for the web ha hahahaha ha ha he. O.k. that wasn't so funny. Everything's o.k. right. This is not boring yet. Two girls who smoke a lot of pot, who can smoke more pot than any man, and a pretend macho urban surfer tattooed skateboarding vegetarian type dude. Hmmmmm! (mounch). Salsa. That's good salsa.

I met them with an open room and that peculiar smell. Not a totally open room. But it wasn't a crack-like thing, the door open a crack, the door was open, very open. Not totally. And that *peculiar smell*. I peeked in. I did, "I peeked in." Heeee haa haa ha hoho hoah ha. Peek-a-boo!. Boo!! No. I didn't do that. I peeked in. "Hey can I join you," somethinc like that. Or "Can I smoke some too," or whatever. They were, I'm not good with a description, or I don't like it, it always seems fake, but they, they need some description. They're very descriptive. THEY ARE A DESCRIPTION. They are descrip-tion itself. That's how I wanna describe them. They're very describable. So anyway, they were there and they weren't alone.   Um, yeah. Um.   Um.

They weren't alone. They were . . .

There was this girl with them. She was straight. In every way. Basically, that's it. She was straight. She had a nice face. She was sitting very straight in a straight chair. Her clothes were straight. Her hair was, o.k., o.k. (cough, cough). 'Nuff sead. She was straight. In every way, basically, 'cept she was a lesbian.   Do ya have anything else to eat, thanx?   She had an Australian accent. And I identify this, I guess everybody does really, with some kinda laid-back thing. You know they're very relaxed, the Australians. But this was the thing. She wasn't! She was not relaxed! Ya know that whole Australian thing, "No Worries, Mate," well she was all "Yes Worries," lotsa worries ya know. I guess not worries exactly. She wasn't Australian, you see, she just had the accent. Ya know when I was in Australia . Um. Ah er. There was this. It's um. It's another hotel story really. Everythinc's a hotel story I guess.

When I was in Australia I stayed in this hotel on the coast not far from Sydney, to go to the beach. They're called pubs, and they are, they're pubs, but they also have rooms, like inns. Ya know, exactly. And um there was like a courtyard. And my room had a veranda on the courtyard. In Australia there's always a veranda. Everybody has a veranda, some kinda outside thing, I think. I guess most countries where it's hot do, duh. I was sitting on the veranda looking out over the courtyard, as you do. That's an inside joke, Australians say that, "as you do." I was looking out over the courtyard, as you do, and there was a band, a pub band, of course "a pub band," and they were warming up, doing a sound check. The same drill. "Check, check, 1, 2, 1, 1,2," etc.

They were amateurs, what a stupid word, whatever. They were kids. It was probably one of their first gigs. And they kept doing this check. "Check, check, check," etc. "1, 2,   1, 2,   1, 2," and so on. "O n n n n n n n n n n n n n n n n n n n n n n n n n n n n e , Twooooooooooooooooooooooooooooo." I mean look it was getting annoying. It did seem like it was going on and on. There was no way it was going to stop. Ya know this salsa is really good. Are we gonna need some more? And um when   I   was   in   Australia   . There was this guy, also, that lived in the pub, that lived in the hotel. A permanent resident. He lived next door to the room I was in. He was sitting out on the veranda too, next door. He was trying to work. Do something. Something with papers on a table, a round table. A round table with like two or three wicker chairs 'round it. He was a businessman of some kind. He was listening. He was being annoyed. By this band's sound check. The constant, "1, 2   1, 2." So he got up. In a very relaxed way. Walked slowly, without seeming purpose, to the edge of the veranda. We were like on the second floor, not very high up. He leaned over the railing without really bending and said loudly, firmly, and very "laid-back":

"If ya don't stop this right this second I'm gonna take out me gun and shoot ya."

Why was I telling you this   story. The girl. The Australian girl. And the two girls. Two girls who smoke a lot of, o.k., o.k., right. This Australian girl was not Australian. She just had the accent. She was from somewhere else.

Somewhere in Europe. I don't know. Somewhere. Somewhere Northern Europe or somewhere. I don't know. You know. What. Well I don't know. They do it to us all the time. They talk about America and they've never even been here. It's a big country. SO Europe's a big place. I don't know. I didn't ask. The point is, or was, or whatever, that she had this laid-back <u>accent</u> but she wasn't   laid-back. She had never smoked pot. I know big-deal. She was cool 'bout it. She was honest which is really cool. She just said it. She was sittin' there in the chair, in that straight chair, in a room full of that smokey greeney smell, very up-right ya know, very there and serious sorta, ya know, and said:

"I've never smoked."

The two girls were great.   Two girls who smoke a lot of pot. They didn't. They didn't make a big deal. They were mid-driff at that moment. They were always very mid-driff.   Even when their mid-driffs weren't showing, their mid-driffs were showing. Ya know. And she liked being there. The girl who had never smoked. She was relaxed in her straight way. Things were happy. Oh yeah there was another guy too. He was another guy. He wasn't the guy. He wasn't the guy with the tattoos who I knew when I saw him would be in trouble. This was another guy. The guy with the tattoos doesn't come into this yet. This other guy. This other guy was there. O.k. there.

The two girls were outta pot. The pot was gone. This was not good. This was bad. Two girls who smoke a lot of pot need a lot of pot. Two girls who smoke a lot of pot need a lot of pot to smoke. Two girls who smoke a lot of pot need a lot of pot to smoke and need to get a lot of pot. Two girls who smoke a lot of pot need a lot of pot to smoke and need to get a lot of pot to smoke. They were outta pot. This was not good. They decided, we decided, to go out to a coffee shop (in Amsterdam they have coffee shops, you know where you can, whatever, blah, blah, blah) to buy some grass, smoke some grass, buy some grass. Again, it was me, the other guy who was there (not the guy with the tattoos), two girls who smoke a lot of pot, and the girl who never smoked.

Me, the other guy who was there, two girls who smoke a lot of pot, and the girl who never smoked went out in Amsterdam to a coffee shop to buy some grass, to smoke some grass, to buy some grass. I was already lost, but I'm always lost, I have no sense of direction, basically, especially in Europe. In a European city. We bought some fries with some mayonnaise-curry dip kinda stuff. They were good. We walked past this big cinema that I'd gone to the night before. It was really cool that place. It's not like a fuckin' 8,000 plex. With 'lil screens the size of yer finger nail. Ya know I was sittin' like in the last seat. Like, really, the last seat. In the high-most, top-most, balcony, I was as far away from the screen as you can possibly get, do ya get what I'm saying, I was far fuckin' away, and the screen was so close, THE SCREEN WAS SO CLOSE, sorry I didn't mean to shout, the screen was so close   'cause THE SCREEN WAS SO BIG. Oops, sorry again.

Um,   hmmm,   hmmm,   um. You, um   ,   ,   ,   you get into the coffee shop,that'swhereIwasright,   and   ya   get   a   menu, it's   funny ya   know   I was   like   cool   'n   everything, stupid, like, really,   there was this whole thing who should get the pot, I, mean, ya, wanna, go, uh, yeah, no, uh, yeah, do, ya, wanna, go, ya get a menu and ya go up to the counter and order it, and, goofy names, and such, Dr. Kervorkian The Marquis de Sade Flipper ("for a whale of a time") huh, yeah, right I guess you're right, Flipper was a dolphin, whatever and, um, what did we order? I think we got, we got some Kervorkian, we had to, and some, um, um, um, actually, that's it, um, we got some "UM", yeah that's what it was called, that was the basic one, basically, and, um god she sat there, ... oh wow shit you have Wheat Thins, pass 'em over, ... (mounch, mounch). She sat there, like I first saw her.

She sat there, like I first saw her. Straight. I could say frozen but it wouldn't be right. Too many. What's that word. Too many connotations. She wasn't cold. Just straight. Her head fixed on some some, upright, some spot, ahead of her, like her head was, um, in a guillotine on its side. You know what I imagine. Youknowwhatiimagine. I imagine one of those things. Those things. What are they. Like, ruffles. Ruffles have r-r-r-r-ridges. Hee, ehe, ha, ha, hee,hee. No. Around their necks. No. You know!! Yeah, in the movies. Whatever century queen whatever whatever. Whatever. No! Not the guillotine again. That meant something else. That was quite poetic when I said it. Why'd you have to spoil it. Oh, you're jokin'. Oops. Sorry. Um. But actually, ya know think 'bout it, I am making, what's that word, illustrative, allusions, comparisons, no, not, connotations, shut up, about queenliness, regalness, beagleness. Snoopy. Hee, hee, hee. She was nothinc like Snoopy.

She sat there in her chair, and we rolled the stuff. Well the two girls did. Two girls who smoke a lot of pot. Man they looked beautiful. In their metier. In their skill. At it. Ya know just at it. At what they did best. Oh, wait, who was in the chair. You didn't get that. The girl who didn't smoke. The Australian who wasn't Australian. There were four of us right, four of us. No wait a minute. There was   me   girl who didn't smoke   two girls who smoke a lot of pot   and um   the other guy, just the other guy, the other guy who was just there   that's four.   There were four of us. Oops, hold on. Wait. That's five. I'm sorry. Right. Five. There were five of us. Right?

They rolled these amazin' joints. They were like ice-cream cones. Big, beautiful, European ice-cream cones. Look I like a B.R. chemical sundae as much as the next guy, but in Europe they have that Belgian shit, big wafer Belgian ship, shit, dipped, in whatever, ya know dip, chocolate, oh,man,shit   yeah their   joints   were   like   that   their joints were like that   their joints,   shit,   like, torches,   each one was like the fuckin' Olympic torch   when they lit them it would set yer eyeballs ablaze   . . .   .

We took our tokes, hee, hee, hee, toke us tucks, ticks are tax, hmm,h,,hhee,hhooooohh,hee, we took (cough, cough), yeah we smoked, and it felt good. , It's   so   funny   'bout   feelin'   god,   good, I mean   we, um, yeah we smoked the UM, and the Kervorkian, mixed, uh, huh   and um I began to tell this story, I told this story 'bout what happened to me in Paris ya know where Jim Morrison is born, not born, buried, ya know where's he buried right?, ya know like Paris right, of course, right, well in this cemetery which has this French name, 'cause I guess like it's in France, ha, ha, yeah, you know that Steve Martin joke, "in France they have a different word for everything, like 'hat', ya know is, 'chapeau'", hee, hee, hee, (cough, cough), well anyway they have all these famous people there, dead people, famous dead people, they have a map and like everythinc, it's weird, but you get excited, you get kinda excited, it's weird, it's strange, but true, strange but true,

so this girl, sorta loopy, pale, sorta like made of straw, what do I mean, I don't know, just, she hands me this thing, not this thing, she hands me a rose, SHE HANDS ME A ROSE,   of   all   the   the   the the   things, not things   of all the not things things   a flower,   it's so   stupid   any-way but it's true   a rose   she says "here"   that's it   "here" yeah, in English, she knew I spoke English   "give it to someone"   so of course you know what that means, that means, I have a chore now, gawd, I've got to "give it to someone"   so I says, 'cause, the girl is made of straw for christ'ssake, I say, "o.k., um, I'm gonna give it to, um, Maria Callas,"   I just saw her name on the big map posted on the big post of all the dead peo-ple, famous dead people who were there, I don't even know who the fuck Maria Callas is really, but now I gotta do it, now I gotta find her goddamn fuckin' grave and give it a rose.

So I'm telling this story. The Australian girl who's not Australian is lookin' at me. That's the only way I can describe it. She's lookin' at me. She's giving me that lookin' at me look. Ya know the kind. The kind that is just that kind

47

of look. The look that isn't about what's it's lookin' at, but is just 'bout lookin'. She's lookin'. She's lookin' like "wha da fuck," ya know. There's another reason tho. There's 'nother reason why she's lookin'. She's lookin' 'cause she's thinkin'. She's thinkin' 'bout being stoned. "Is this it" "Am I feeling anything?" "C'mon isit workin'?" and my favorite, my personal favorite "What am I s'pposed to feel?" The two girls, two girls who smoke a lot of pot, are also lookin'. Their eyes are different. They have a look and are lookin'. They know and are trying to find out. O.k. I'm sorry that sounds a little, a little dramatic. They're high o.k. that's all. They're high.

But is she high?

I'm tellin' the story. I'm in the French cemetery with the French name carrying a rose given to me by a girl made of straw that I promised to put on the grave of Maria Callas. Guess what?   Oh, turn that up, I love that song, yeah   Yum, yeah, er, what, where was I, Callas, Callas, Callas, oh yeah, guess what, MARIA CALLAS DOESN'T HAVE A GRAVE, uh huh, uh huh, uh huh, she was buried there, I mean she wasn't buried there, she was there, she was in that cemetery, but she was cremated so she was in this special crematorium place, uh huh, that's right, can you believe it.   I   gotta   tell ya   and   ya gotta   believe me. There were 10,100. That's ten thousand one hundred little boxes full of cremated former people. Each one   a   a   a   little drawer. (As I'm tellin' this she's beginnin' to look at me even more than she was lookin' at me before.)

As I'm tellin' this she's beginnin' to look at me even more than she was lookin' at me before. Like she's mad. "Cremated former people?" she's saying. Like I'm kinda being. You know being, what's that, I'm being, outrageous. Right. Ho. Ho. Outrageous, moi? Runnin' 'round like an electrocuted, an electrocuted, ...   like someone electrocuted, maybe that's not what I was doing, you get it, there were a lot of boxes. A LOT OF BOXES. With names. A big bank vault kinda thing. Avoid the pigeon shit. Climb the stone steps. Look at the names on the drawers. Isadora Duncan. Etc., etc., etc. But no Maria Callas!

The thing is we're all laughing. We're all laughing 'bout it. Two girls who smoke a lot of pot are smelling beautiful with their smiles. Does that make sense? Their lips were their laughs. I wanted to kiss their laughs. ANd evEn her. UEP. YEP she was. (cough, burp, splutter, cough, cough). EVEN HER. But of course even her. SHe waS. She WAS. She was. High. Hi!. Just stopped the story and looked at her. I looked at her! And said:

"Hi."

And then she did it. She did it. She laughed. O.k., she giggled. But you know she did it. She looked smiled giggled. LOOKED SMILED GIGGLED. "You see," I said. "You're high." "No, I'm not," she said. "Yes, you are," I said. "What do you mean," she said. "I mean I don't know it's no big deal, I'm saying, I'm just saying, you asked me before, would you feel anything, or anything, and you do, you're high, that's all, I'm explaining." "What do you mean," she said again, slowly, very slowly. "What you're feeling that's all, you're feeling high, right?" "What," she said. "You're happy 'n stuff," I said.

49

"Well I can feel this way without drugs," she said.

"Great," I said. "I can't."

Hee, hee, hee, hee, hee, hee, hee, hee, hee, hee, hee, hee, hee, hee, hee, hee, hee, hee, hee, hee, hee, hee, hee, hee, hee, hee, hee, hee, hee, hee, hee, hee, hee, hee, hee, hee, hee, hee, hee, hee, hee, hee, hee, hee, hee, hee, hee, hee, hee, hee, hee, hee, hee, hee, hee, hee, hee, hee, hee, hee, hee, hee, hee, hee, hee, hee.

Then we had to find our way back home.

European cities. Some of 'em. To me, at least. They seem. They are. They're centrifugal. Am I using that right. I feel like a sock in a dryer, do you know what I'm saying. I don't know where the fuck I am, when I am. When I am there. And plus, o.k., I was stoned. We're standing outside the coffee shop. I have no Rjfsdl;k idedkflj;adjkfl (cough, couch) f-f-f-f-f-uckin' idea where I am. Right? Have I said that? Two girls Whosdf smeoksdfalot ofpot are laughin' bUt wIThout makin' any noise. Laughing   quietly   to   them-selves.   Hmmmmmmmmmmmmm.   Hmmmmmmmmmmmmmmm.   No more chips, huh?

Hmmmmmmmmmmmmmm.

50

We're lost.

Oh yeah we start to walk and I'm sure of the direction I'm really sure I'm really really sure 'cept like everybody that's really sure really really sure of anything I'm not really sure you know I am sure I am sure that I don't want to say anything that I don't want to say which way to go because I'm afraid I don't really know even though I'm really really really sure I do know so I just follow but who am I following. There's nobody to follow.

Oh, oh, oh, oh, then the most amazing thing happens. The Most Amazing Thing!! The guy. The guy. The guy. The guy who was there. The guy who was there. The guy who was just there. That guy. That guy just started leading. I mean takin' us. Taking us, but taking us, really taking us. Tellin' us. Just going. Going and shouting: "THIS WAY, THIS WAY, I KNOW, I KNOW, I KNOW, THIS WAY, THIS IS THE WAY TO THE HOTEL." And we followed him, but mygod,   mygod, mygod, mygod   he was going the wrong way, I knew it, I knew he was going the wrong way, but you know I wasn't sure, I wasn't, I didn't know, I mean maybe, but no, there was no way, we were going 'gainst the fuckin', away from a canal, or towards a canal, somethinc, I just knew we were going wrong.

I kept following. This way. This way. I know. I know. This way. He kept saying. Finally, I knew it. We were totally lost. He'd taken underneath tunnels, old medieval gates, etc. etc. Two girls who smoke a lot of pot who were kinda keeping up with him stopped and looked back at me and the Australian who wasn't really Australian and who hadn't smoked before tonight and who still wasn't sure if she was high and who everybody else said might not be because you know your first time you don't really get high or whatever although I did although I don't remember my first time and who I was trying to convince was high and who I'm pretty sure was, high. Two girls who smoke a lot of pot looked back at me and the Australian who wasn't really Australian and said: "Save yourselves, we have to go on. He's our friend. You don't. Go back while you still have a chance." Then I realized that we were there. That he was right. He did know. Up ahead was our hotel.

(cough, cough). So this guy had tattoos. Remember the tattoo guy, yeah right. This guy, man, wow. So he was there in the room. This time it was me, two girls who smoke a lot of pot, and him. This was when the myth was about to hit right into place. Right into place. I'd heard it all before. Ya know news of him before. He'd really come on strong. He'd really come on strong to one of the two girls who smoke a lot of pot. Which was alright, in a way, I mean sure, why not. Of course. Once I was in this cab with them. I kid you not. The driver just like went insane. I mean fell in love. That's all I can say. But the thing was. He kinda figured out what hotel we were living in. And he waited. Well he was crazy. He was crazy in love. These girls did that you know. 'Cause they just were so stoned, ya know what I'm sayin'. He left this note right, for one of the girls, actually the same one that the tattoo guy was crazy 'bout, this note was in invisible ink, wait, I'm sorry not in invisible ink, it was um backwards, that's right he wrote it in the mirror. Ya know call me whatever. revetahw em llac wonk aY. Gawd, I dunno why he did that. I remember this one time we came back late, from somethinc, dancin' or somethinc, and he was like waiting outside the hotel, like I said. As we came in and closed the door shut, I heard this like lame yodel of some kind, ya know, "hey, two girls who smoke a lot of pot, hey, hey!!" We just went up to our rooms, and smoked. It was paradise.

It was paradise. In the morning they would come with these breakfast doobies, I mean weed filled croissants. I mean forget a Blunt. This was ridiculous. Oh man it was just, it was just, beautiful. The girl that the tattoo guy liked, and the cab driver, I liked the other girl. I don't even wanna talk 'bout it. But god wow. We'd all get stoned and they'd like be playin' 'round on my bed, ya know, I swear pillow fights and everythinc. Oh man, wow. Unbelievable. So, no, it was o.k. really. Ya know like this guy had come on to her. I liked one of them and he liked one of them, and ya know, there were two of them, and there were two of them, I mean there were two of us. So it was like. Um   even.   Yeah   . 'Cept I knew somethinc. I respected something, or suspected somethinc, or somethinc. There was somethinc 'bout the combination, it had to be, ya know, it was tricky. Well it always is. Girlfriends 'n shit. I don't know if he knew this. In fact I'm sure he didn't. That was his thing. It wasn't that he was like being too cool, or anything, or that he was being stupid. Ya gotta respect shit, ya know what I'm

53

saying. And um, I know this. He didn't respect what they could do with pot. I mean they absorbed the fuckin' shit like it was nothinc. I mean they fuckin' secreted it. They uh, they uh, they took weed baths. I mean they breathed the shit in. They inhaled.

I'd heard 'bout him. He'd come onto her. Heavy. He'd taken them to a con-cert or somethinc, and said stuff like, ya know said stuff like, "you're the most beautiful girl in the world" "I've never met anyone like you" shit like that. I was like alright, o.k., you know fine. But you know, um, um, um. So he sat down. He was like all friendly and shit. So was I. Hee, hee, hee, hee, hee, hee, hee, hee, hee, hee, hee, hee, hee. Like. I'd ask him. Uh. I asked him, what it was like to be the ah, to be the ah, I forgot the term I used, drawing board or somethinc, ya know for the tattoo artist's designs. 'Cause he was like, he was like covered in tattoos. I told you that right? But there's some other word for it. Drawing board is not the right word, and he told me kinda snottily.

Two girls who smoke a lot of pot were rolling meanwhile. As always, oh. It was beautiful. It always seemed to take hours. There was a method. No, not a method. A method is wrong. There was a way. There was ah, ah, ah, ha, ha, ha, hee, hee, hee. No. Wait. Wait. Wait. What. What. What. What am I saying. I'm hungry. What else ya got.

(mounch, mounch, mounch, mounch, mounch, mounch, mounch, mounch, mounch, mounch)

Um. The joints were ready. They were big. I mean you could look at them and you could figure out. They were big. Of course they were cut. They cut them in Europe with tobacco, which I don't know they just do. But there still was a lot of fuckin' shit. And they were like, well they weren't perfect. I mean I've seen joints that were made like, like that were factory made, you know they almost came in colorful boxes with a surgeon general's warning. But these did have filters, they do that in Europe too. They weren't perfect, but they were beautiful. Anyway they lit 'em up. They were, they were, there were so mid-driff. Not the joints, the girls. Ha, ah, ha, eh, hee, hee. They took these, big, big, beautiful, puffs. They shotgunned. They made pipes outta their fists and they shared it with each other. They took their time. They loved to smoke.

Then they passed a joint. Ya know to the tattoo guy. (Okay it took them a little bit of time, I mean they loved to smoke.) I looked at the guy, and he wasn't my favorite guy right, but still I was thinkin' c'mon buddy, alright bud, take it slow, ya got it, don't down it, man, look at what you're smokin', I don't care if you've been smokin' everyday of yer fuckin' life since birth, this is a special joint man, these are special girls, ya know, use it man, caress it, treat it with respect. But he couldn't. He liked pumped up. Got all big. And filled up his lungs with a big big big reverse lugie of pow pow pow. And. He dropped MAN. He D*I*E*D. He starting laying down, on my fuckin' hotel bed by the way, and crying out, "oh, oh, oh." The girls tried to help 'cause they're like experts man, two girls who smoke a lot of pot, they had they had the stethoscope out, telling him to eat and shit, and rest and take it easy and all this but he kept sayin' "no, no, I'm o.k." and "it's just you put tobacco in it and I don't smoke that, ya know tobacco just fucks up the body ya know." We left him lying on my bed to cool out, and everybody was really cool to him, and everythinc, but then when we got outside the girls started to laugh, first just a little, and then really a lot loud. At the concert earlier he'd bummed a cigarette off them.

You know how groups get together. Groups, families, friends, workers, bowlers, lynch mobs, ya know.

A GOOD MAN

"A good man is fuckin' hard to find." Verne was answering a question that wasn't asked. O.k. the question was being asked, but it was being asked with eyes not voice (suddenly I'm talkin' in that English Northern working-man talk, ya know where they drops the "the's", like "goin' down pub.") Well the guy that was askin' had the eyes for that kindof talkin', bartender eyes, 'cause um he was a bartender. W.B., tall with a pounch (a pounch?), leaned forward in that leaned forward with rigid bottom-half kinda way that people who are tall with pounces and who lean forward with rigid bottom-halfs do. And asked the question loudly loudly loudly with direct brown eyes of worried wonder. The question was:

"Why?"

A lot of people asked that question of Verne, and she was gettin' a little annoyed. There's really no difference 'tween gettin' a little annoyed and being fucking crazy like out-of-what-little-of-your-mind-is-left angry as shit. So she was, she was pissed off. Not so much 'bout the people. More about her. 'Cause she was askin' the question too. And that was what was really annoying her. Like it annoys anybody. Everybody. Everybody who asks it, which everybody does. Everybody asks themselves. Why. Why. Why. Why. Why. Why. Why. Why. Why. Why. Why. Why. Why. Why. Why. Why. Why? He was a good man. Victor was a good man. He was. He definitely was. Victor was. Victor was a good man.

Victor was late. He wasn't late. He was just in a hurry. Which you always are when you're going to catch a train (that's so funny that expression, like you're squatting in front of an on-rushing loco with a kid's baseball mitt). It doesn't matter if you've got hours. Hours. Hours. Hours. You've got hours! You've got hours before your train leaves, you're still gonna rush. 'Cause you never know. You never know. He didn't have hours but he wasn't late and he hurried. When he got to the platform his train wasn't even there. He had to wait.

Franklin had solved an essential problem. It's "the world as dirty dishes" theory. "The world as dirty dishes" theory is the theory that the world is a dish. And this dish exists in two states. Sometimes it is dirty. Sometimes it is clean. When it is dirty it must be cleaned. When it is cleaned it is used and then gets dirty. What to do with this dish, meaning what to do with the world, has to do with what state the dish/world is in when you are asked to do something with it. When it is clean you use it. When it is dirty you clean it so you can use it. You cannot think about the world unless you understand that it is constantly changing and you are the force of its change. Or another way to put it is is things must be done so you do them. Or still another way to put it would be to put it this way: keep busy. Keep busy. Keep busy. Keep busy. This was Franklin's form of Why. Why. Why?

"I learned an interesting thing the other day," Franklin was tellin' Verne in Franklin's office in the restaurant SOCKS where they both worked. "NOT!"

They both laughed. It was an in-joke among all (United States of)

Americans that the only thing beyond the horizon you were staring at was the horizon you were staring at. Days were to be repeated efficiently. And effort, huffing and puffing, was important for its own sake. Franklin then went on to bring up the topic that was then topical being a topic of discussion for her and Verne.

"So what. What. What da ya think. Do you. Um. How 'bout. Well. O.k. Are you sure?"

"No I'm not sure!!" Verne snapped.

Franklin wanted to fix-up Verne with someone she knew, alright somebody that somebody she knew knew. Verne, had a boyfriend, Victor, but Franklin didn't approve.

"Victor's a good man ya know." Verne continued.

"Yeah, yeah, Victor is a good man." Franklin agreed.

The United States of America sits right in the continent called America. Canada is near it which speaks English, and a part of Canada that doesn't even call itself Canada, Quebec, speaks French. There are some islands and places like islands that speak English and some that speak French. Brazil speaks Portuguese. There are native tongues too, of course. But mostly, everybody else, in America (the continent), speaks Spanish. Victor, Verne's boyfriend, a good man, speaks Spanish, as well as English.

Culture, is another one of those words that has a lot of meanings, but still means a lot. There is such a thing as "pretty girl culture" for example. Women have a nefarious vaporous relationship with P.G.C. which I think, even though the words I've used (nefarious vaporous) are kindof interestingly chosen and not totally precisely exactly what I'm trying to say (more in sound than in ya know that other word that begins with sub), is a good example of almost everybody's relationship to a culture. That is that a culture is both us and outside of us. It is something that is totally whole and also only a part. It is not the earth and it is not the soul (actually I can't say this, earth and soul are such ridiculous terms, however I can say that there is an interesting connection in earth AND soul, funny I like that, so I can say this:) It is not earth and soul, but culture is as windswept and flat and total and strewn with strange-armed spiny creatures that give you that odd feeling of total completeness and complete totalness as any desert anywhere. That's it. It's anywhere. It's not everywhere.

Victor, Verne's boyfriend, a good man, speaks Spanish, as well as English. He is Puerto Rican. Well not really. I mean. Puerto Rican - American? Does that make sense. No. No. No. Definitely not!! So, ah forget it, it's so complicated. It's um. Well let's put it this way: Puerto Rico is somehow a part of the United States but is not a state. That "somehow" is kinda important. Victor, when he was younger, he's now 48, was a terrorist. He wasn't a terrorist. "All my friends were terrorists," was how he put it. They wanted, and he still does want, independence for Puerto Rico.

"I didn't place the bombs but if you asked me where they were I might have been able to tell you," Victor didn't wink but if he did wink there would have been exactly the same effect as his face was having currently.

She smiled.

Victor was talkin' on the train to a person he'd never met before. A woman. The train is the most romantic place in the world. And I am saying this banal phrase on purpose. The train is the most romantic place in the world. It's simply stated and it's true. In fact, quite frankly (these two words are always usually followed by the most hideous lies) the truth of it is gonna rise up 'n smite the lingering malaise of meaningless repetition of this phrase and give it meaning again. All praise the phrase! Gawd the train is romantic. There's the rhythm, the motion, the chug-a-chug-chugga. There's the interior, like a hotel room on wheels. There's the landscape changing like a movie made by surrealists with a Hollywood budget. And you can only see it through the slightly smudgy glass of slightly smudgy glass. There's the men and women in uniform, the conductors, who possess the most amazing kindof authority but have no way to abuse it. There's the screeching of power pulling you in one direction and one direction only: away.

Victor and the person he'd never met before, a woman, were bumping in the nondescript commuter car across from each other on somewhat lumpy seats. She was tall and pretty and shy and also in her 40's. She had a long grey skirt and a dully shimmering almost fuzzy black, perhaps very dark brown, sweater. It was hard to tell what her body was like. Yet the clothes weren't misshapen or ill-fitting or lumpy or oversized. They were very tasteful, with once again actual meaning to this phrase. That was the problem. That was the problem with very tasteful clothing, Victor thought. It was hard to tell what the body was like that was wearing them.

Bodies were important to Victor. But to keep on the meaning thing, what did that actually mean? He liked to talk about bodies and in a way look at them, but there were other things more important. How can I put this so it sounds like I'm telling the truth. How can I put this so I am telling the truth. Bodies were almost an excuse. He used bodies, talk of bodies, looking at bodies, touching bodies, as a cover, a pleasurable one a lot of the time, as a cover for his real purpose. His real purpose? His real purpose was to cheer people up. His real purpose was to cheer women up.

"I'm just not being able, being able to handle things at the moment."

It was Franklin. Franklin with her chin pushed into the blotter (blotter?) that her old desk, it was really old not "faux old," had as an accouterment. The restaurant she managed, SOCKS, had these touches, these flourishes, to provide the mounchers of steak with the appropriate ambience for the mounching of steak. SOCKS was a steakhouse. It had famous socks of famous people in glass cases. It was funny it was Franklin. Franklin with her chin in her blotter. It would really make more sense if it was Verne. Franklin was the kindof character that only exists in stories in the sense that she is the kindof character that doesn't exist. Or in an interesting thought, we, who do exist, that can exist, exist by making ourselves this

64

kindof character. This kindof character is the kindof character that never finds herself with her chin on her desk. Down. Outta control. Or maybe another way. This kindof character does put her chin on her desk. Does, occasionally, is, every so often, down, outta control. But we never think of them like that. They do it in front of us. It's not that we don't see them. Do it. But we come to them continuously. We come to them continuously with our problems. They're the stable ones. They're the ones that can help. They seem to be o.k. We forget immediately anytime we see them not the way we see them.

Verne never had her chin in a blotter. Of course she didn't have a blotter. She didn't have a desk. She was an assistant manager. Franklin was the manager. Dr. G.O. Best who owned SOCKS had just called SOCKS and had made Franklin cry. Franklin did not cry much, at all, I mean not to her boss. At least that's what everybody thought, including Franklin. That's what everybody said, including Franklin. But was it true? I dunno. She cries. More/less? than other people. I dunno. Right now she was, or had been. Now she had her chin in her blotter. Verne didn't know what to do. It was almost like, it was like, Verne couldn't see Franklin like this, didn't see Franklin like this. She started to talk to Franklin 'bout bottles of wine that needed to be ordered. Franklin elevated her chin from the blotter but kept it pushing forward, ya know juttin' out, her eyes, mascara racoon circles, were dewy, beautiful.

"Yes." She said.

In the suburban house of Brand Sammy, Brand Sammy was as usual not perplexed. Not perplexed was how she went through her day. It was sorta perplexing. She was so totally, fully, to the other side from being perplexed, that her face looked kinda perplexed. It was like since nothing perplexed her she was always being perplexed. Does this make any sense (am I always asking this question?). She had no way to properly parse life (ooh god, ooh god, I hate that last sentence). No way to make sense of it 'cause it always made sense. Even on the craziest nights, the craziest bizarrest nights, the strangest weirdest, most notoriously out-of-wack occurrences, didn't make anything occur to her that anything was in any way, perplexing. So the next day, following one of these evenings, one of the most wacked out nights you can possibly think of, she was looking out her kitchen window holding a long tall wide thick wine glass fulla wine, just some wine that was sittin' 'round, it was good tastin', it was good ya know, lookin' out at her wading pool that her boyfriend, who also was a good man, had put in her garden, and was thinkin' not 'bout much, not 'bout anything. She was worried. Yeah, she had been worried. She was still kinda worried. But she wasn't as worried. She wasn't really worried now. She wasn't as worried as she had been last night. And she certainly wasn't perplexed.

Slope was Canadian. From the English speakin' part, thus the expression, "Canadian." Well he wasn't Canadian. He was American (United States of) now. He'd moved south (is it?) in North America. He'd married Franklin in what they joked was a "green card marriage." Slope was a successful person. He was called "the most successful lazy person in the history of the world," by Jesse James Joyce (J.J.J.), a young kid English painter of cartoons on walls. But lazy is an insulting word and Slope didn't like it. Or maybe he didn't didn't like it. He didn't like it when he heard it, when J.J.J. said it, but then he'd forget it. He was an easy-going guy our Slope. J.J.J. almost had an affair with Piper ("almost had an affair?") but didn't, so almost is appropriate. Affair is not appropriate. It's a stupid word. By the way stupid words, are words in my opinion, that aren't appropriate. 'Cause they don't sound right. Piper was a pretty girl. Oh boy. She was a lot older than J.J.J. Piper was from the South.

"Who the fuck da ya think you are J.J.J.?" Piper would say.

Victor was mad at Piper, not out out mad, like out-in-the-open mad, but that hidden sorta not hidden kinda bitchy way mad. It was the kinda mad that a handsome man has for a beautiful woman when she didn't succumb to his advances (lotsa inappropriate words here). Piper didn't need cheering up. She was very sad. She was very sad and her beauty was black and tan. Her beauty was a Guinness. She was married and sometimes the banns were bummers. She didn't need cheering up. She got married 'cause she needed cheering up. She needed somethinc else, maybe. Maybe, she needed a baby. Baby, maybe, she needed a baby. J.J.J. did not want a baby, he was young, blah, blah, blah. Probably a good idea was for her to have a baby with her husband. That would seem to make sense. Did she really want J.J.J.? What does that even mean to really want someone. Something was making her sad though. She was very sad. J.J.J. did cheer her up, but she didn't want cheering up. Why couldn't I cheer her up, Victor thought.

"Did I cheer you up?" J.J.J. asked.

"Who the fuck da ya think you are J.J.J.?" Piper said.

Victor met Verne when Victor was helping Slope to make a 'lil extra money doing a 'lil extra painting at the restaurant SOCKS where Slope's wife was the manager. Victor and Slope both worked for the same guy Knot. Knot won't appear in this story. And you won't find out where Slope and Victor work here. Verne hated Victor immediately when she saw him. O.k. not to be really really irritating but hate is the wrong word. What's the word, or better, what'd be the word for that thing when you kinda like someone so you hate them. That thing. That's the thing that Verne had when she saw Victor. Verne needed cheering up. Pushing away at Victor, even if it was only taking place in her own head, of course it did present itself in kindof hostile behavior towards Victor, like calling him "idiot" to his face in about the first three minutes she met him, made Victor like her.

"What are you an idiot?" She said to him after she stopped him from painting a molding that didn't need to be painted.

The first time that Verne and Victor did it was when Victor found out that Verne had been raped when she was younger. The first time people do it or are about to do it or are thinking about doing it or are talking about doing it or are in the middle of doing it is usually the first time people find out about things like that. Victor had heard it before and Verne had told it before. Not exactly this way. Although everybody is the same and societies create the friction that causes the need for the fiction that people are different, combinations of people are not the same. How it's separate, combinations of people and societies, is too troublesome for me to trouble with. Together, Victor and Verne, did make a difference. They made a combination that was different, than um, other combinations; other combinations in other places and times of other people, and other combinations of other places and times in their own lives. Although it was hard. It was hard to believe it was different. So you force believed it. You made yourself through talk, talk, talk to believe/say it was different. You didn't have to, 'cause it was different. Luckily, none of this matters.

Victor, a good man, was excellent at truth 'n consensus. Truth 'n consensus is the idea that truth is also a lie. When you are nagged by nagging naggs. When things seem not what they seem. When it seems that it's not really right, but it is right. Or you're not sure but you're sure. When you can't have orgasms from intercourse because you say you were raped when you were younger and tried your best when you were being raped and you succeeded to not have an orgasm, to not enjoy it, and so now you can't enjoy it, when you're not being raped, when you say that to someone, it's good when that someone is someone like Victor, a good man, someone who wants to cheer you up, someone who is good at truth 'n consensus, someone who can kinda make things o.k. by not really caring too much about the exact absolute exact absoluteness of everything.

"You cheer me up," Verne said soft sweaty not with an orgasm but with a sex flash of lovemaking closesivity.

"Ah, good," Victor said.

Slope and Franklin had to do their green card shit. Their green card shit, although I'm not sure of the details exactly, had to do, at least as far as they told me, with someone in a bureaucracy (and I'm trying not to use this expression in a bad way, like not using it as an expression, but as identification) meeting with them and making sure they were in love. That they weren't faking it. That they were really married. That they ... etc., etc., etc. What a job! Franklin always said that all anybody would have to do in order to believe they were really married would be to see the two of them in their mini-van, Slope driving, Franklin navigating, and uh, you can guess the rest.

J.J.J. and Piper almost had an affair. He was really annoying her. I suppose this is 'lil bit like Verne here, but different. Piper was a pretty girl. Not that Verne wasn't. Victor would say and believed that she was beautiful. He said it with that accent of his. That accent of his that Verne liked so much. He would say that about a lot of things. The word, "beautiful." He would say it with that accent of his. And he would say it about Verne. He would say:

"She's so beautiful."

Piper was a pretty girl. Sometimes pretty girls are beautiful sometimes they're not. They are all apart (not apart, I'm sorry, a part) of the pretty girl culture. Sometimes they have pretty girl disease (P.G.D.). Piper had pretty girl disease. She had P.G.D. For more on this, please refer to the next story. The next story is appropriately titled Pretty Girl Disease. Piper doesn't appear in it. Piper had brown hair, long, straight, brown, hair and a beautiful ass. "Her ass is so beautiful," Victor would say, but of course not to Verne, except maybe once when he was drunk. She did have a beautiful ass. There's a certain beauty to a woman's ass that is just so certain — so certain to get you hard. Curves are . . . it's all geometry isn't it. I mean what we like. Sexually. Ya know if you're gay or straight or whatever, boy or girl, etc., it has something to do with that, something with shape, something with the kind of shapely shapes you like that pulls your trigonometry. The shape of things that make you cum.

Piper was married and she was not married to J.J.J. J.J.J. was a young kid English painter of cartoons on walls. There's something about spray paint. There's something about spray paint, being able to use it, having it, being able to use it and having it, using it. All of this. There's something about spray paint. There's something sexy about spray paint. J.J.J. first saw Piper where she worked and he annoyed her. Then he would come to visit Piper where she worked and it would annoy her. He knew he was annoying her but he didn't know it. He kept visiting her and finding excuses (stupid phrase!!) to visit her. At her work. Not at her home. Piper was married. Piper was married and she was not married to J.J.J. Piper had pretty girl disease (P.G.D.). Piper and her husband had just bought an old run-down thing (a place to live) to fix-up and make it a place to live. To live. A place to live. To live. A place. Piper wanted a place to live, but that's not exactly what I mean, not that I know, or she knows, really, what I mean, or what she means.

Brand Sammy put her feet into the wading pool that her boyfriend, also a good man, had put in her garden. As the water was disturbed by her entrance so was the neighborhood by the . . . no I can't, I can't write this sentence this way. Let me say this. The wading pool had started a sortof revolution in her little neck of suburbia. Wading pools suddenly started going in everywhere. All sorts of all sorts of different kinds of different ways. There was, yes there was, a wading pool mania. Notes were compared. Catalogs consulted. Fences looked over. Money spent. Her boyfriend thought this was really hilarious, 'cause you know it was really hilarious. He didn't spend hardly anything for his wading pool. He put it in himself basically with odds and ends. Like the net that covered the pool from the falling leaves. That was nothing. He bought that at the five 'n dime (not that there is actually a store anymore any-where that is a five 'n dime but you understand). His neighbors were buying special like, well, special nets. That cost a bundle.

"That net is so beautiful," he said to one of his neighbors although he didn't really mean it, but still he wasn't really trying to be nasty.

For a brief second (what is briefer than a brief second) before they went out on their "date" J.J.J. and Piper lay together. You should always put "date" in quotes (why, why?, I dunno, you just should, should!!). It wasn't really a date (oh, that's why). It wasn't really a date because oh, one thing, Piper was mar-ried and J.J.J. wasn't. To her. Also they had a pretend reason to meet, it could have been the real reason, I don't know. The pretend reason or the real rea-son or whatever it was was that Piper needed some graphic help on a com-puter and J.J.J., well, J.J.J. would help. After they finished their work they were going to go out and have some dinner. After they finished their work and before they went out to have some dinner J.J.J. lay down on the bed in his room. He looked at Piper sittin' at the computer. She looked at him.

"Come here. Here. Come here." He said.

Without saying anything but I want this to be obvious, really obvious, she didn't say anything, she lay down next to J.J.J. Stiff, her back to him, he put his arms around her. That's it, for a few minutes. Then. Then they went out. They had Japanese food which is, you know what Japanese food is. Wooden bar. Saki. Fish. Not cooked. Green hot mustard. This was not a date. A "date." That's good because it sucked. It was not going well. But it sucked in a strange way. It wasn't really that bad. It was really kindof good. No it wasn't that. But it was something. There was something. They had to wait for a table. Then they didn't wait for a table and ate at the bar. Snuck ahead somehow in front of some other people on a strange scratched list that a waiter/manager made but didn't seem to have real names on it. Their part of the bar where they ate was also where food was put for the waiters to take to tables. It was cramped. Speaking of cramped, wait, I'll explain that in a sec. While they were waiting. While they were waiting . . . by the way to set this up better, Piper had some strange obsessive phone call thing to make, and she kept trying to make it, but could never get through. It wasn't to hubby. Hubby was out of town (what? yep.). It was someone, a girlfriend or somethinc, that was having a party, or something like that, or was housesitting somewhere nearby, or somethinc like that, anyway she was trying to reach her, or something like that. But she couldn't.

While she was trying once. In the phone booth, after dinner, trying again to have, ya know, figure out a place to go next. Whatever. What to do next, etc. There was a guy on the phone. She had to wait for the guy to get off the phone. She began to poke him. Then kinda flirt with him. She did flirt with him. Sorta hit his ass playfully. Then he got off the phone. She got on the phone. But she couldn't get through. To her friend. What would they do next. Her n' J.J.J. But this was after dinner. Right before dinner. Right when they were heading to the wooden bar to have their dinner, she didn't go to the wooden bar. J.J.J. went to the bar and Piper went to the bathroom. They had saki, as I said. It was hot. It was good. It made them feel. That's it basically not better or worse, made them feel, that's all. It got less hot. They got some more. They didn't really get very high but they felt the need to get really high. That's it, they felt the need. They kinda bickered. Sometimes they laughed. They liked each other I guess. In the middle of the dinner, or somewhere near the middle, she went to the bathroom. And then again before the dinner was over she went again. Then she told him. She was really upset. Upset is a good word, and it has to have the right meaning. She was upset. She had her period, she told him. She got it. Just.

Piper was the kinda girl that could have a beer for breakfast. She could, and did, sometimes, have a beer in her hand 24 hours a day. A beer in her hand and tight jeans on her butt. That was Piper. They left the restaurant with nowhere to go. Everything was kinda upset. The feeling that dare not speak its name was dare not speaking its name. J.J.J. was very young. Piper felt very old. J.J.J. got a glimpse of her beauty which was very powerful 'cause it was only a glimpse. He was carrying his skateboard with him. She hailed a cab. It was a peck. The kiss. O.k. more than a peck. Deep nothing. Shallow something. Something. She got in. He left on his skateboard. The taxi drove. She pushed her head out.

"Who the fuck da ya think you are J.J.J.?"

Victor was mad at J.J.J. Yeah. Yeah. Yeah. He wasn't mad at J.J.J. He was more. Um. You know the drill. Victor was mad at J.J.J., not out out mad, like out-in-the-open mad, but that hidden sorta not hidden kinda bitchy way mad. It was the kinda mad that a handsome man has for an attractive younger guy when a beautiful woman who didn't succumb to his advances succumbs to his advances. He wasn't mad at J.J.J. but he gave J.J.J. sarcastic eye-brow raises when ever he saw J.J.J. and Piper together which wasn't a lot. I mean especially not alone. I mean J.J.J. and Piper alone. There was always a group. You know how groups get together. Groups, families, friends, workers, bowlers, lynch mobs, ya know. There was this group that got together that sometimes included J.J.J., Piper, and Victor and Verne, Franklin, Slope and others, and sometimes Piper's husband too. It was a big group and so there wasn't anything obvious about J.J.J. and Piper. Not not that there was anything obvious about J.J.J. and Piper anyway really. They had nothing to be obvious or not obvious about. Victor would always give them these looks, well to him, to J.J.J., sarcastic eye raises, 'cause Victor thought he knew better, and probably did, about what was going on, with things like that, things that were going on, or not going on.

Brand Sammy's boyfriend was very calm (is calm and very calm the same thing? no.) and started up the car. Brand Sammy's daughter, she was divorced, Brand Sammy was, so was the daughter, Brand Sammy's daughter's daughter, her grandchild inotherwords, Brand Sammy's granddaughter, a baby, was sick. The baby had eaten some pills that Brand Sammy's daughter's friends had laying 'round da house. They had these pills laying 'round da house?! Laying 'round da house? LAYING 'ROUND DA HOUSE?! Maybe it wasn't Brand Sammy's daughter's friends. Maybe it wasn't Brand Sammy's daughter's friends who left the pills laying 'round da house. Maybe it was Brand Sammy's daughter's (ex) husband's friends who left the pills laying round da house. Whatever.

She was worried. Yeah, she had been worried. She was still kinda worried. But she wasn't as worried. She wasn't really worried now. She wasn't as worried as she had been last night. And she certainly wasn't perplexed. This was the day after. The baby was o.k. There was a lot of questions. Of course. There was. There were? Brand Sammy was looking out her kitchen window holding a long tall wide thick wine glass fulla wine, just some wine that was sittin' 'round, it was good tastin', it was good ya know, lookin' out at her wading pool that her boyfriend, who also was a good man, had put in her garden, and was thinkin' not 'bout much, not 'bout anything. Her boyfriend, the good man, came up to her and I wish I could say put his arm around her. Because he did. He did put his arm around her. But I can't say that. I can't say that because if I did say that, it would sound inappropriate. Not the action, not the gesture, not the . . . not the, you get it, it was fine, him, doing that to her. But it wouldn't sound right. You wouldn't see it right. It would just be talk. What it meant. And even that is stupid. When meaning becomes meant (I don't really know what I just said there, really). The thing is the thing is this. He cheered her up. Her boyfriend. Her boyfriend came up to her and put his arm around her and it cheered her up.

"Oh," she said.

If you heard the way she said it, you'd um, you'd see.

The mania resides in a special place. The only possible way to use the word special is in a sentence where mania resides. Mania is the theory of everything. Or. Not the theory. But is. Is. But mania burns. And burning ends. And in the mania is also its inability to reproduce. It will always exist. But never repeat. It will always exist. But never repeat. Flame is singular, different. Diffidence, the art of ignoring the mania, is important. The mania resides in a special place because as everything it locks the jaw of speaking which is nothing. Speaking is nothing but without speaking we cannot say "I love you." I cannot say it. When I write it it looks dumb. I do. I do. I do. I do believe the mania. I do believe the mania resides in a special place. That's all I can say.

There was this group that got together that sometimes included J.J.J., Piper, and Victor and Verne, Franklin, Slope and others, and sometimes Piper's husband too. It was a big group, mixed up, and various variousness. Some people worked here or there, some people knew people from people that worked here or there or from some people that knew people. Also the job where Victor and Slope worked, and where Knot worked and managed, along with Deer (yes, Deer!, his father and mother named him after a deer), well on that job, a lot of people passed through. As I told you, I'm not going to tell you yet, where Victor and Slope worked, or where Knot and Deer managed. At this place, Ivy was getting married. Well o.k. she wasn't getting married at this place, but she worked at the place, along with (yeah, yeah, yeah, Victor, Slope, Knot, Deer and some others) and she was getting married. So like everybody was invited. Not everybody but you know. Well actually a lot of people were. A lot of people were invited. Not everybody could come. Not everybody could come for various reasons. This big group did go. Tho. J.J.J., Piper, and Victor and Verne, Franklin, Slope and others, and Piper's husband too. Knot and Deer too. Although Knot won't appear in this story, not even passing through.

About passing through, I'd just like to pass through this. The details, and the people, that appear in these stories might have a familiar ring to the (very) few people that they have a familiar ring to. These people are people I know, some of these people, many of these people are my friends. That is the people that might find the details to have a familiar ring to them. Not the people in the stories. The people in the stories are not my friends. Not that they couldn't be if they were real. But they're not real. Sometimes I take the details of people I know, and a lot of times I play with names and stuff, but it is almost like naming a turnpike or somethinc. (What is a turnpike? For that matter, what is a thoroughfare? Actually I think I know what a thoroughfare is, I think.) There's an honoraryness to this, and arbitraryness. I want to say something that has nothing to do with the details I'm using to say them with. The coathanger is important not the coat. If you recognize your coat in these stories or somebody else's coat, think again you're not actually recognizing anything. The humane beans, whose coats I've stolen, are alive and well, and very very different than the fictional characters I've hung their coats on.

"We're off to see a wedding! A wonderful, wonderful, wedding."

And someone added:

"That's odd!!"

"Odd that we're going to a wedding or that the wedding is odd, which one?"

"I was trying to make it sound like the song, you know, odd, Oz, etc."

"Oh."

There's about 18 people in Slope's minivan. He's driving and Franklin's navigating. He's a good driver for what it's worth. What is it worth? There's uncomfortable groupings and pairings. Verne is not there. How do you form an uncomfortable grouping and pairing when you're not there. Very easily. (However, to form a comfortable groping and panting you would have to be there.) Of her current feud, and by this I would just like to make perfectly clear to the best of my recollection that I am not a crook in saying that we are going to bomb Hanoi to smithereens that current feud does not mean that there was only one feud going on at this moment. Verne was not a serial feudist. But she kept many harsh and twisting juggling batons of feuds in the air and in the wings ready to once again ascend the air at any given moment. A given moment. You know I'd like to be given a moment. 'Scuse me buddy, hey buddy, could you give me a moment. Jus' a moment. A moment's moment.

Movement, which is what a car, even the new-fangled big-fanged muthas that patrol the highways like tanks and you almost don't even feel like you're on the road, does, does get one moving. And the 18 or so people were moving. Deer was there, and like I was saying, he was oddly partnered with the absent Verne, who was currently involved in a feud with him. She wasn't going to the wedding because he was going. She wasn't!! He wasn't going to the wedding either if she was going but then she wasn't going so he was going. Victor was there too but he didn't want to be. He didn't want to go because he had to be somewhere else and anyway what did it matter if Verne wasn't going. Anyway he couldn't go even if Verne, his girlfriend, was going, because he had to be somewhere else. The only reason he was going was because Ivy made him by making him cheer her up by agreeing to go. Slope, as I said, was going 'cause he was driving the van. He was going pretty good. Until. Until the first direction on the list of directions that Franklin had in her hand came up.

"We're supposed to turn here. We're supposed to turn here! We're supposed to turn here!!"

Slope turned there, very quickly 'cause he had to.

Brand Sammy's boyfriend had mentioned something about him being late. It didn't really bother her really, o.k., really, sorta, kinda, well, o.k., maybe, a little. It bothered her a little. She only got to see him on the weekends afterall. Afterall that wasn't a lot. That wasn't a lot to see a person. To expect. To expect a person. But she did expect him. And he did expect her. I mean respect her. He was there. He did come always. Sometimes. Very very rarely. Sometimes very, very rarely he would have something he would have to do. Sometimes he wouldn't be able to come. But that was very rare. Rarely, rare. This time. This time might not be one of those times, 'cause he just said he might be late, come late Saturday night instead of the morning or Friday night. He still was coming. Afterall.

Piper, in the backseat, with her husband, and J.J.J., another odd grouping, began to cry out to pee. I gotta pee. I gotta pee. Let me pee. I need to pee. Time to pee. Let's stop to pee. I need to pee pee. Slope pulled the ton of steel into a parking lot of a Taco Bell. Piper's husband stayed in the van and thought. He remembered this one time he had had with Piper before, before ya know they got married. Not that they weren't ever really not married ya see. They got together right away and it was good. But this time he remembered. He thought about it now. While his wife was pee-peeing:

It was her friend. This strange chick. Not really though. Underneath. Normal as all fuck. That was the thing. The thing thing thing thing – THING. Try to find the underbelly of the beast and all you get is the underbelly of the beast. We are kindof soppy. All of us. How to find sensuous cutting. Sensuous cutting among the soup? Soap. She was clean too. Scrubbed, ivory, flakey, clean. She came across as dirty, dirty as in distraught, 'cause she was clean. That's the thing 'bout the sensuous cutting, the serious, sensuous cutting. When we see one maybe who has. When we see one maybe who has cut from the vine and hung the grape-colored leafless strands on the high bay windows greying out the light. When we've seen these. We think. My gawd how dirty. Not dirty like we think it. Like we think it 'cause we're told it. We really think it. What a shame. What a pity. We feel this. They just seem distraught. Who wants to seem distraught.

She was wearing a wig, made of orange fake pigeon feathers (but pretty real looking for orange fake pigeon feathers). She was talking to two fucking idiots. My wife was jus' sittin' there massaging her beer glass. The two fucking idiots were converting their pity their shame into some kindof commodity, some kindof method of exchange. They were gonna own my wife's friend if they could. Show her the light of slavation. I walked up to the table and heard what they were saying. Respect yourself or some shit. I let loose. A cannon of bang. Shut the fuck up, I said. Just shut the fuck up. She respects herself plenty. And you people are shit. And then I got a big visual whiff of that wig again, and I just fuckin' cracked up. My wife too, I mean my girlfriend then whatever, and her friend. We laughed and the idiots left.

Later she scored some heroin for us, she'd gotten beaten up a couple of weeks ago doing it, but this time it was o.k., she could do shit like that. We went back to my place and all lay on the bed. She was really ugly. She was. Strange. I don't mean ugly in a strange way. She was just ugly. She was really normal too. She just was. It was dark. The lights out in my room. My girlfriend in my arms, and she began touching my dick. Not my girlfriend, my girlfriend's friend. It felt good but I had her stop.

82

"You gotta keep going, you 'just gotta keep going," no one was saying this.

They were doing it. They had been going and they were going. They'd rest-stopped. They'd food-stopped. They'd rest-stopped and food-stopped. They'd heard noises and seen new things. Outof windows. Outof the van. Franklin and Slope had argued. Victor drank out of a flask. J.J.J. had giggled. Piper's husband had thought. Piper had made J.J.J. giggle but then sorta tried not to, sorta. Deer whistled. The whole moving parade of engines, plastic, and rubber moved. They were a part of it. Going. Going. Going on. Their friend, Ivy, was getting married. They were tired when the van pulled in. They'd arrived. They were tired in that way that only a "they" can get when a "they" arrives. Together. Enmasse. Everybody was tired.

"I'm tired," Slope said.

"You've been driving, Honey," Franklin said.

Deer had his own room. J.J.J. was sharing with Victor. Franklin and Slope had their own room. Piper and her husband were together in another. The smell in Piper and her husband's room was strong. Not strong 'zacktly, but bad.

"A skunk?" Slope had said when he smelled it.

But it wasn't. It was just bad. A bad, bad, smell. It was a good room though.

Besides the smell. Piper felt close a little bit allofasudden, maybe. Close to him. Close to her husband. Sexy almost. Sexy. Yes. It's so funny isn't it. Ha, ha, ha. When we, or how we, or what we, when we, feel sexy. A hotel room. Even if it smells bad, really, really, bad, but is still kinda cool, I mean just like a hotel room, is so cool, as far as, well you know: PEOPLE LIKE TO FUCK IN HOTELS. Of course it could've been just the smell. I mean the smell could've been what was doing it. It's amazing, funny, ha-ha, what um, ya know, um, get's people going. ("You gotta keep going, you 'just gotta keep going.") This time Piper and her husband, well, from this time, anyway, she got, you know, um, pregnant, then, right here, I mean in the bad smelling hotel room just after, just after, they'd arrived. Pregnant, yup, Piper.

J.J.J. who'd almost had an affair with Piper was off in his room that he was sharing with Victor getting ready for the Wedding. He actually had some-thinc to get ready for. He had been asked to do a live cartoon, a performance, well, art, during the ceremony. He would begin the thing. A large, big, big, large, ok not that large, banner, flag, sheet kindof thing, would drape, hang, fly, well sorta like be there, ya know, 'tween two big poles, flappin', that's right flappin', in the breeziness. He would paint on it, and what he would paint, that would be, that would be the backdrop for the rest of the thing. In his room, Victor had left somewhere, J.J.J. was busy. J.J.J. was busy sketching.

Different things happened to him in different ways at different times, but in this case different is not the right word. He wasn't different when he was sketching. When he was busy. Furious is a word that could be used here:

busy, furious, sketching etc. And it might even be o.k. Furiously sketching. Yeah so maybe it's o.k. He felt contained by the giant container that he couldn't be contained by. Ya know? (Probably not.) Actually, you know probably yes. The thing is he felt this big thing usually. And this big thing that he felt usually wasn't that usual. But it was usual that he felt it. Da ya know what I'm saying. So when he drew. When he drew. So when he drew, nancy, (huh?), when he drew, he um. He drew.

When he drew he drew. And this was a moment, one of those things, um. He uh. Yeah uh. Uh. Uh. Um. He . . . It was okay.

It was o.k. Brand Sammy thought to herself (who else can you think to really?). It was o.k. Something strange was happening (brrrrrrrr!). Something perplexing. Can I be getting perplexed, she thought to herself. Of course she didn't. She didn't think that to herself. That would be ridiculous. She did wonder, sorta. She did wonder sorta what she was feeling. Sorta. The wine, a new bottle, she'd bought it this morning, and already opened it (how else was she going to drink it), in her glass lapping 'gainst the sides. It was o.k. right. Things. The way she lived. She wasn't deep. She said that deeply. It's amazing how people say that, say anything, say things like that 'bout themselves. They like it. You sum yourself up. It's like. It feels good. You feel real. This is, ya know. I am, right? But is it. Right. Right? She wasn't deep, was she? No. She was deep. I think. I don't even know what deep means. She was a good woman. I don't even know what that means.

But I said it. Morality as a language loses what it is. At the hospital her gentleness pervaded. At the hospital her gentleness pervaded. They had left pills around. It doesn't even matter who. And her baby granddaughter had taken the pills. Eaten the pills. Take, is for adults. Eaten the pills. And got sick. They had to go to the hospital. Her good man, her boyfriend, had calmly drove the car. Calmly. And got them there. There were lots of worries. What does deep mean. There were lots of worries. What does deep mean. At the hospital her gentleness pervaded. At the hospital her gentleness prevailed.

Some people say you know when you get pregnant. I mean when it happens. The minute, less than a minute, it happens. Some people do know, or say they knew, or did know, or some people say they didn't know, or maybe they did know, or didn't think about it, or maybe they didn't know. Maybe nobody knows. Piper was lying next to her husband and somethinc had happened.

And together they did somethinc. And that was what made somethinc. Later. Later could be felt then.

Deer had his own room. He thought about getting a drink. He thought about getting a drink with Victor. He thought about getting a drink with Victor and then he thought about not getting a drink with Victor. He thought about not getting a drink with Victor because even though thinking about gettin' a drink with Victor was a good thought it was also a bad thought. It was also a bad thought because Victor 'n Verne were ya know, and um, Deer and Verne were, well, exactly. So he wasn't gonna go drink with Victor. Deer had his own room. He thought about getting a drink.

Victor was having a drink. A drink was having Victor. They had a relationship. Together. They felt right. Victor was having a drink with Slope and Franklin. Slope was happier now. Then again, he was pretty happy anyways. He was happier now then right when they first arrived, when he was tired, when he had been driving. He was caring, Slope, that's why he was happy. Or let me put this this way. He wasn't happy. But he seemed happy. He seemed happy 'cause he was caring. He cared about other people. He knew they liked him to seem happy. It almost made him happy. Sometimes it made him angry. Angry. ANGRY AT FRANKLIN.

Victor was tense. The past a long future for him that he always tried to forget. He seemed to be this way before. In this type of thing. Always in this type of thing. But this type of thing was even stranger, or maybe this is just a matter of degree. Victor didn't want to go to the wedding. He didn't want to go to the wedding because he had to be somewhere else and anyway what did it matter if Verne wasn't going. Anyway he didn't want to go even if Verne his girlfriend, could go, because he had to be somewhere else. The only reason he came was because Ivy made him by making him cheer her up by agreeing to go.

He had to go. Go. Go. Go.

As soon as the ceremony was over.

The wedding was the most beautiful thing ever in the whole world there ever was ever. Everything was just like wow. It was just wow. It all worked ya know. Like things just worked. Like the weather. The weather worked. Well worked isn't right. The weather did its thing and that's not work that's somethinc else. Like, um, special. The weather was special. The weather was a special delivery from, whatever. It was beautiful. The day. The sun. The leaves. The colors but not just that, how they decided to fall. Like they were choreographed. The leaves and their colors knew when to take off, knew the time to take off, knew how to take off and in what order. They fell as the b 'n b (bed and breakfast, bride and groom) stood there sta-bilized by glory. The balance that the chaotic accident of perfection brings out of balance. The shooting star against the boring sky.

Afterwards somethinc happened afterwards. But before that somethinc happened beforewards.

Verne showed. Just as the first words were spoken. Just as J.J.J. began his crazy spraypaint performance painting his madcap banner proclaiming the soft indestructibility of love. Just as the first leaf took its leap. Just as all this, Verne showed. She had decided to come afterall. Victor was going to be there, and why shouldn't she. Sure. Yeah. Right. That giant duck of a per-son that had quacked his last quack in her book, Deer, was there, but yeah, but so what. Yeah. Sure. Right. She has every right to be there. She will be there. Too. So there. Dressed in a warm, brown, maleish suit she strode over the hill and down (not really down, it's a real gradual hill) into the garden of the B 'n B where the B 'n B were. Victor felt her, saw her, felt/saw her, first.

"Verne." His lips softly saying her name drowsily automatic. "She's here."

Slope was up taking pictures and moved around to get a snap of her coming to a seat behind Victor.

"Hiya Verne," Slope said.

"Hey girl!," Franklin smoothed, she had known, the possibility, they'd talked 'bout it, she'd really encouraged her, really told her, she should really, really should, come.

The ceremony ended and Victor left.

"Why are you leaving. I don't understand. I just got here. And."

"Verne, I have to go, you know that." And,

"You looked beautiful coming up, um, down that hill you know."

To find the key, to figure it out, to think how it works, to know how it works, some kinda magic, but magic based on an understanding, a learning, through experience to know: this is something that Victor always avoided.

"I didn't place the bombs but if you asked me where they were I might have been able to tell you," Victor didn't wink but if he did wink there would have been exactly the same effect as his face was having currently.

She smiled.

Victor was talkin' on the train to a person he'd never met before. A woman. The train is the most romantic place in the world. And I am saying this banal phrase on purpose. The train is the most romantic place in the world. He said goodbye to the woman. Smiled. Got off the train. In the suburbs. He'd left the wedding. He'd made it here. She was waiting for him. He'd called and told her what time he'd arrive, what train he was taking. She was there. With her car. Victor got in and drove.

"Hi, Brand, honey. You look beautiful."

"You're a good man, Victor," Brand Sammy said smiling, cheered up, "you're a good man."

She felt a kindof bubble a soft soap bubble roll bobb up and down her arms

PRETTY GIRL DISEASE

Ivy who worked in a hotel (and as a chef in a restaurant!) had a cousin, Palace, who worked in a word processing department of a law firm, and fuck, she was pretty. She'd come into work, hurry into the Center (word processing that is), put her stuff down and hurry out. She was the first one in, well taking over for the night shift, but she'd only be in for that second and then she'd be out again. There wasn't really anything to do in the morning, I mean right away, and if there was, shit, she didn't want to do it. Who would want to do it. She was just honest 'bout it that's all. She'd do it. I mean she did it if she had to. But she didn't like to. And most of the time she'd find some way out. The cute white boy that worked the night shift she'd really flirt with, but not really, 'cause she wasn't ready quite yet. She had some stuff to do, then she'd come back and flirt.

Then again when she was ready she didn't really flirt. I mean she did really but not really. He was a little scary this white boy, strange, but sexy, and um, but ya know, she was kinda tired of that too. She hadn't had sex in a year, over a year. That was alright. She knew like her girlfriend at work who was like married well she had to put out I mean that was like all. She had to do it. That's all. She didn't want to or nuthinc. You know. But she did. Well she didn't have to, Palace didn't, so why should she. Still it wasn't like things didn't occur to her occasionally 'n shit, ya know, jus' stuff, feelings 'n stuff, that's all, things.

She was sorta seeing this guy, ya know, jus' seeing him. Nothing was happening or anything yet, and that was fine by her. Actually, it was funny,
there was this one time, she was ready, she was all set 'n stuff, she, well, I
dunno, it just didn't happen. He came on to her too strong, like too buck
wild, and, he like made her all prepared for what was going to happen, and
she knew what was going to happen, she didn't need to get all prepared, he
should've just done it. That's all. Gently 'n everything, but just done it. He
turned off the lights, he turned music on, he looked at her in this certain
way. That was wrong. But she liked him, and everything, good enuff. Still.
Could happen again. She was taking her time. She wasn't going to rush into
anything. That was all. You know. Take it easy. Take it slow.

When she'd rush in to the Center and rush back out first thing in the morning, barely laying her bag down (and what a bag, designer, beautiful, leather,
with the logo in full effect), but taking her purse, where was she actually
going to? Well where she was actually going to was the bathroom. Not to
go to the bathroom, she'd done that before she left the house, but to use the
mirror. You could say it was a ritual because it was a ritual. She'd slowly,
carefully, make-up her face, and check out her body, which was um, uh,
yeah, ah, something. She was a small girl, "petite," which was her size, and
the floor and store, in the malls, boutiques, and department stores where
she'd shop. Not that that was the only place she'd shop, she liked catalogs
too, but that's not what I mean, what I mean is she didn't like to be sec-
tioned off either, she didn't really think of herself as small, really, she was-
n't, she was but, um, not like ah, yeah, um, in um, ah, uh, certain places.

Her last boyfriend was a cop. And the thing was, the thing was, she could never get it right. I mean not that she could never get it right. It never seemed to get right. She wanted to be one thing to one person. She didn't want to say that right away. Let it be known. Known. It was almost like (it was! like) she wanted them to figure it out. And they couldn't, didn't, or whatever. It's like Marty in the mailroom, he'd come by, slidin' 'round, he was sweet really, but he couldn't let that out. She wasn't that you know whatever. She wasn't that special. Of course she was. But she wanted some kind of combination. I'm special. I'm special, yeah o.k., but I'm also there. You know, be there with me. "I'll be there. I'll be there." That's all. In the mailroom, every Friday in the afternoon they'd play the same song, that went like this, somethinc like this: "I Don't Wanna Work, I Wanna Bang On The Drum All Day."

She'd go in there, chill with Marty, hang out with the fellahs. It was fun, ya know, it was relaxed. But don't let Marty think nothinc, no, no, no. I mean not that he couldn't. She didn't really mind him thinkin'. She just. He was-n't for her. She knew he liked him. It was obvious. She let him have some sometimes. Not some. Not anything. She got all nice lookin' n' stuff. She always did. When she was in there. Gave him a little smile every so often. Made him happy. He knew what wuz up. She knew what wuz up. She had booty and breasts. And for a tiny girl. Whoooo boy! She worked it in the mailroom. And the fellahs finished up their work and went home.

Home for Palace was her Mom's house. She hadn't moved since a kid. She was 29. Okay she was thirty. She didn't lie about her age. She was thirty and she knew it. I'm thirty she said. Pretty girls have confidence. It's never that that gets them down. They don't know it really. If you asked them, do you have confidence, they might say yes, they might say no. Sometimes they get really down, and they say I'm so insecure, I'm so insecure, but they're not, that's not it. Pretty girls are pretty. They are pretty damn pretty. People are pretty nice to them 'cause they're pretty. People are pretty not nice to them 'cause they're pretty. But no one ever says why they're being nice, or not nice. It's a great big wide large huge, you know, big, whatever, huge, large, taboo. You know to say things like that. To mention it. To say, ah, she's a pretty girl, so my behavior is changed because of it. I mean you ignore it right. Or you come on to it. Anyway, how you do it, you front. You don't fess up. You don't say hey, wow, that's a pretty girl, you're a pretty girl, I'm going to treat you in a certain way 'cause you're a pretty girl. And especially pretty girls can't say it. Can't say it. What are you like? Oh, I'm a pretty girl.

The cute white boy was like she's a pretty girl. Shit fuck damn god ooh. You're a pretty girl, he said, and right away she got like weird. He can't say that. Like that. I'm a pretty girl. What da hell does he mean. Coming out right out right out out like that. But then later on she thought about it: "I am a pretty girl."

She had smoked for awhile and she was stopping now. It was sorta I guess a kinda part of the general thing of self-improvement that she was involved in. Self-improvement was all well and good and shit but shit she was jittery. She didn't even smoke that much damnit. She didn't even know what was real anyway. Fuck self-improvement. Then she got all quiet. Thirty, being thirty, made you jittery anyway. It all seemed to go and not very slow. It was a year now. More than a year. Since, you know, since. She was alright with that. She was upset. Not that anybody would know. Not that anybody would know outside. On the outside. Know she was upset. But she was. She didn't even know if she was.

She did the same thing everyday. She'd go to work. Rush. She was almost always sometimes late. Jump in, don't wait, put stuff down, cause she wanted to do her bidness, get her face together, before, well before she talked to anyone. She could be comfortable after. It was important to be comfortable, relaxed. Relaxed. She wasn't that relaxed. Maybe she was, you know, not relaxed. She liked to chill 'n everything but maybe she didn't. She smoked weed, have a few occasionally, drink like Melon Balls or Long Island Ice Teas, but really only one; those Ice Teas could mess you up. She did it less and less though. She didn't really go out. She was never that big on going out anyway. Hangin' 'round the way. She went home, thought about stuff. Whatever.

She loved to shop. That was her thing. That was it. Read catalogs. Spend money. That was it. She loved it. I do. She said. I do love to spend money. She liked. She liked nice things. That was one thing. That was one thing why she didn't move out of her mother's. She paid no rent. She had mo' money. She had mo' money to spend. I like it. That's all. I do. She did look good. She didn't like to wear a lot of the same stuff. She didn't see something on somebody else and then wear it. Sometimes in the magazines she'd see something, but never like a whole outfit or anything. She'd mix 'n match, pick her stuff out, different designers, then come up with different stuff to wear everyday. She prided herself on that. On making an effort. It was like, sometimes, she didn't know. She did not know, what wuz up with other people, the way they came to work.

I mean not that she didn't have her problems with that. She dressed really nice, but it was her idea of really nice. Her supervisor, complained, made a fuss a couple of times. Anyway they did not get along anyway. Palace had been there longer than her, almost 8 years, yeah, 8 years now, and, I don't know, why did she need a supervisor anyhow. You know dressing like an old bag. She could tell her how to dress, 'cmon. There was a dress code, and she couldn't wear jeans. But jeans, c'mon, she didn't wear jeans. She wore designer jeans. They were tight yeah and they look good on her. So what. Jeez, she didn't look like an old bag.

One day she came in in the morning, and she didn't flirt with the cute white boy, and she didn't go into the bathroom and make-up her face, she had done it at home. She had heard some news the night before. The night before she had heard some news. She did not want to be at work, but she didn't not want to be at work in the same way she usually didn't not want to be at work.

The cute white boy started up wit' his stuff and she jus' looked at him. Plain 'n simple. Not now.

"Didya hear about Alice?"

"No. What. No."

"Her son killed hisself."

For awhile they were worried 'bout Alice, and that awhile lasted a long time. Alice stopped working in the Word Processing Center.

Soon tho Palace and the cute white boy were flirting again. He told her about the car he took to get home the day before. You see they got a free car the word processors to take them home if they worked weird shifts like the one the cute white boy worked (the "graveyard"). The night before (the morning before really) he'd flirted with Palace and then he got in his car. It was pouring, rain emptying bucketing from the sky, he got in his car, and the driver was crying. Tears dropping down his hard cheeks just like the rain was falling outside the car. He'd gotten a ticket. For waiting. Which of course wuz what he wuz s'pposed to do. But still he wuzn't s'pposed to too. Not according to the cops. They had quotas ya see. It was near election. And right before election, ya see the cops were told not to really give tickets, so that people wouldn't take it out on the current pols at the polls. But they still had their quotas to fill. So right near election, before they stopped, they did it big time, and of course after election. So they would ticket things that they might not otherwise ticket. Like drivers of car services waiting, not parking, for their customers/clients to come out.

The cute white boy's driver was crying, and then he took off. Driving in the rain, a gray dank morning, water everywhere, sloppy streets, and drooling rooftops, and drenching skies, his tires and windshield wet, he concentrated, agitated, and tried. He started across a green light and a big car broke its light trying to beat the startup of traffic and hit the cute white boy's driver's car and turned 'round and took off.

"Aeiyyayakdfjidyeeeeeeeeee"! The cute white boy's driver yelled.

"Get him," the cute white boy said.

In the slop from the heavens someone from another country from his own country in his own country kinda an anonymous ticketed man tears dried took off after someone that had took off. He chased him.

"Get him, get him, get him!"

Swerving, derving, dwerving, slithering through slow cars, lane moving, fast, the one, the one he was chasing made another quick turn, so he had to follow.

BOOM.

His quick turn, his following quick turn, was not quick 'nuff. He bounced up and onto the sidewalk and into some scaffolding, wet and slithering, against a building being built.

"How are you. Are you o.k.?"

"Car no work."

Vroom. Vroom.

"Car no work."

Palace was in hysterics hearing this story, part pretend part real, hysterics. Which Everything Is. Part real. Part pretend. When you're laughing you're also laughing, laughing. Aware that you're laughing, doing it, pushing it out. But it's not exactly an intersection, but it is, when pretend and real meet. You have . . .

She felt a kindof bubble a soft soap bubble roll bobb up and down her arms 'round her neck underneath her chin in 'n out of her ears on her forehead down her nose tease her nostril stay perfect and round in between the space her lips make when they close but still only barely touch. She kissed the bubble and her mouth became moist and even slightly soapy. Her eyelids flashed and her eyes looked. He looked back.

A little bit of a fear, o.k. a great big of a fear, then took. Hold. She could feel herself shake but she didn't actually do it. She. She. She. The badly plastic phone alarmed.

"Word Processing. Hello."

She got on the phone wit' her girlfriend at home, later.

"Who you doing. I can't believe it. Really."

Her girlfriend was doing a ballplayer. She didn't really understand her girl-friend. She was crazy 'n shit. She always had this or that going. A lot of girls didn't like her. Said she was sleazy. But ya know, so what, really. But ya know she jus' fucked 'round like crazy. She was crazy. No question. No doubt. She was alright too. She had orgasms like easily 'n stuff n' shit. You know she said she wouldn't be wit' a guy if he couldn't get her off. And um, she did some wild shit. Took Ecstasy and went to like parties where every-body switched partners 'n everything. Like she went to this party and she didn't like know this was going on 'n stuff and she liked this one guy and then he like went into the bathroom with another girl and then this girl came out and then said like now it's your turn to go and she didn't under-stand but then she went in and the girl stayed too 'n everything. And she had sex this one time, her girlfriend, on an airplane. She went down on her boyfriend right there in the plane, also in the bathroom. She like, well like, Palace, she liked to go the bathroom, A-LONE.

Palace was talkin' to her girlfriend on the phone looking into a very clean, her room in her mother's house was very clean, full length mirror. She was lookin' at herself up 'n down, sorta listening or hearing, she definitely was hearing but not exactly listening, the drama of her girlfriend's current thing with this big money-making big guy (his tabloid nickname was "Xtra

102

Large"). She liked what she looked like in her clean mirror. She did. She was petite yeah but she thought that was kinda nice yeah. She was thirty but she might even have looked better than she ever did. She took care of herself. She did wear a lot of makeup, but she always did, and it wasn't like she wore makeup like that it was obvious or nothinc, she wasn't into that look! Her skin was nice, the browns beautiful, and her eyes, her eyes, yeah, her eyes sparkled.

She got off the phone. She lay on the peach comforter. She picked up her fuzzy dinosaur and began to smooth out its almost sheep dog like mane. She thought about her friend at work, this gay guy, not that tall but kinda built, and handsome. She thought about how she could get so physical with him. About how she would push up against him. And sit in his lap. And how he'd put his strong arms around her. How he'd squeeze her. How he would sometimes almost kinda grab her. How it kinda made her feel good. Like good. Ya know. Good. Like good. Good. Good, down there. Good down there at the top of her legs, 'round from her ass. She could tell he felt good too sometimes. She knew he had a kid, but that happened a long time ago. Actually she could sometimes be physical with Marty too. Marty, phuet! What's up wit' him really. He should just come out sometimes and say somethinc. 'Stead of all that stuff. All that slidin' 'round. Still he was kinda fine.

The poems began to appear on her desk, her very clean desk, one Monday morning. She had a very clean desk. She had a thing 'bout her very clean desk. Lots of people used her very clean desk when she wasn't there. That's the way a Word Processing Center in a law firm works. Lawyers, for rea-sons (change that to Lawyers, for reasons **seemingly**) Lawyers, for reasons seemingly obscure to be found somewhere (change that to be **possibly** found) to be possibly found somewhere in the obscure (change that to **somewhat** obscure) Lawyers, for reasons seemingly obscure to be possibly found somewhere in the somewhat obscure annals (add **(both researched and unresearched)**) in the somewhat obscure annals (both researched and unresearched) of time and history of social standing and human factors have developed a system (implied and structured) that is in essence (**(its essence as defined as its base and implied purposeful (ital) purpose)**) have developed a system (implied and structured) that is in essence (its essence as defined as its base and implied *purposeful* purpose) of reward that contains no reward, (change to **;** semi-colon) of reward that contains no reward; the donkey moves without a carrot (note: think about relationship to stick). Lawyers, for reasons seemingly obscure to be possibly found somewhere in the somewhat obscure annals (both researched and unre-searched) of time and history of social standing and human factors have developed a system (implied and structured) that is in essence (its essence as defined as its base and implied *purposeful* purpose) of reward that con-tains no reward; the donkey moves without a carrot.

That is they've worked very tediously long hours all their lives so they can work very tediously long hours all their lives. (Change to That is**,** comma) That is, they've worked very tediously long hours all their lives so they can work very tediously long hours all their lives. They're professionals with jobs like sharecroppers, and without the jugs of malt wine at the end of the day (check with library to see if sharecroppers actually drank jugs of malt wine).

Lots of people used her very clean desk when she wasn't there. That's the way a Word Processing Center in a law firm works. Lawyers are professionals with jobs like sharecroppers. They work long hours. So support staff is on call all the time. When Palace wasn't working at her very clean desk, someone else would be working there. It was like the cute white boy. The cute white boy worked at a different time than her (the middle of the night) but they would run into each other, and flirt, as the shifts changed. The cute white boy was a poet. Many word processors did other things or said they did other things or hoped they did other things than word processing, even if it was running a side business from home or raising a family etc. Work wasn't the word processors' lives. It was hard for Palace to keep her very clean desk clean with other people working at it. Also lawyers are slobs. They spill thing and have stacks and stacks of stacks in their offices. They're always trying to remember something, and keep something in their head, and that makes them forget stuff. It's hard to keep things clean even a kinda spiritual clean in a law firm.

Every morning before she started work, and after she had done her makeup, settled herself, and flirted with the cute white boy before he left, she would clean. She would clean her very clean desk at work. She'd remove the plastic, almost like the proverbial slip cover that proverbially goes over the proverbial suburban couch, molded covering that she used (she was the only one that used) to place over her keyboard to her computer, and cleaned it thoroughly, inside and out. She dusted, she sprayed (she kept cleaning products in her drawer, locked), washed and air-freshened. After she was certain that everything was clean she set up her little pocket mirror, took one more look at herself, maybe applied a little something more, some lipstick or something, somethinc new maybe she just bought, Avocado Red, or Street Nitro Metal, and settled in, smellin' good.

This morning, Monday morning, like when she found out 'bout Alice and her son, she did somethinc different. She didn't clean, well right away. And when she did she didn't do it that thoroughly, somewhat distractedly, that's how, she didn't even bother with the plastic molded covering that she used to place over her keyboard to her computer. This morning, resting with its bottom edge in 'tween two rows of the keyboard, and its top carefully taped to the fuzzy dusty statically CRT glare screen that she had gotten specially through supply and used on her computer monitor, was a beige paper, like resume paper almost, a good paper, and on this good paper, also carefully printed, in a fancy but not wack font, was a poem.

Beauty breaks over me/waves over a stranded/seashell in the sand/I hear the sound/of these waves/every time I'm near you/listening to you/your beauty/you/you also, a seashell/stranded in the sand.

There is clutter. There is so much clutter that we almost walk through it clean, clear. But in doing so we lose track of our own. We lose track of our own clutter. Our inside noise. Noise is good, if it's ours. When we still ourselves, push away our melting, and leave only the hard cone, we are pretend.

Pretend in the most sickenly real way. We have stopped to B. because we don't want to C. the A to Z. Palace could never do it. Although she tried. She could never still herself, stop herself, the clutter, the real big beautiful clutter of her pride, and hope, that someone would desire her, really desire her, really want her, not for them, not so that she would be some sorta reflection on them, but that because, just because, she was, she was her. And now this poem. This poem on her desk out of nowhere. By who knows who. Hey, who did send it, I mean put it, on her desk. Who did?

"Hey _____." She tried to call out to the cute white boy to catch him before he left but he'd already, already left, out the doors of the Center, down the elevators, and into his waiting car service car.

Sometimes Palace's mind overtook her. Overtook her to a deeper level than she was even prepared to stand on. Like some weird going through turnstiles continually going through turnstiles of a strange subway system that you kept going down and down to. Standing on each level. No train. Go down and down. No train. She felt some sense of some lack of tools. She thought about the cute white boy. He seemed to have them. A sortof articulateness. Like he could express himself, well I guess that's what a sortof articulateness would be. She thought about Marty. You know Marty, also, well Marty also. I dunno, she thought (and this is not exactly a thought, in the sense of it being an articulate thought, it was just in her head, in her body, in her "heart," in various ways) what Marty thought. But sometimes she thought he knew. She felt this feeling of his knowing. His knowing something about her.

Her friend at work, the gay guy, with the nice body, hmmm!, there was somethinc sexy 'bout him, but why, he wasn't interested in her, I mean not really, he liked men (duh!). Her friend at work, her friend at work exhibit- ed a kinda, another way, of, well another way. Her friend at work exhibited another way of knowing. Almost a knowing but a not showing. Her friend had things hidden, wasn't worried, wasn't worried about the difference between what he knew and what he could say.

But Palace wanted wanted wanted. Palace wanted to say. She wanted to say, not even words, she wanted to breath her passion, to express herself through the movements of her body. And who was that passion for. That was the question. Who was leaving her these poems? 'Cause there had been another one.

Star light/Lights up the sky/But what lights up the star/Its own light/Or the light it brings out/In others?

It sounds so strange. The feeling of something so strong, but not knowing where this feeling will go to, who was it for. It was exactly what she always wanted. She wanted to love. But she didn't want to pick. She wanted to love. But she didn't want to choose. She wanted to have it chosen for her. By the power and weight and majesty of the power and weight and majesty of someone else's power and weight and majesty. Of someone else's lust. Of someone else's lust, and love, and desire, and passion. Passion for her. HER. Who was writing those poems? Who was writing those poems and typing them up on a computer and printing them up on such nice paper and carefully leaving them for her. Who? That was who she loved. She loved him (and yeah she was pretty sure it was a him) more than anybody she had ever loved. She loved him in a way that could not even be contained within herself. She loved him. She didn't know who he was.

She was gettin' all feely feely feely. She knew that soon, soon it would be her period. She would get all just feely feely feely when she got her period and maybe it was like a little stronger now. She was breakin' out a little bit now, too. She had this one zit right to the right of her nose. She remembered with her last boyfriend, she used to like to pop his zits. It made her laugh a little, not really laugh, that sortof obvious smile thing at a recollection, thinkin' 'bout it, kinda for a second got her outta her grumpy mood.

Alice had started work again and Alice seemed better. As better as better as you could expect better to be in this kinda better situation. But better was better than worse. Her gay friend, her married friend, even the cute white boy, all took their turns taking their turns, in that work kinda way, but still in a way, to make her know that she wasn't in the way, the opposite really, that she was wanted. That what happened was something that happened. Yeah, that she was wanted. But was Palace wanted? There was no poem on her desk this morning, on her very clean desk. And she had to admit it, she did admit it, she looked forward to them. There had been five in all. The fourth one was the one she had at the moment in her head.

Together/We create togetherness/Like the word didn't exist/Until we did/Together

When she first read it, and really still when she thought about it she read one of the lines as *Like the _world_ didn't exist.*

She watched her gay friend, and then she thought about it, why is she always thinkin', that way, describing him that way, her gay friend, it's not like she really thought about his sex life, when she thought about him, or the cute white boy, why did she, but wha da fuck, it was her mind, she could think anyway she pleased. But who was her boo? Who was her boo? She watched her gay friend jokin' 'round with Alice, doing the same things he did with her, squeeze her n' all dat stuff, poke her, and laugh, and make her laugh, have her sit on his lap, press up 'gainst her, it made her a little, dunno a little, well still it was good to see Alice laugh. Jeezus, she needed to. She watched as Alice almost, well actually did, catch herself, and stop, like, stop, having fun, like she shouldn't be, 'n junk.

It was all good, yeah? She went out to lunch with her married friend. Her married friend was happy, in fact she was pregnant again, just.

"Everything's fine," her married friend said. "Fine 'n dandy. You ever found out who been given you those rhymes?"

Palace felt something, like oh you know that, the warmth the squishiness, looked at her leg, just casually, she was wearing a real, mini, skirt, and she saw this blood on it. Oh my god. Oh my god. Oh. Oh my god. Wow, that's like the biggest flow of my life. Oh wait, oh no, then she looked down more and saw that it was just some kinda cherry ice stuff, she looked back and she saw this cherry ice on the ground melting 'round its wooden stick, her friend must have stepped on it or somethinc and it must have splashed her.

She found out who gave her the poems and she had a drink with him after work she never did that had a drink with someone after work but she did this time she did and had an Ice Tea two of them and she and she and she and she was so horny she was just so horny that was all she could say about herself if there was something that someone asked her about herself and that particular time that's all she could say she would say I'm horny and she and she and she was happy he was here the man she loved no matter what it sounded like even in her own head it didn't matter she loved him she love love loved him the only thing she was worried about she was worried about was was was whether she was going to get her period she hoped it would-n't happen but she didn't even care she wanted to be with him right now sleep with him now none of the other things that were in her head that would usually be in her head none of those other things were in her head she just wanted him to kiss her and he did he did he did and his kisses were like his poems they were they were they were full up full up to the top flowing over with a passion for her she felt it she felt it everywhere he was beautiful his eyes were forceful and immediate and looked at her and looked at her and looked at her she felt it in her breasts in her breasts she felt it her breasts had never been that sensitive before she'd never felt it like that like that before she she she oh my god her nipples were hard her nipples were so hard how can I if I'm feeling this how can I if I'm feeling this how can I feel anything else do anything else I love him I love the way he makes me feel I love the way he was talkin' to her low and throaty and soft and murky and touched her with the sounds from his tongue and so sweet and so damn sweet about how beautiful she was about how wonderful about how much he wanted her about how he couldn't even see straight really with her beauty in his eyes dazzling him her girlfriend her wild wacky girlfriend told her later yo when your body says that to you yo you gotta listen to your body she went home with him to his apartment and she liked the way it was clean she was surprised it was so clean like he almost cleaned it for her and they kissed each other and their moist mouths tongued and their bodies felt the impact of their bodies and they took their clothes off and their touches were like rubber bands of softness swacking on every sensitive spot and making every spot that wasn't up till then sensitive sensitive and then he started licking her licking her 'round her neck crazily without even thinkin' or knowing licking her in places that didn't even matter and then did all of a sudden oh lick me again there oh there lick me again there and he licked her breasts all around her nipples closer closer then her nipples oh god oh god oh their breathing their breathing her nipples were like they were like oh oh oh he bit them licked them sucked them squeezed them hard between his lips and teeth oh yeah oh yeah he licked down her belly oh your breasts are so beautiful oh your belly is so beautiful he kept at it he kept talkin' oh licking he started licking the top of her hair that started the between her legs wet spiral of fluids flowing up on her lips she had shaved it cared carefully trimmed it this morning how did she know she knew how did she know this was going to happen oh it felt so good she felt so beautiful she felt her pussy so wet and beautiful and open oh he started to lick her oh he did he did he was he was he was licking her he was doing it oh god oh yeah oh it felt so good oh what's that? what's that? he got up he got up straightened

112

up oh god what happened he was holding his hand to his face oh god oh god oh no he was covered in blood his face covered in blood oh no she thought oh no oh no she almost was crying it's me it's me I got my period I bled on him oh no not that anything but that

But he wasn't crying he was laughing. Oh jeez can you believe this. My nose is bleeding. It's just so beautiful. You're so beautiful. I got so excited. My nose started to bleed. And then she laughed and they both laughed and laughed and

Τηε βεαυτιφυλ, ολδερ ωομαν ωασ τουχηεδ βψ αν αγγελ. Α ηελλ σ αγγελ.

SEXUAL RETARDS

(translation follows text)

Πεοπλε λικε το φυχκ ιν ηοτελσ.

Πεοπλε λικε το φυχκ ιν ηοτελσ βεχαυσε α ηοτελ ισ νοτ α ηομε. Ηομε ισ ωηερε τηε ηεαρτ ισ, βυτ ιτ ισ νοτ ωηερε τηε φυχκινγ ισ. Βαβιεσ χομε φρομ ηομεσ ανδ ηοσπιταλσ (ωηιχη αρε λικε ηομεσ, ωηιχη αρε νοτ ιν ανψ ωαψ λικε ηομεσ, βυτ αρε λικε ηομεσ, λικε) ανδ βαβιεσ χομε φρομ φυχκινγ. Βυτ φυχκινγ δοεσ νοτ τακε πλαχε ατ ηομε. Ιν "Τηε Πηιλοσοπηψ οφ Εϖερψδαψ Λιφε" τηερε ισ α διφφερενχε βετωεεν φυχκινγ ανδ μακινγ λοϖε. Ψου μακε λοϖε ατ ηομε. Βαβιεσ χομε φρομ μακινγ λοϖε.

Ωηερε δο βαβιεσ χομε φρομ?

Νο ονε εϖερ τηινκσ (ανδ βψ τηισ Ι'μ προβαβλψ φυστ ταλκιν' 'βουτ με) τηερε ωιλλ εϖερ βε ανψβοδψ ψουνγερ τηαν τηεμ. Υντιλ τηεψ γετ ολδερ. Τηεν εϖερψβοδψ ισ ψουνγερ τηαν τηεμ. Βυτ ωηατ δοεσ ιτ μεαν. Δο ψου αλωαψσ ηατε τηε γρουπ ψου δον'τ βελονγ το? Βυτ ψου αλσο ηατε τηε γρουπ ψου βελονγ το. Ηοω χαν ψου εσχαπε τηισ ηατε.

Ολδερ πεοπλε τηινκ ψουνγερ πεοπλε αρε βαβιεσ. Ψουνγερ πεοπλε τηινκ ολδερ πεοπλε αρε βαβιεσ. Τηεψ δον'τ υσε τηε ωορδ "βαβιεσ", τηε ψουνγερ πεοπλε. Τηεψ δον'τ υσε ανψ ωορδσ φορ τηεμ, εξχεπτ "τηεμ."

"Τηε Πηιλοσοπηψ οφ Εϖερψδαψ Λιφε" σαψσ τηερε ισ α διφφερενχε βετωεεν ολδερ ανδ ψουνγερ, ανδ τηισ διφφερενχε ισ ηεαλτηψ. Ιφ ψου κνοω τηε αγε ψου'ρε ιν, ψου'ρε ιν.

Α βεαυτιφυλ ωομαν σαιδ τηισ. Ι κνοω ωηψ σηε σαιδ τηισ. Σηε ωασ βεαυτιφυλ. Ι χουλδ ηαϖε σαιδ α βεαυτιφυλ, ολδερ ωομαν σαιδ τηισ. Ιτ σουνδεδ φυννψ. Φυννψ, ωρονγ.

Βεαυτψ ισ νοτ ιν τηε εψε οφ τηε βεηολδερ. Ιτ ισ ιν τηε εψε οφ τηε βεηολδεε. Τηε βεηολδεε κνοωσ. Ηοω δο ψου γετ τηισ κνοωλεδγε?

"Τηε Πηιλοσοπηψ οφ Εϖερψδαψ Λιφε" αλσο βελιεϖεσ ιτ ισ ιμπορταντ το βε ψουνγ. Ιτ ισ ϖερψ χοντραδιχτορψ. Ψεσ, κνοω ψουρσελφ, βυτ αλσο κνοω οτηερσ, "Τηε Πηιλοσοπηψ οφ Εϖερψδαψ Λιφε" σαψσ. Ιν κνοωινγ οτηερσ, ψου αλσο κνοω ψουρσελφ, κνοωινγ ηοω τηεψ κνοω ψου. Ιφ ψου κνοω ηοω τηεψ κνοω ψου, τηεν ψου χαν κνοω ωηατ το δο.

Ωηατ το δο?

Τηε βεαυτιφυλ, ολδερ ωομαν ωασ τουχηεδ βψ αν ανγελ. Α ηελλ'σ ανγελ. Τηατ σ ηοω σηε δεσχριβεδ ηιμ. Ιν δεφερενχε το ηερ ψουτη. Μεανινγ: λεατηερ γυψσ ωερε τηοσε κινδ. Ηε ωασν'τ ζαχτλψ α λεατηερ γυψ. Βυτ ηε ηαδ α λεατηερ φαχκετ. Σηε φελτ τηε χοω, βλαχκ ανδ ταννεδ, ανδ σηε σμελλεδ βεερ. Ορ τηουγητ σηε διδ. Σηε διδ. Ιτ

116

μιγητ νοτ ηαϖε βεεν τηερε. Ηισ ηανδ ωασ λικε α λεατηερ φαχκετ. Τηε ρουγηνεσσ αππεαλεδ το ηερ. Ηε ρυββεδ ιτ πρεττψ ηαρδ ον ηερ, τηε βαχκ οφ ηισ ηανδ, ον τηε φροντ οφ ηερ φαχε. Σηε σηυτ. Ηερ εψεσ. Βυτ εϖερψτηινχ ελσε σεεμεδ το δο διφφερεντ. Σηε χουλδ βρεατηε ιν τηε λαχκ οφ τενσιον σηε φελτ – τενσελψ. Ηισ λιπσ ωερε χραχκεδ ανδ ηαρδ. Τοο. Σηε αλωαψσ ηαδ δρψ λιπσ. Βυτ τηατ ωασν᾽τ ωηατ τηε "τοο" ωασ 'βουτ. Τηε τοο ωασ αβουτ τηε χραχκεδ ανδ ηαρδνεσσ οφ ηισ ωηολε τηινγ. Ιτ ωασ φιερχε. Τηε πηψσιχαλ πυλλ οφ ηισ λοωερ αρμ πυσηιν', πυλλεψ–λικε, λεϖερ–λικε, 'γαινστ τηε βροαδ οφ τηε βαχκ οφ ηερ νεχκ, πυση. Α λοχκ φολτ. Σηε ωασ σοφτ. Βρεατηψ, ασ α συβστανχε, νοτ ασ αν αχτιον. Ωισπψ ανδ ωηισπερινγ. Οοη. Γοοδ. Τηε ωορδ ιτσελφ βροκε οϖερ ηερ λικε ψοκε δροππινγ ουτ οφ α φυστ χραχκεδ εγγ. Ιτ ωασ ηερε τηατ σηε ωασ υνλικε οτηερσ. Τηατ τηινγσ μοϖεδ λικε χλοχκωορκ. Ἑπτ τηατ νοτηινγ λικε χλοχκωορκ χουλδ δσχριβε τηε ωαψ τηινγσ μοϖεδ. Σηε βεγαν το ηολδ ον. Ηοω α βαβψ γραβσ ον το τηινγσ. Ηερ ηανδσ σομεωηατ λυμπψ, χοοκεδ ϖεγετα-βλεσ, πρεσσεδ υπ ανδ οντο τηε χηεστ᾽σ σηιρτ. Ηερ ηανδσ. Τηεψ, τηε φεελινγ τηινγσ, φεελινγ, νοτ σενσινγ, βεινγ τηε τηινγσ σενσεδ. Σμυσηεδ. Ἑωεεν ηερσ ανδ ηισ. Οωη. Τηε βρινγινγ.

Ατ τηε διννερταβλε ηερ δαυγητερ γοτ συρπρισεδ. Σηε ενφοψεδ συρ-πρισεσ βυτ σηε αλωαψσ ηαδ το κνοω τηεψ ωερε χομινγ. Λικε, ετχ., ψου κνοω, τηε ωηολε τηινγ οφ τηε διννερταβλε. Τηερε ωασ νο συχη τηινγ. Ανδ ηερε τηεψ ωερε. Εατιν'. Σηε λικεδ τηατ. Αρχηαιχ. Χοολ. Βυτ τηισ οτηερ τηινγ. Τηισ δροππιν' οφ σομετηινγ, φυστ δροππιν᾽ ιτ ουτ τηερε, φυστ λεττιν᾽ ιτ φυστ ηανγ τηερε, φυστ ποπ τηερε, φυστ

117

βανγ ριγητ ιν τηερε ηεαϖιλψ, βυτ ινδιρεχτλψ, σο λικε νοτ ηεαϖιλψ, ατ αλλ. Αλλ. Αλλ σηουλδ ηαϖε λιστενεδ. Βυτ αλλ διδν'τ. Νοβοδψ ηεαρδ.

"Διδ ψου ηεαρ τηατ, 'μεμβερ I ωασ τελλινγ ψου αβουτ τηατ, I μεαν φυστ ψου κνοω ωηενεϖερ, I δυννο ωηερεϖερ, ψεστερδαψ, τηισ ωασ ηερ γρεατ λοϖε. Ηερ γρεατ λοϖε! Ανδ σηε φυστ τελλσ με. Σηε φυστ τελλσ με. θυστ λικε τηατ. Ηε'σ δεαδ. Σηε φυστ σαψσ ιτ. Ωηεν ταλκιν' 'βουτ σομετηινχ ελσε."

Σηε ωασ ιν α ηοτελ ροομ ωιτη α στρανγερ ωηο ωασ φαμιλιαρ. Αλμοστ φαμιλιαρ. Τηερε αρε μανψ στρανγερσ τηατ χαν βε φαμιλιαρ. Μοστ χαν. Εϖερψονε ψου κνεω ψου ονχε διδν'τ κνεω. Βυτ τηατ'σ νοτ ωηατ I μ ταλκιν' 'βουτ. Τηατ'σ σο οβϖιουσ. Ιτ'σ στυπιδ. Ωηατ I'μ ταλκιν' 'βουτ ισ τηισ. Τηε αλμοστ βοψφριεδ. I μεαν βοψφριενδ. Τηε αλμοστ γιρλφριενδ. ψου χαν αλμοστ βε βορεδ. ψου χαν αλμοστ βε βορεδ ωιτη. Ψου χαν αλμοστ βε βορεδ ωιτη τηεμ. Ηοω βεαυτιφυλ το βε. Ηοω βεαυτιφυλ το βε βορεδ ωιτη. Ηοω βεαυτιφυλ το βε βορεδ ωιτη τηεμ.

Σηε ωασν'τ βορεδ ωιτη ηιμ.

Ιν "Τηε Πηιλοσοπηψ οφ Εϖερψδαψ Λιφε" βορεδομ μεανσ α διφφερ−εντ τηινγ. Ιτ μεανσ βορεδομ. Ιτ δοεσν'τ μεαν φαμιλιαρ. Ιτ μεανσ βορεδομ 'χαυσε τηε οπποσιτε οφ βορεδομ ισ τηε οπποσιτε οφ βορε−δομ. Ιτ ισ νοτ βορεδ. Ιτ ισ νοτ βορεδ ιν τηε ωαψ σηε ωασν'τ βορεδ.

118

Σηε ηαδ σαιδ σηε διδν't λικε ηισ πενισ. Ωηατ δοεσ τηατ μεαν. Τηε λψινγ τηατ γοεσ ον αλλ τηε τιμε ισ τρεμενδουσ. Ι λιε αλλ τηε τιμε. Ι νεϖερ λιε. Οφ χουρσε, ιτ ωουλδ μακε σενσε. Ιτ ωουλδ μακε σενσε ιφ σηε διδν't λικε ηισ πενισ. Ψουνγ γιρλσ, ιν τηε μοστ υνβελιεϖαβλε χλιχηεδ τψπε οφ ψουνγ γιρλνεσσ, α κινδοφ χυτενεσσ ρεαλνεσσ, αλμοστ λικε, λικε ιτ ωουλδ βε τοο ηαρδ το βελιεϖε, 'χαυσε ιτ'σ σο χυτε, λικε, ωελλ, υμ, λικε α μαν μαδε ιτ αλλ υπ, ηα, ηα, ψουνγ γιρλσ, ηοο, ηοο, τηεψ αρε σχαρεδ οφ ουρ πενισεσ, βυτ τηεν τηεψ γετ το λικε τηεμ, ηα, ηα, τηεμ, ηα, ηα, ψουνγ γιρλσ γετ σθυεαμιση 'βουτ πενισ– εσ, βυτ τηεν σομε γιρλ, αλσο, α ψουνγ γιρλ, βυτ φυστ ηαϖινγ βεεν αρουνδ α πενισ, ορ τωο, ορ ονε, ωε αλλ λιε, ωελλ αλλ εξαγγερατε, ιτ ισ ιν τηε λανγυαγε, ιτ ισ ιν τηε λανγυαγε, δοεσ ανψβοδψ εϖεν κνοω ωηατ τηεψ're σαψινγ, δοεσ ανψβοδψ εϖεν κνοω, α ψουνγ γιρλ ωιλλ σαψ το νοτηερ, ψου κνοω, ιτ'σ ο.κ., ψου γετ υσεδ το τηεμ. Τηεψ're ο.κ.

Ηερ μινδ ωασ α σλιδε σηοω. Τηερε ωασ τηε εμπτψ δυλλ χλασσροομ ωιτη τηιχκιση ποστερσ ωαρνινγ 'βουτ σμοκινγ χορνερσ ποππινγ φρομ τηε ταπε γλυε χυρλινγ οφφ τηε ωαλλ. Σουνδ οφ σηοεσ. Τηε λιγητ οφφ βαρελψ βρεακινγ τηε ποωερ λιγητ φρομ ουτσιδε, τηε βριγητ. Σηαδεσ νοτ υπ ορ δοων. Δοων βυτ νοτ σταψινγ σο. Σο, ιτ βεγινσ.

Χλιχκ.

Χλιχκ.

Χλιχκ.

Ηερ μινδ ωασ α σλιδε σηοω. Εαχη σλιδε. Διφφερεντ. 'Χαυσε α σλιδε ισ τηατ, φυστ διφφερεντ, νοτ φυστ, διφφερεντ. Νοτ α μοϖιε. Σλιδεσ αρε νοτ μοϖιεσ. Τηε φραμεσ δο νοτ χοννεχτ.

Ιτ ωουλδ μακε σενσε ιφ σηε διδν'τ λικε ηισ πενισ. Ωηψ ωουλδ τηατ βε α λιε? Λατερ, σηε σαιδ ηοω μυχη σηε λικεδ ηισ πενισ.

Χαν ψου. Ιμαγινε. θυστ ωηατ ιτ ωουλδ βε λικε. Ι δον'τ κνοω. Ι δυννο. Χαν Ι. Χαν ψου. Ωηατ'σ ηε λικε. Ι δον'τ κνοω. Ι δον'τ ρεαλλψ λικε ηισ πενισ. Ορ. Ηοω'σ ηε δοινγ. Ηισ πενισ ισ δοινγ φυστ γρεατ. Ωομεν ηαϖε τηεσε χονϖερσατιονσ αλλ τηε τιμε. Ψου δον'τ νεεδ ιμαγινατιον.

Τηε δαυγητερ'σ μοτηερ στοοδ ατ τηε βασε οφ Ροχκεφελλερ Χεντερ ανδ λοοκεδ υπ.

"Μομ. Ψου ρε συχη α τουριστ."

Α μαν γοτ ουτ οφ τηε συβωαψ ανδ σταρτεδ το γετ τοωαρδσ ωορκ. Ανοτηερ μαν λοοκεδ ατ ηιμ ανδ ηε λοοκεδ ατ ηιμ. Τηεψ ταλκεδ ανδ ωεντ το α νεαρβψ ηοτελ τηατ τοοκ "σηορτ σταψσ."

Τηεψ πυτ τηισ δρυγ ιν ηερ δρινκ ατ α παρτψ.

Ιτ ωασ τηε φιρστ τιμε σηε ηαδ α πενισ ιν ηερ.

Σηε ρεμεμβερσ. Σηε ωασ νοτ συρε ιφ ιτ ωασ τρυε. Ιτ ωασ τρυε. Σηε ωασ ραπεδ.

Μανψ βοψσ ραπεδ ηερ.

Ωηεν σηε ωροτε λεττερσ το ηερσελφ σηε ωουλδν'τ ωριτε τηεμ δοων. Ωηεν σηε ωροτε λεττερσ το οτηερ πεοπλε τηεψ σουνδεδ λικε τηε λεττερσ σηε ωροτε το ηερσελφ. Αλασκα ισ χολδ. Βυτ νοτ χολδ λικε τηε ωαψ ψου τηινκ ιτ ισ ιν Αλασκα. Πεοπλε τηινκ οφ χολδ ασ χλεαν. Σομετιμεσ χολδ ισν'τ χλεαν. Σομετιμεσ χολδ ισ δανκ 'ν διρτψ. Ανχηοραγε ισ α νοιρ τοων. Ονλψ α νοιρ τοων χαν γετ αωαψ ωιτη βεινγ χαλλεδ α "νοιρ" τοων. Τηεψ παιδ ψου μονεψ το λιϖε ιν Αλασκα. Ιφ ψου λιϖεδ ιν Αλασκα φορ α λιττλε ωηιλε τηεψ ωουλδ παψ ψου μονεψ. Τηεψ ωουλδ παψ ψου μονεψ το λιϖε τηερε μορε. Ανχηοραγε ισ ιν Αλασκα.

Αλασκα ισ συχη α μεταπηορ τηατ ιτ'σ α μεταπηορ. Τηερε'σ α πιπελινε. Ιτ ισ φαρ αωαψ. Τηε οτηερ στατεσ. Τηε οτηερ στατεσ οφ τηε οτηερ στατεσ οφ τηε (Υνιτεδ Στατεσ οφ) Αμεριχα ωερε χαλλεδ τηε λοωερ 48. Τηε οτηερ στατεσ οφ τηε οτηερ στατεσ οφ τηε (Υνιτεδ Στατεσ οφ) Αμεριχα ωερε χαλλεδ τηε λοωερ 48 βψ τηε πεοπλε οφ Αλασκα. Ωηο ωερε τηε "πεοπλε" οφ Αλασκα. Τηεψ παιδ ψου μονεψ το λιϖε ιν Αλασκα. Ηερ δαδ ηαδ χομε τηερε φορ ϖαριουσ ρεασονσ.

121

Σηε γρεω υπ τηερε. Ηερ παρεντσ διϖορχεδ. Ηερ παρεντσ διϖορχεδ ανδ σηε σταψεδ ωιτη ηερ φατηερ. Ονε ψεαρ σηε σταψεδ ωιτη ηερ μοτηερ. Ηερ φατηερ ηαδ χαλλεδ ηερ μοτηερ. Ηερ μοτηερ ηαδ χομε βαχκ το Αλασκα. Ηερ μοτηερ ηαδ χομε βαχκ το Αλασκα ανδ λιϖεδ νεαρβψ. Ηερ μοτηερ ηαδ χομε βαχκ το Αλασκα ανδ λιϖεδ νεαρβψ ηερ φατηερ. Ονε ψεαρ σηε σταψεδ ωιτη ηερ μοτηερ.

Ηερ μοτηερ ηαδ λεφτ βεχαυσε ηερ μοτηερ ηαδ λεφτ.

Τηισ ισ α χυλτυραλ πηενομενα. Ωηατ ισ? Τηισ ισ. Ωηατ Ι αμ αβουτ το ταλκ αβουτ. Ωηατ αρε ψου αβουτ το ταλκ αβουτ? Α χυλτυραλ πηενομενα.

Ηερ δαδ ηαδ ρεμαρριεδ. Ρεμαρριεδ ισ α φυννψ ωορδ. Σηε ηαδ στεπ–βροτηερσ ανδ στεπ–σιστερσ. Τωο. Ονε οφ εαχη. Ι τηινκ. Ιτ δοεσν'τ ματτερ ρεαλλψ. Ιτ ρεαλλψ δοεσν'τ ματτερ.

Σηε ωασ ιν λοϖε ωιτη τηισ γυψ ναμεδ Τομ. Τομ ωασ ιν ηερ μινδ. Ιν ηερ δρεαμσ. Ιν ηερ ωριτινγ. Τομ. Τομ. Τομ. Σηε ωουλδ ωριτε ιτ αγαιν ανδ αγαιν. Ιτ. Ιτ. Ιτ. Τομ. Τομ. Τομ. Νοτ Τηομασ. Οη νοτ Τηομασ. Ηισ ναμε ωασ νοτ Τηομασ. Τομ. Τομ. Τομ. Ονχε τηεψ ηαδ σλεπτ τογετη–ερ ονχε. Ονχε τηεψ ηαδ. Βυτ οη. Βυτ Οη. Τηε στρανγε ανδ υνκνοω–ινγ. Τηε στρανγε ανδ υνλοϖελψ ανδ υνκνοωινγ. Τηε χιπηερ τηατ ωασ ηερ. Τηατ ωασ ηερ. Ηισ. Ηισ γιρλφριενδ. Ηε λικεδ ηερ. Ηε διδν'τ λικε ηερ. Οη. Οη. Οη. Τομ. Τομ Τομ.

Ρενατα ωασ ηερ ναμε. Ρενατα. Ρενατα. Ρενατα. Ηε λικεδ Ρενατα. Ηε διδν't λικε ηερ.

Ηερ στεπ–σιστερ γοτ α χαρ ωηεν σηε ωασ σιξτεεν. Σηε διδν't γετ α χαρ ωηεν σηε ωασ σιξτεεν. Σηε ωασ λιϖινγ ωιτη ηερ μοτηερ. Ηερ φατηερ ηαδ χαλλεδ ηερ μοτηερ. Σηε χουλδ νοτ βε χοντρολλεδ. Σηε ωασ ουτ οφ χοντρολ. Χοντρολ ωασ ωηατ σηε χουλδ νοτ βε.

Βοψσ. Βοψσ. Βοψσ. Βοψ. Βοψ. Βοψ. Τομ. Τομ. Τομ. Βοψ. Τομβοψ. Σηε ηαδ βεεν α τομβοψ. Υπ το α χερταιν τιμε σηε ηαδ βεεν α τομβοψ. Σηε ωασ στιλλ κινδα ωελλ κινδα φλατ. Σηε ηαδ α νιχε ασσ τηουγη σηε διδ. Σηε ωουλδ σταρε ατ ηερσελφ . Σηε ωουλδ. Σηε ωουλδ σταρε σταρε ατ ηερσελφ. Σηε διδ ηαϖε α νιχε ασσ σηε τηουγητ. Ανδ νιχε εψεσ. Ανδ λιπσ. Ανδ νιχε λιπσ. Σηε χαταλογεδ ηερσελφ. Σηε κεπτ νοτε. Σηε τοοκ νοτεσ. Σηε τοοκ νοτε. Σηε σαω Τομ ονχε. Σηε σαω Τομ ονχε λοοκ ατ ηερ. Λοοκ ατ ηερ ασσ. Ηε ηαδ τολδ Χηαρλιε. Ηε ηαδ τολδ Χηαρλιε. Χηαρλιε ωασ Μελανιε'σ βοψφριενδ. Χηαρλιε ωασ Μελανιε'σ βοψφριενδ ανδ Μελανιε ωασ ηερ φριενδ, τηεψ ωερε βοτη, βοτη ωερε ηερ φριενδσ. Ηε ηαδ τολδ Χηαρλιε σηε ηαδ α νιχε ασσ.

Σηε ωασ ιν α ηοτελ ροομ ωιτη α στρανγερ ωηο ωασ φαμιλιαρ. Αλμοστ φαμιλιαρ. Τηερε αρε μανψ στρανγερσ τηατ χαν βε φαμιλιαρ. Μοστ χαν. Εϖερψονε ψου κνεω ψου ονχε διδν't κνεω. Βυτ τηατ'σ νοτ ωηατ I'μ ταλκιν' 'βουτ.

Τηεψ ηαδ φυστ χομε βαχκ φρομ α χλυβ. Ιτ ωασ α χλυβ ωιτη βλαχκ

123

πεοπλε. Τηερε ισ α διφφερενχε βετωεεν βλαχκ πενισεσ ανδ ωηιτε πενισεσ. Ιτ'σ νοτ τηε σιζε. Ιτ'σ τηε χολορ. Βλαχκ πενισεσ αρε βλαχκ. Ωηιτε πενισεσ αρε ωηιτε. "Τηε Πηιλοσοπηψ οφ Εϖερψδαψ Λιφε" φεελσ ψου αρε αττραχτεδ το στυφφ ψου αρε διφφερεντ φρομ.

Α ωηιτε γιρλ ιν τηε χλυβ ωιτη βλαχκ πεοπλε ωασ χρψινγ. Νοτ εξαχτλψ. Σο ψου χουλδ σεε ηερ τεαρσ. Σο Ι γυεσσ σηε ωασν'τ. Σηε ωασν'τ χρψινγ. Σηε ωασ φρομ ανοτηερ χουντρψ. Σηε ωασ νοτ φρομ τηε λοωερ 48, (τηε Υνιτεδ Στατεσ οφ) Αμεριχα. Σηε ωασ νοτ Αμεριχαν. Υνιτεδ Στατεσ οφ. Σηε ωασ χρψινγ (αλτηουγη νοτ σηοωινγ ιτ) βεχαυσε ιν ηερ χουντρψ τηερε ωερε νοτ α λοτ οφ βλαχκ πεοπλε. Σηε τηουγητ σηε διδν'τ λικε βλαχκ πεοπλε. Σηε ωασ ιν α χλυβ ωιτη βλαχκ πεοπλε.

Χηαρλιε ανδ Μελανιε'σ φριενδ διδ νοτ νοτιχε τηισ γιρλ. Σηε ηαδ χομε το τηε χλυβ ωιτη α στρανγερ ωηο ωασ φαμιλιαρ. Αλμοστ φαμιλιαρ. Τηεψ ηαδ χομε υπ το τηε χλυβ ανδ τηερε ωασ α λονγ λινε. Α λονγ λινε οφ ψουνγ βλαχκ μεν. Βοψσ. Βλαχκ βοψσ. Σηε ωεντ το τηε βαχκ οφ τηε λινε. Ηυρριεδ. Τηε δοορμαν χαλλεδ ηερ. Χομε ον. Σηε ωεντ ιν. Σηε ωασ ωηιτε. Σηε ωεντ ιν. Σηε ωασ νερϖους. Σηε δρανκ. Ανδ ιμμεδιατελψ. Οη ωοω. Σηε ωασ. Τηατ ψου κνοω. Ψου δο κνοω. Ιτζιτ ρεαλ. Σηε ωασ φυστ ηαππψ. Ψου κνοω ηαππψ το βε ωιτη ηιμ, τηε στρανγερ ωηο ωασ φαμιλιαρ. Ιν τηε χλυβ τηατ ωασ στρανγε. Σηε διδν'τ νοτιχε τηε γιρλ ωηο ωασ χρψινγ σορτα. Βυτ ωηερε σηε ωασ φρομ, Αλασκα, Ανχηοραγε Αλασκα, τηερε ωερεν'τ α λοτ οφ βλαχκ(σ). Ψου κνοω ειτηερ.

124

"Τηε Πηιλοσοπηψ οφ Εϖερψδαψ Λιφε" σαψσ ψου αρε ψουρσελφ ωηεν ψου ρε δρυνκ.

Βλαχκ(σ) δανχε υπ το ψου ωηεν τηεψ δανχε. Τηεψ δανχε υπ το ψου ωηεν τηεψ δανχε. Υπ το ψου. Βεηινδ ψου. Φρομ βεηινδ. Βεηινδ ψου. Σηε ωασ ρεαλλψ ρεαλλψ ρεαλλψ ρεαλλψ ρεαλλψ ρεαλλψ ρεαλλψ ρεαλλψ ρεαλλψ ρεαλλψ ρεαλλψ δρυνκ. Σηε δανχεδ ωιτη α γυψ. Τηεψ ωεντ το τηε βαχκ οφ τηε χλυβ τογετηερ. Τηερε ωερε σομε πιλλοωσ τηερε. Τηεψ φυχκεδ.

Σηε ραν ουτ οφ τηε χλυβ. Σωεατιν.

"Χ'μον. Χ'μον. Χ'μον. Χ'μον.!"

Ιτ ωασ τιμε φορ α ρομαντιχ στρεετ χορνερ κισσ ωιτη τηε στρανγερ ωηο ωασ αλμοστ φαμιλιαρ.

"Οημψγοδ. Ωηατ διδ Ι δο? Ωηατ διδ Ι δο? Οημψγοδ."

Σηε τριεδ το κισσ ηιμ. Ηε διδν'τ. Ηε διδν'τ υνδερστανδ.

"Ι διδν'τ κισσ ανψβοδψ. Ορ συχκ τηειρ χοχκ ορ ανψτηινγ."

Σηε ωασ ιν α ηοτελ ροομ ωιτη α στρανγερ ωηο ωασ φαμιλιαρ. Αλμοστ φαμιλιαρ. Τηεψ ηαδ φυστ χομε βαχκ φρομ α χλυβ. Τηεψ ωερε κισσινγ. Τηεψ ωερε μακινγ. Λοπε. Σηε ωασ σαψινγ ηισ ναμε οπερ ανδ οπερ αγαιν. Οπερ ανδ οπερ αγαιν. Οπερ ανδ οπερ αγαιν.

Ωηεν σηε ωροτε λεττερσ το ηερσελφ σηε ωουλδν'τ ωριτε τηεμ δοων. Ωηεν σηε ωροτε λεττερσ το οτηερ πεοπλε τηεψ σουνδεδ λικε τηε λετ-τερσ σηε ωροτε το ηερσελφ. Σηε ωασ ωριτινγ λεττερσ το τηε στρανγερ ωηο ωασ αλμοστ φαμιλιαρ.

Σηε ωασ ωριτινγ αλλ αβουτ Τομ.

Τομ. Τομ. Οη. Τομ. Ηε. Ι δον'τ κνοω. Ηε κνοωσ. Ηε κνοωσ. Ι λοπε ηιμ. Ι λοπε ηιμ σο. Τηε στρανγε ανδ υνκνοωινγ. Τηε στρανγε ανδ υνλοπελψ ανδ υνκνοωινγ. Τηε χιπηερ τηατ ισ ηερ. Τηατ ισ ηερ. Ηισ. Ηισ γιρλφριενδ. Ηε λικεσ ηερ. Ηε δοεσν'τ λικε με. Οη. Οη. Οη. Τομ. Τομ Τομ. Ρενατα ισ ηερ ναμε. Ρενατα. Ρενατα. Ρενατα. Ηε λικεσ Ρενατα. Ηε δοεσν'τ λικε με.

Ηερ μοτηερ ωασ α βεαυτιφυλ ολδερ ωομαν. Σηε ηαδ το βε αν ολδερ ωομαν βεχαυσε α μοτηερ ισ αλωαψσ ολδερ τηαν α δαυγητερ. Τηισ ισ α φαχτ. Α φαμουσ φιλμ διρεχτορ ονχε σαιδ τηατ ηε ωιλλ αλωαψσ βε ψουνγερ τηαν τηε τιμε ωηεν ηε ωιλλ βε ολδερ. Φιλμ υνδερστανδσ τιμε. Λιτερατυρε δοεσν'τ. Τηισ ισ νοτ τρυε. Αλλ τηε τιμε.

Βεαυτψ ισ σεξψ. Ωε μισυνδερστανδ τηισ 'χαυσε ωε τηινκ σεξ ισ υγλψ. Σηε ωασ σεξψ, ηερ μοτηερ σιττιν' ατ τηε διννερταβλε ωιτη, ηερ δαυγητερ.

126

Ιν τηε 60σ εϖερψβοδψ ωασ σεξψ.

Τηισ ισ ηαρδ το υνδερστανδ βυτ ιτ ισ ριγητ. Λοοκ ατ τηε πιχτυρεσ ωηιχη ισ αλλ ωε ηαϖε. Ωηιχη ισ νοτ αλλ ωε ηαϖε. Λοοκ ατ τηε πιχτυρεσ. Λοοκ ατ αλλ τηοσε. Λοοκ ατ αλλ τηοσε σεξψ πεοπλε.

Σηε ωασ σεξψ, ηερ μοτηερ σιττιν' ατ τηε διννερταβλε ωιτη, ηερ δαυγητερ, ανδ ηερ μοτηερ. Ηερ δαυγητερ σ γρανδμοτηερ.

Σομετηινγ ηαδ χηανγεδ. Τηε σκψ ηαδ φαλλεν. Νοω ωηεν ψου λοοκ υπ αλλ ψου χουλδ σεε ωασ τηε σκψ.

Ατ τηε διννερταβλε ηερ δαυγητερ γοτ συρπρισεδ. Σηε ενφοψεδ συρπρισεσ βυτ σηε αλωαψσ ηαδ το κνοω τηεψ ωερε χομινγ. Λικε, ετχ., ψου κνοω, τηε ωηολε τηινγ οφ τηε διννερταβλε.

Ηερ δαυγητερ'σ γρανδμοτηερ, ηερ μοτηερ. Ηερ δαυγητερ'σ γρανδμοτηερ λιϖεδ ιν Θυεενσ. Ιν α σεχτιον ωηερε αλλ τηε σιγνσ αρε ιν ανοτηερ λανγυαγε. Σηε ηαδ λιϖεδ ιν Θυεενσ ωιτη ηερ ηυσβανδ ωηο ρεχεντλψ διεδ. Σηε ηαδ λιϖεδ ιν Θυεενσ ωιτη ηερ ηυσβανδ ωηο ρεχεντλψ διεδ ανδ ανοτηερ μαν ωηο αλσο ρεχεντλψ διεδ. Σομε μαν ωηο αφτερ Ωορλδ Ωαρ ΙΙ λιϖεδ ωιτη τηεμ. Λιϖεδ ωιτη τηεμ αλλ ηισ λιφε. Ηερ δαυγητερ μαρριεδ α μαν. Α παιντινγ οφ τηε μαν ηερ δαυγητερ μαρριεδ ωασ ον τηε ωαλλ οφ ηερ ηουσε ιν Θυεενσ. Ηερ δαυγητερ μαρριεδ α μαν ανδ τηεψ ωεντ το λιϖε ιν Αλασκα. Ηερ δαυγητερ

127

μαρριεδ α μαν ανδ τηεψ ωεντ το λιϖε ιν Αλασκα ανδ τηεψ γοτ διϖορχεδ. Τηεψ ηαδ α δαυγητερ ανδ τηεν τηεψ γοτ διϖορχεδ.

Τηισ δαυγητερ, ηερ μοτηερ, ανδ ηερ γρανδμοτηερ, ωερε νοω ατ ηερ γρανδμοτηερ'σ ηουσε ιν Θυεενσ ηαϖινγ διννερ. Τηεψ ηαδ α γυεστ.

"Διδ ψου ηεαρ τηατ, 'μεμβερ Ι ωασ τελλινγ ψου αβουτ τηατ, Ι μεαν φυστ ψου κνοω ωηενεϖερ, Ι δυννο ωηερεϖερ, ψεστερδαψ, τηισ ωασ ηερ γρεατ λοϖε. Ηερ γρεατ λοϖε! Ανδ σηε φυστ τελλσ με. Σηε φυστ τελλσ με. φυστ λικε τηατ. Ηε'σ δεαδ. Σηε φυστ σαψσ ιτ. Ωηεν ταλκιν' 'βουτ σομετηινχ ελσε."

Σηε ωασ ιν α ηοτελ ροομ ωιτη α στρανγερ ωηο ωασ φαμιλιαρ. Αλμοστ φαμιλιαρ. Τηεψ ωερε ταλκινγ αβουτ τηε διννερ τηεψ φυστ ηαδ ατ ηερ γρανδμοτηερσ ιν Θυεενσ, ωιτη ηερ μοτηερ. Τηεψ ωερε γοινγ το γο το α χλυβ τηατ νιγητ. Τηεψ ωερε φυστ ηανγινγ ουτ α λιττλε βιτ ρεστινγ. Ηερ μοτηερ'σ γρεατ λοϖε αχχορδινγ το ηερ δαυγη–τερ ωασ τηε ϖικερ γυψ τηατ σηε ταλκεδ αβουτ ατ διννερ. Ηε'δ διεδ ιτ τυρνσ ουτ. Σηε εξπλαινεδ τηισ το ηιμ βεχαυσε ηερ μοτηερ τολδ τηε στορψ αβουτ τηε ϖικερ γυψ ανδ διδν'τ μεντιον ηε'δ διεδ. Τηεν ιν α τοταλλψ διφφερεντ παρτ οφ τηε χονϖερσατιον σηε μεντιονεδ α μαν'σ ναμε, ανδ σαιδ τηισ μαν ηαδ διεδ.

Τηισ δροππιν' οφ σομετηινγ, φυστ δροππιν' ιτ ουτ τηερε, φυστ λετ–τιν' ιτ φυστ ηανγ τηερε, φυστ ποπ τηερε, φυστ βανγ ριγητ ιν τηερε

128

ηεαπιλψ, βυτ ινδιρεχτλψ, σο λικε νοτ ηεαπιλψ, ατ αλλ. Αλλ. Αλλ–
σηουλδ ηαπε λιστενεδ. Βυτ αλλ διδν'τ. Νοβοδψ ηεαρδ.

Ωηεν σηε τηουγητ αβουτ ιτ σηε διδν'τ ρεμεμβερ, βυτ τηισ ωασ α
μεμορψ. Τηισ ισ α χυλτυραλ πηενομενα. Ωηατ ισ? Τηισ ισ. Ωηατ I αμ
αβουτ το ταλκ αβουτ. Ωηατ αρε ψου αβουτ το ταλκ αβουτ? Α χυλ–
τυραλ πηενομενα. Ο.κ. ιτ'σ νοτ α ωιδεσπρεαδ χυλτυραλ πηε νομενα.
Ιν τηε σενσε τηατ ιτ ωασ επερψωηερε βυτ ιτ ωασ σομεωηερε. Τηεψ
ηαδ α ναμε φορ ιτ, α σλανγ ναμε φορ ιτ, ανδ τηε μεδια ("τηε μεδια"?
"τηε μεδια?" "τηε μεδια?" διδψαηαπετασαψ "τηε μεδια!"). Ψεαη I διδ. Τηε
μεδια χαλλεδ ιτ τηε "δατε ραπε" δρυγ. Ιτ ωουλδ πυτ τηε περσον ουτ βυτ
τηεψ'δ στιλλ βε αωακε, ανδ ψου χουλδ δο α λοτ το τηεμ. Ανδ τηεψ
ωουλδ κινδα κνοω ιτ ωασ ηαππενινγ βυτ τηεψ ωουλδν'τ. Τηατ σ ωηψ
ωηεν σηε τηουγητ αβουτ ιτ σηε διδν'τ ρεμεμβερ, βυτ τηισ ωασ α μεμορψ.

Ηερ στεπ–σιστερ γοτ α χαρ ωηεν σηε ωασ σιξτεεν. Σηε διδν'τ γετ α
χαρ ωηεν σηε ωασ σιξτεεν. Σηε ωασ λιπινγ ωιτη ηερ μοτηερ. Ηερ
φατηερ ηαδ χαλλεδ ηερ μοτηερ. Σηε χουλδ νοτ βε χοντρολλεδ. Σηε
ωασ ουτ οφ χοντρολ. Χοντρολ ωασ ωηατ σηε χουλδ νοτ βε.

Τηεψ πυτ τηισ δρυγ ιν ηερ δρινκ ατ α παρτψ.

Ιτ ωασ τηε φιρστ τιμε σηε ηαδ α πενισ ιν ηερ.

Σηε ρεμεμβερσ. Σηε ωασ νοτ συρε ιφ ιτ ωασ τρυε. Ιτ ωασ τρυε. Σηε
ωασ ραπεδ.

Μανψ βοψσ ραπεδ ηερ.

Ηερ μινδ ωασ α σλιδε σηοω. Τηερε ωασ τηε εμπτψ δυλλ χλασσροομ ωιτη τηιχκιση ποστερσ ωαρνινγ 'βουτ σμοκινγ χορνερσ ποππινγ φρομ τηε ταπε γλυε χυρλινγ οφφ τηε ωαλλ. Σουνδ οφ σηοεσ. Τηε λιγητ οφφ βαρελψ βρεακινγ τηε πωωερ λιγητ φρομ ουτσιδε, τηε βριγητ. Σηαδεσ νοτ υπ ορ δοων. Δοων βυτ νοτ σταψινγ σο. Σο, ιτ βεγινσ.

Χλιχκ.

Χλιχκ.

Χλιχκ.

Ηερ μινδ ωασ α σλιδε σηοω. Εαχη σλιδε. Διφφερεντ. 'Χαυσε α σλιδε ισ τηατ, φυστ διφφερεντ, νοτ φυστ, διφφερεντ. Νοτ α μοϖιε. Σλιδεσ αρε νοτ μοϖιεσ. Τηε φραμεσ δο νοτ χοννεχτ.

Ιν χλασσ σηε ωασ τηινκινγ 'βουτ ωηατ ηαππενεδ. Εϖερψ–βοδψ σεεμεδ το κνοω ωηατ ηαππενεδ. Σηε διδν't κνοω ωηατ ηαππενεδ.

Πεοπλε λικε το φυχκ ιν ηοτελσ.

Α μαν γοτ ουτ οφ τηε συβωαψ ανδ σταρτεδ το γετ τοωαρδσ ωορκ. Ανοτηερ μαν λοοκεδ ατ ηιμ ανδ ηε λοοκεδ ατ ηιμ. Τηεψ ταλκεδ ανδ ωεντ το α νεαρβψ ηοτελ τηατ τοοκ "σηορτ σταψσ."

Ιν "Τηε Πηιλοσοπηψ οφ Εϖερψδαψ Λιφε" τηερε ισ α διφφερενχε βετωεεν φυχκινγ ανδ μακινγ λοϖε.

"Τηε Πηιλοσοπηψ οφ Εϖερψδαψ Λιφε" σαψσ τηερε ισ α διφφερενχε βετωεεν ολδερ ανδ ψουνγερ, ανδ τηισ διφφερενχε ισ ηεαλτηψ.

"Τηε Πηιλοσοπηψ οφ Εϖερψδαψ Λιφε" αλσο βελιεϖεσ ιτ ισ ιμπορταντ το βε ψουνγ.

Ψεσ, κνοω ψουρσελφ, βυτ αλσο κνοω οτηερσ, "Τηε Πηιλοσοπηψ οφ Εϖερψδαψ Λιφε" σαψσ.

Ιν "Τηε Πηιλοσοπηψ οφ Εϖερψδαψ Λιφε" βορεδομ μεανσ α διφφερεντ τηινγ.

"Τηε Πηιλοσοπηψ οφ Εϖερψδαψ Λιφε" φεελσ ψου αρε αττραχτεδ το στυφφ ψου αρε διφφερεντ φρομ.

"Τηε Πηιλοσοπηψ οφ Εϖερψδαψ Λιφε" σαψσ ψου αρε ψουρσελφ ωηεν ψου ρε δρυνκ.

People like to fuck in hotels.

People like to fuck in hotels because a hotel is not a home. Home is where the heart is, but it is not where the fucking is. Babies come from homes and hospitals (which are like homes, which are not in any way like homes, but are like homes, like) and babies come from fucking. But fucking does not take place at home. In "The Philosophy of Everyday Life" there is a difference between fucking and making love. You make love at home. Babies come from making love.

Where do babies come from?

No one ever thinks (and by this I'm probably just talkin' 'bout me) there will ever be anybody younger than them. Until they get older. Then everybody is younger than them. But what does it mean. Do you always hate the group you don't belong to? But you also hate the group you belong to. How can you escape this hate.

Older people think younger people are babies. Younger people think older people are babies. They don't use the word "babies", the younger people. They don't use any words for them, except "them".

"The Philosophy of Everyday Life" says there is a difference between older and younger, and this difference is healthy. If you know the age you're in, you're in.

A beautiful woman said this. I know why she said this. She was beautiful. I could have said a beautiful, older woman said this. It sounded funny. Funny, wrong.

132

Beauty is not in the eye of the beholder. It is in the eye of the beholdee. The beholdee knows. How do you get this knowledge?

"The Philosophy of Everyday Life" also believes it is important to be young. It is very contradictory. Yes, know yourself, but also know others, "The Philosophy of Everyday Life" says. In knowing others, you also know yourself, knowing how they know you. If you know how they know you, then you can know what to do.

What to do?

The beautiful, older woman was touched by an angel. A Hell's Angel. That's how she described him. In deference to her youth. Meaning: leather guys were those kind. He wasn't zactly a leather guy. But he had a leather jacket. She felt the cow, black and tanned, and she smelled beer. Or thought she did. She did. It might not have been there. His hand was like a leather jacket. The roughness appealed to her. He rubbed it pretty hard on her, the back of his hand, on the front of her face. She shut. Her eyes. But everythinc else seemed to do different. She could breathe in the lack of tension she felt - tensely. His lips were cracked and hard. Too. She always had dry lips. But that wasn't what the "too" was 'bout. The "too" was about the cracked and hardness of his whole thing. It was fierce. The physical pull of his lower arm pushin', pulley-like, lever-like, 'gainst the broad of the back of her neck, push. A lock jolt. She was soft. Breathy, as a substance, not as an action. Wispy and whispering. Ooh. Good. The word itself broke over her like yoke

133

dropping out of a just cracked egg. It was here that she was unlike others. That things moved like clockwork. 'Cept that nothing like clockwork could describe the way things moved. She began to hold on. How a baby grabs on to things. Her hands somewhat lumpy, cooked vegetables, pressed up and onto the chest's shirt. Her hands. They, the feeling things, feeling, not sensing, being the things sensed. Smushed. 'Tween hers and his. Owh. The bringing.

At the dinnertable her daughter got surprised. She enjoyed surprises but she always had to know they were coming. Like, etc., you know, the whole thing of the dinnertable. There was no such thing. And here they were. Eatin'. She liked that. Archaic. Cool. But this other thing. This droppin' of something, just droppin' it out there, just lettin' it just hang there, just pop there, just bang right in there heavily, but indirectly, so like not heavily, at all. All. All should have listened. But all didn't. Nobody heard.

"Did you hear that, 'member I was telling you about that, I mean just you know whenever, I dunno wherever, yesterday, this was her great love. Her great love! And she just tells me. She just tells me. Just like that. He's dead. She just says it. When talkin' 'bout somethinc else."

She was in a hotel room with a stranger who was familiar. Almost familiar. There are many strangers that can be familiar. Most can. Everyone you knew you once didn't knew. But that's not what I'm talkin' 'bout. That's so obvious. It's stupid. What I'm talkin' 'bout is this. The almost boyfried. I mean boyfriend. The almost girlfriend. you can almost be bored. you can

134

almost be bored with. You can almost be bored with them. How beautiful to be. How beautiful to be bored with. How beautiful to be bored with them.

She wasn't bored with him.

In "The Philosophy of Everyday Life" boredom means a different thing. It means boredom. It doesn't mean familiar. It means boredom 'cause the opposite of boredom is the opposite of boredom. It is not bored. It is not bored in the way she wasn't bored.

She had said she didn't like his penis. What does that mean. The lying that goes on all the time is tremendous. I lie all the time. I never lie. Of course, it would make sense. It would make sense if she didn't like his penis. Young girls, in the most unbelievable cliched type of young girlness, a kindof cuteness realness, almost like, like it would be too hard to believe, 'cause it's so cute, like, well, um, like a man made it all up, ha, ha, young girls, hoo, hoo, they are scared of our penises, but then they get to like them, ha, ha, them, ha, ha, young girls get squeamish 'bout penises, but then some girl, also, a young girl, but just having been around a penis, or two, or one, we all lie, well all exaggerate, it is in the language, it is in the language, does anybody even know what they're saying, does anybody even know, a young girl will say to 'nother, you know, it's o.k., you get used to them. They're o.k.

Her mind was a slide show. There was the empty dull classroom with thickish posters warning 'bout smoking corners popping from the tape glue curling off the wall. Sound of shoes. The light off barely breaking the power light from outside, the bright. Shades not up or down. Down but not staying so. So, it begins.

Click.

Click.

Click.

Her mind was a slide show. Each slide. Different. 'Cause a slide is that, just different, not just, different. Not a movie. Slides are not movies. The frames do not connect.

It would make sense if she didn't like his penis. Why would that be a lie? Later, she said how much she liked his penis.

Can you. Imagine. Just what it would be like. I don't know. I dunno. Can I. Can you. What's he like. I don't know. I don't really like his penis. Or. How's he doing. His penis is doing just great. Women have these conversations all the time. You don't need imagination.

The daughter's mother stood at the base of Rockefeller Center and looked up.

"Mom. You're such a tourist."

136

A man got out of the subway and started to get towards work. Another man looked at him and he looked at him. They talked and went to a nearby hotel that took "short stays."

They put this drug in her drink at a party.

It was the first time she had a penis in her.

She remembers. She was not sure if it was true. It was true. She was raped.

Many boys raped her.

When she wrote letters to herself she wouldn't write them down. When she wrote letters to other people they sounded like the letters she wrote to herself. Alaska is cold. But not cold like the way you think it is in Alaska. People think of cold as clean. Sometimes cold isn't clean. Sometimes cold is dank 'n dirty. Anchorage is a noir town. Only a noir town can get away with being called a "noir" town. They paid you money to live in Alaska. If you lived in Alaska for a little while they would pay you money. They would pay you money to live there more. Anchorage is in Alaska.

Alaska is such a metaphor that it's a metaphor. There's a pipeline. It is far away. The other states. The other states of the other states of the (United States of) America were called the lower 48. The other states of the other states of the (United States of) America were called the lower 48 by the people of Alaska. Who were the "people" of Alaska. They paid you money to live in Alaska. Her dad had come there for various reasons. She grew up there. Her parents divorced. Her parents divorced and she stayed with her father. One year she stayed with her mother. Her father had called her mother. Her mother had come back to Alaska. Her mother had come back to Alaska and lived nearby. Her mother had come back to Alaska and lived nearby her father. One year she stayed with her mother.

Her mother had left because her mother had left.

This is a cultural phenomenon. What is? This is. What I am about to talk about. What are you about to talk about? A cultural phenomenon.

Her dad had remarried. Remarried is a funny word. She had step-brothers and step-sisters. Two. One of each. I think. It doesn't matter really. It really doesn't matter.

She was in love with this guy named Tom. Tom was in her mind. In her dreams. In her writing. Tom. Tom. Tom. She would write it again and again. It. It. It. Tom. Tom. Tom. Not Thomas. Oh not Thomas. His name was not Thomas. Tom. Tom. Tom. Once they had slept together once. Once they had. But oh. But Oh. The strange and unknowing. The strange and unlovely and unknowing. The cipher that was her. That was her. His. His girlfriend. He liked her. He didn't like her. Oh. Oh. Oh. Tom. Tom Tom.

Renata was her name. Renata. Renata. Renata. He liked Renata. He didn't like her.

Her step-sister got a car when she was sixteen. She didn't get a car when she was sixteen. She was living with her mother. Her father had called her mother. She could not be controlled. She was out of control. Controlled was what she could not be.

Boys. Boys. Boys. Boy. Boy. Boy. Tom. Tom. Tom. Boy. Tomboy. She had been a tomboy. Up to a certain time she had been a tomboy. She was still kinda well kinda flat. She had a nice ass though she did. She would stare at herself. She would. She would stare stare at herself. She did have a nice ass she thought. And nice eyes. And lips. And nice lips. She cataloged herself. She kept note. She took notes. She took note. She saw Tom once. She saw Tom once look at her. Look at her ass. He had told Chaz. He had told Chaz. Chaz was Melanie's boyfriend. Chaz was Melanie's boyfriend and Melanie was her friend, they were both, both were her friends. He had told Chaz she had a nice ass.

She was in a hotel room with a stranger who was familiar. Almost familiar. There are many strangers that can be familiar. Most can. Everyone you knew you once didn't knew. But that's not what I'm talkin' 'bout.

They had just come back from a club. It was a club with black people. There is a difference between black penises and white penises. It's not the size. It's the color. Black penises are black. White penises are white. "The Philosophy of Everyday Life" feels you are attracted to stuff you are different from.

A white girl in the club with black people was crying. Not exactly. So you could see her tears. So I guess she wasn't. She wasn't crying. She was from another country. She was not from the lower 48, (the United States of) America. She was not American. United States of. She was crying (although not showing it) because in her country there were not a lot of black people. She thought she didn't like black people. She was in a club with black people.

Chaz and Melanie's friend did not notice this girl. She had come to the club with a stranger who was familiar. Almost familiar. They had come up to the club and there was a long line. A long line of young black men. Boys. Black boys. She went to the back of the line. Hurried. The doorman called her. Come on. She went in. She was white. She went in. She was nervous. She drank. And immediately. Oh wow. She was. That you know. You do know. Izit real. She was just happy. You know happy to be with him, the stranger who was familiar. In the club that was strange. She didn't notice the girl who was crying sorta. But where she was from, Alaska, Anchorage Alaska, there weren't a lot of black(s). You know either.

"The Philosophy of Everyday Life" says you are yourself when you're drunk.

Black(s) dance up to you when they dance. They dance up to you when they dance. Up to you. Behind you. From behind. Behind you. She was really really really really really really really really really really really really drunk. She danced

140

with a guy. They went to the back of the club together. There were some pillows there. They fucked.

She ran out of the club. Sweatin.

"C'mon. C'mon. C'mon. C'mon.!"

It was time for a romantic street corner kiss with the stranger who was
almost familiar.

"Ohmygod. What did I do? What did I do? Ohmygod."

She tried to kiss him. He didn't. He didn't understand.

"I didn't kiss anybody. Or suck their cock or anything."

She was in a hotel room with a stranger who was familiar. Almost familiar.
They had just come back from a club. They were kissing. They were making.
Love. She was saying his name over and over again. Over and over again.
Over and over again.

When she wrote letters to herself she wouldn't write them down. When
she wrote letters to other people they sounded like the letters she wrote to
herself. She was writing letters to the stranger who was almost familiar.

She was writing all about Tom.

Tom. Tom. Oh. Tom. He. I don't know. He knows. He knows. I love him. I love him so. The strange and unknowing. The strange and unlovely and unknowing. The cipher that is her. That is her. His. His girlfriend. He likes her. He doesn't like me. Oh. Oh. Oh. Tom. Tom Tom. Renata is her name. Renata. Renata. Renata. He likes Renata. He doesn't like me.

Her mother was a beautiful older woman. She had to be an older woman because a mother is always older than a daughter. This is a fact. A famous film director once said that he will always be younger than the time when he will be older. Film understands time. Literature doesn't. This is not true. All the time.

Beauty is sexy. We misunderstand this 'cause we think sex is ugly. She was sexy, her mother sittin' at the dinnertable with, her daughter.

In the 60s everybody was sexy.

This is hard to understand but it is right. Look at the pictures which is all we have. Which is not all we have. Look at the pictures. Look at all those. Look at all those sexy people.

She was sexy, her mother sittin' at the dinnertable with, her daughter, and her mother. Her daughter's grandmother.

Something had changed. The sky had fallen. Now when you look up all you could see was the sky.

At the dinnertable her daughter got surprised. She enjoyed surprises but she always had to know they were coming. Like, etc., you know, the whole thing of the dinnertable.

Her daughter's grandmother, her mother. Her daughter's grandmother lived in Queens. In a section where all the signs are in another language. She had lived in Queens with her husband who recently died. She had lived in Queens with her husband who recently died and another man who also recently died. Some man who after World War II lived with them. Lived with them all his life. Her daughter married a man. A painting of the man her daughter married was on the wall of her house in Queens. Her daughter married a man and they went to live in Alaska. Her daughter married a man and they went to live in Alaska and they got divorced. They had a daughter and then they got divorced.

This daughter, her mother, and her grandmother, were now at her grand-mother's house in Queens having dinner. They had a guest.

"Did you hear that, 'member I was telling you about that, I mean just you know whenever, I dunno wherever, yesterday, this was her great love. Her great love! And she just tells me. She just tells me. Just like that. He's dead. She just says it. When talkin' 'bout somethinc else."

She was in a hotel room with a stranger who was familiar. Almost familiar. They were talking about the dinner they just had at her grandmothers in

Queens, with her mother. They were going to go to a club that night. They were just hanging out a little bit resting. Her mother's great love according to her daughter was the biker guy that she talked about at dinner. He'd died it turns out. She explained this to him because her mother told the story about the biker guy and didn't mention he'd died. Then in a totally different part of the conversation she mentioned a man's name, and said this man had died.

This droppin' of something, just droppin' it out there, just lettin' it just hang there, just pop there, just bang right in there heavily, but indirectly, so like not heavily, at all. All. All should have listened. But all didn't. Nobody heard.

When she thought about it she didn't remember, but this was a memory. This is a cultural phenomenon. What is? This is. What I am about to talk about. What are you about to talk about? A cultural phenomenon. O.k. it's not a widespread cultural phenomenon. In the sense that it was everywhere but it was somewhere. They had a name for it, a slang name for it, and the media ("the media"? "the media?" "the media"? didyahavetasay "the media"!). Yeah I did. The media called it the "date rape" drug. It would put the person out but they'd still be awake, and you could do a lot to them. And they would kinda know it was happening but they wouldn't. That's why when she thought about it she didn't remember, but this was a memory.

Her step-sister got a car when she was sixteen. She didn't get a car when she was sixteen. She was living with her mother. Her father had called her mother. She could not be controlled. She was out of control. Controlled was what she could not be.

They put this drug in her drink at a party.

It was the first time she had a penis in her.

She remembers. She was not sure if it was true. It was true. She was raped.

Many boys raped her.

Her mind was a slide show. There was the empty dull classroom with thickish posters warning 'bout smoking corners popping from the tape glue curling off the wall. Sound of shoes. The light off barely breaking the power light from outside, the bright. Shades not up or down. Down but not staying so. So, it begins.

Click.

Click.

Click.

Her mind was a slide show. Each slide. Different. 'Cause a slide is that, just different, not just, different. Not a movie. Slides are not movies. The frames do not connect.

In class she was thinking 'bout what happened. Everybody seemed to know what happened. She didn't know what happened.

People like to fuck in hotels.

A man got out of the subway and started to get towards work. Another man looked at him and he looked at him. They talked and went to a nearby hotel that took "short stays."

In "The Philosophy of Everyday Life" there is a difference between fucking and making love.

"The Philosophy of Everyday Life" says there is a difference between older and younger, and this difference is healthy.

"The Philosophy of Everyday Life" also believes it is important to be young.

Yes, know yourself, but also know others, "The Philosophy of Everyday Life" says.

In "The Philosophy of Everyday Life" boredom means a different thing.

"The Philosophy of Everyday Life" feels you are attracted to stuff you are different from.

"The Philosophy of Everyday Life" says you are yourself when you're drunk.

146

She was having an awful conversation. A horrible conversation. She was having an awful conversation with herself.

a very confusing story with way too many characters that's somehow 'bout a dog named
BIJOU

She had lost the fucking plot. It was blue. She was blue. The water was a link. A kindof flat, engulfing lever. By falling into the splash she could reverse everything that had happened. Make it all go away. She had left the loft with nothing. No keys. No money. No cards. No jacket. It was cold. It was cold in Montreal. She left because she had to. She had to because she had to. She just left. Walked to the water.

A friend went looking for her. Found her. Called out after her. She ran. He lost her. She hid in a construction site. Then slept in a park. She ate city-park fruit off a tree, and wondered if it would hurt her in some way. She was dry, the lips, the tongue, the mouth. All dry. She didn't drink. She didn't eat. She left because her mother told her. Her mother told her her father was sick. Her mother told her her father was sick and they were getting a divorce. Her mother told her her father was sick and they were getting a divorce and it was all because of her. It was all because of her because of the problems with the loft. The loft was bought and then Wit left.

Wit was weak. He had all the attractive qualities that weakness brings. Weakness, in a boy, brings with it a kindof cuteness, but softens the cuteness so it's less annoying. Wit, not purely cute, was confidant but doubtful, oops what I should say is he was confident and filled with doubt, and full of bursts of energetic fear and then kinda dizzying downward moods, that altogether were kinda sweet. He was sweet and charming and you wanted to hug him.

Bernice wanted to hug him and did. At this time she wanted to kill him or herself, more herself. She almost did it. Kinda close. Kinda scarily close. More than almost. Almost doesn't really cut it. She really came pretty damn fucking close. Bernice disappeared.

(In Montreal the girls were cultured from birth in pretty-girl culture. They were pretty those pretty girls in the pretty-girl culture. Oooooh! Every interaction, getting a fucking croissant, whatever, wow, boys fell in love. The boys were insane with desire. Every interaction, etc. Oooooh! They were overcome. They were overcome the boys. They could not overcome. They never overcame that they could not overcome. They were tired. They were tired. They were tired with being allured all the time. They were always being allured. And. They were tired.

They had "desire fatigue.")

Bernice was one of the mothers of the dog Bijou. Wit had liked the other mother of the dog Bijou. But, and this is where it gets confusing, the other mother of the dog Bijou could tell that Bernice liked Wit. So she didn't. She didn't. She let Bernice have him. Did she?

Wit was a photographer. Bernice was a photographer. He made photographs. She taught photography to children. She walked home from work.

One night she walked home from work and the moon was out. The moon was very bright. Very, very, bright. It lit up. It made light. Montreal in the winter is really wintry. It wasn't winter yet. It got dark. Though. It got dark fast. She had been working in the darkroom at her school. Developing some pictures. Developing some pictures for Wit. The moonlight lit her up. The moonlight lit her up and she hurried with a shine, a moonshine.

A boy is in possession of a tremendous need. The need is not what you think it is. It's also not not what you think it is. The other mother of the dog Bijou knew about this tremendous need. She knew about it not up in her head, right up there, like she could say it back to you. But she knew it. She might have learned it, she might not have learned it and just knew it. She might have learned it "the hard way."

Bernice was in possession of a tremendous need.

"I feel her. I feel her need." Wit said unhappily.

Bijou was "the prettiest dog in the world." Everybody loved Bijou. People that didn't love Bijou loved Bijou. She was too small. Somehow she was too small. She was a small dog, and somehow she was too small. Lots of people don't like small dogs. These people loved Bijou. The other mother of the dog Bijou had found Bijou. She had found Bijou on the street. She had found Bijou on the street and had taken her home. Sometimes there were arguments about who was the mother of Bijou. Between the two mothers.

Bernice had this look. It is hard to describe what this look is like. Actually it's not hard to describe. It's just that there's no point. You know the look. It's just that. A look. When she felt Bernice's look the other mother of the dog Bijou felt Bernice's look. It could make her do things sometimes. She would do things, so Bernice's look would stop or something like that. Bernice knew the power of her look. It didn't feel like a power to her. It wasn't.

The two mothers of the dog Bijou were different with the dog Bijou. When they held her. To Bernice, the dog represented something. To Bernice the dog, Bijou we should call her, Bijou would demand it, just by being Bijou, that she be called by her name, to Bernice, Bijou was a symbol, something separate from herself, something different from herself, something better than herself. Something Bernice could hold up and say, hey, look, look, hey, I'm o.k. Perhaps, this is unfair. I apologize for using the word "perhaps."

Bernice did take care of Bijou often. It could be argued ("it could be argued?" what is happening here), that taking care of someone is always about show-ing off. And taking care of someone is important. That we would have to agree on. Do we have to agree though that taking care of someone is always about showing off? If that is true do we have to agree that taking care of someone is important? People, and other kinds as well (I am afterall talking about a dog), do need to be taken care of. They also need not to be taken care of.

Doreen Snow, whose story is not in this story but in another story, wanted to be taken care of but didn't appear to want to be taken care of. And didn't know it herself. And maybe didn't even want it herself. To be taken care of. Take care.

Take care. The other mother of the dog Bijou took care. She might not have always taken care of Bijou but when she did take care of Bijou she took care. Great care. She held her not as a thing, but as a thing loved, not as a symbol, but as an expression. There is a difference between a symbol and an expression. My aim is true.

But there were times when the other mother of the dog Bijou wasn't there.

Bernice was always there. Even when she disappeared.

I am now gonna introduce a new character.

There comes a time in every storyteller's life when the story doesn't make sense, gets fucked. Bogart, lying in the Montreal loft on the bed bought by Bernice (one of the mothers of the dog Bijou) was such a storyteller who had come to such a place.

He had lost the plot.

He called this, firmly, distinctly, and strongly, The Idea That He Had No Idea. For Bogart to have no idea was a blow. I mean he prided himself on the idea that he knew nothing. He always did that. But it was a certain kind of nothing. He didn't know things like where certain things were in New York

City, even though he grew up in New York City. Or like Queens, New York City. He went to a bachelors' party that someone from work invited him to, and it was in Queens. When he got out of the subway he had no idea where he was. The ride seemed to take hours, 'cause it did take hours. He almost stopped, and gave up, and went home, but he had been trying to fuck Sue for what seemed like about six months, 'cause it was about six months, okay three, and he wanted to tell her a good story the next day. So he did. I mean he did tell her a good story the next day. But he still had no idea where he was — when he got out of the subway.

No, he didn't know things like that. But he did know things, or at least he did know things until now.

Doreen Snow, who once again is not in this story but in another story, summed up things pretty well once. Summing up things pretty well once she said:

"I know I'm attractive but I also don't know."

That is still a kindof knowledge. The kindof knowledge Bogart didn't have anymore. Doreen Snow is really sexy, but as I said, her story is another story.

Speaking of Queens, Montreal is one of the gayest cities in the world, with some of the faggiest straight men ever. Actually, that's not what I was going to say, what I was going to say was:

speaking of Queens, Bogart, lying in the Montreal loft on the bed bought by Bernice (one of the mothers of the dog Bijou), was thinking about a girl who was his friend when he was 17 and who lived in Queens. She was pretty. She had a boyfriend, and the boyfriend also lived in Queens and was more "her type." Bogart would visit her, the weird elevated tracks that he would go to, that was her stop. The strange outdoors subway station.

The other mother of the dog Bijou was also lying in the same Montreal loft where Bogart was lying, but not on the bed bought by Bernice. She was lying on one of the sofas. The two sofas were the nicest things in the Montreal loft. The other mother of the dog Bijou was "the prettiest girl in the world."

The Montreal loft was in the gay section of Montreal, called (and how did they come up with this one?), "The Village." The loft was fixed up, but not really. It was currently being lived in by some French, I mean not just French-speaking, but actually people from France. And it was lived in by Bernice when she was in Montreal, and by Wit, her ex-boyfriend, when he was in town, although not at the same time. It's a long story.

And I'm gonna tell it.

Bernice and Wit bought the loft, spent all this money, her money, his money, her parent's money, his parent's money, and then Wit broke up with her.

That's it. That's the story.

I'm gonna talk 'bout Bogart again.

It's unfair to say that Bogart had been trying to "fuck" Sue for six months or whatever it was, three, whatever, because of the connotation of the word "fuck." They had a relationship. That is what is so amusing about the connotation of the word "fuck". I just even like that phrase so much. So much I'm gonna say it again. The connotation of the word "fuck." I on purpose above have sometimes put the quotes inside the period ("fuck".) and outside the period ("fuck.") because I always get confused about this, and 'cause I'm not sure which way I like it.

What is so amusing about the connotation of the word "fuck" is that all "relationships" begin with people tying to fuck. O.k. not all, but a lot. Sue was a beautiful girl. And it wasn't that Bogart was too stupid to know she was a beautiful girl. It's that he wanted to fuck not have a relationship. He ended up with a relationship with no fucking. You might want to say here, "ha, ha, Bogart!." Ha, ha Bogart! But a relationship with no fucking is not a relationship. He ended up with nothing. But since *they* were in a relationship. It's better to say "*they* ended up with nothing." They ended up with nothing. What I'm trying to say ipso-facticly cryptically is this, expressed in a poem:

Love is a seeing eye dog
Drunken clarity is not clarity
but at least your drunk

This is the story Bogart told Sue about the bachelors' party he went to:

They were worried about five, actually maybe six things. They were worried about six things. They were worried about the size of their dicks, getting it up, being queer, being fat, minorities taking their jobs, and going bald. These were the five things, actually maybe six things, they were worried about. How I got there is not important but somehow I got there. I was at a bachelors' party in Queens. First off there was a person I hated who was there. This person was being made fun of immediately. They were saying they'd found the black book of a guy at their work who was kinda openly sorta gay and that this guy's name was in it. For some reason I immediately stood up for this guy that I hated. I told the guy that was making fun of the guy that I hated that I had also seen the book and seen that this guy's name, the guy that was making fun of the guy that I hated, was in there, not only that, was in there with four big stars next to his name. There was lots of kiddin'. There was lots of kiddin' about dicks, not getting it up, size, being queer, being fat, minorities, and losing hair. There were even some "minorities" there. There was "Chinese Checkers." That's what they called him. A Chinese friend in their "crew." And there was "Homeboy Pete," a Black friend. Thyme Warner (not his real name, duh, but what he called himself, both here and at work) had organized the party and was making things work. He had died his hair blonde recently and wore three earrings in one ear. He had a motorcycle. He had pictures of the band Kiss, on his wall. He had first called himself Thyme Warner when he had a kindof rapping career. There were a couple of pictures of him on the wall from those days. He had gotten the strippers. They hadn't come yet. He was waiting. They came. Two strippers and two body guards. Sorry lookin' guys. Packin'. Actually sorry lookin' girls with "big fake helium breasts" (one) and (two) "a snotty little girl wit too much of a 'tude." They stripped and danced wit da fellahs, and with each other, the guys felt them up. There was almost a kindof strange orgy at one point. With a lotta big fat bald small dicked impotent angry

157

closeted queers making fun of each other and grabbing each other's asses and kindof
almost jumping on each other. Afterwards everybody jumped in a car to go somewhere else
quickly, quickly, Chinese Checkers began running up to one of the cars, the car with me and
the guy that I hated, and a friend of Thyme's driving, there was room for him, for Chinese
Checkers, but the car waited just until Chinese Checkers got to the door and then sped off
again, finally for good, leaving their friend in the, actually in the, yes, the dust.

"What in the fuck, why did you do that?" I said.

"What the fuck is it your business. You want him to be in the car you get out."

"O.k. I will. Fuck you. Let me out."

"What is this? What is this? What is this? Ahhh. I can't stand this. Who is this guy in my
back seat. This fucking guy."

And in Montreal,

Bijou was beeping around the Montreal loft like a computer game blip. She
was so fast for such a slow creature. She had the energy and drive of digital
code in an analog body. She scampered, scampered, scampered, and got
nowhere. Fast. In a slow way. She had bright eyes. "Bright Eyes" is what the
character was called in the Planet of the Apes films. The human character,
by the apes. I think it was a joke. 'Cause we often call our animals that or
think of them that way. Bright Eyes. But what does it mean? What's behind
the gleaming glow of an animal's bright eyes?

158

Behind Bijou's it was obvious. There was something. An intensity of love and an energy of hope. It wasn't just the small thing's large ambitions. It wasn't cuteness. Funnily 'nuff Bijou wasn't cute. Bijou was sexy. And in that way I guess she was cute. Bijou was a star.

She wasn't no lap poodle puppy dog popcorn sized individual kernel of corny cat/dog. She was no cat. She was elegant, coy, dramatic, silly, — by the way nothinc against cats, it's just that she was no dog posing as a cat, she was all dog — wherewasI, she was coy and dramatic and silly and elegant and startlingly erudite and sometimes vulgar, o.k. not vulgar exactly, but just willing to get down. She was a down dog. She was a down dog for such a charismatic beauty.

Charisma. Pawproppelling herself in her upped, hyper fashion she still managed to exude a kind of exacting, striking balance of reserve and gushing lifeness. When she came down stairs it wasn't your usual animal stampede but almost, in the dog equivalent, a soft striding ball gown-wearing staircase descending debutante.

She was underfoot. She did get underfoot. But even in her getting underfoot it was different than getting underfoot. She wanted to be noticed. And you wanted to notice her. She wanted to be involved somehow. Be a part of it. Maybe even be a major part of it. She was, afterall, Bijou.

"The prettiest dog in the world."

She was underfoot when Bernice and Wit would have those aruguments. You know those aruguments that are had when things end. The air would not be thick because I never really never understood what that description means, but that air would have something in it, the menace of new hate. And Bijou felt it. And ran around with a different disposition. Muddled, strange, some-how, maybe even, worried. Like an ice-skater suddenly forming a question mark in the ice instead of a Figure 8.

It's hard those aruguments that are had when things end. That's it.

Bogart was abosolutely totally positive that he would not fall for Bijou's charms. He'd heard about Bijou's charms. He'd heard all about Bijou's charms. He'd heard more than enough about Bijou's charms.

"I'm not gonna fall for Bijou's charms. That's it." He said.

He fell for her charms big time.

Maybe that was 'cause the first time he met Bijou was when he was lying in the Montreal loft without a clue, or whatever it was, yeah, without the plot.

There is nothing like an animal to give the story a thread, or is it a tail, giving the tale a tail, or somethinc, somethinc to hang on to, or something to wag. Animals are simple, right, not like people, they have nothinc to hide, 'cept a poop or a bone, you know, or summinc, they're not like a storyteller, blabbing

160

on, 'cause he doesn't want to say what he wants to say, or can't say, or does-n't know, or some combination, or maybe nothinc like that at all. The truth is stories with animals are about people. It would be an interesting exercise. It would be an interesting exercise to write a story with animals that really basi-cally was 'bout animals and nothing else, just exactly, to the best of our abili-ty, we wrote what they did, without transposing our stuff, our language, etc., on them. It would be an interesting exercise, for someone else to do.

Bogart was in the middle of a complicated human mess, and he was happy to see the little dog, impossibly little, but not really little in the way that lit-tle ("toy") dogs are, bounce up on the bed; the bed Bernice had bought for the Montreal loft, the bed Bernice had bought for the Montreal loft and that Bogart had went to sleep on the night before, the bed Bernice had bought for the Montreal loft and that Bogart had went to sleep on the night before alone. Bernice, one of the mothers of the dog Bijou, wasn't there. And the other mother of the dog Bijou, "the prettiest girl in the world," was lying on one of the sofas, a very pretty sofa, one of the few pretty things in the loft, which was kinda strangley decorated, not really inotherwords, kinda left to its own devices, kinda undecorated. There were also some French students staying in the one bedroom in the loft. One of them had snarled at Bogart the night before for no apparent reason.

Bijou bounced up on the bed and yapped. Yap! Yap! Yap!. Then kinda made towards Bogart and then backed off. Cutely, coyly, not all the way, not off the bed, just a few little paw steps back, and then stood sorta wobbly but proudly, and with eyes bigening, gave Bogart a peering peer.

"You are my friend aren't you little dog?" Bogart said even though he knew the dog's name. He knew the dog's name was Bijou.

Bijou barked.

On the way back from Montreal to NYC by plane, Bogart and the other mother of the dog Bijou, were stopped, on the Canadian side at the airport. Before they were stopped Bogart had insulted the other mother of the dog Bijou's mother. She had shown him a picture of her mother. Bogart has said she was fat. Insulting 'nuff. Then the other mother of the dog Bijou, "the prettiest girl in the world," said that her mother looked exactly like her when her mother was her age. Bogart grimaced.

Before they were stopped some other people were stopped. A very normal looking family were stopped. Boy. Yowza. Those border people were tuff. Those Canadian, or were they American, customs' people. The had this family. This "normal" family up AGAINST DA WALL!!! If these guys, this family, were doing anything wrong it was only to their stomachs or somethinc. To their own stomachs. But obviously to the crack border patrol they were drugs fiends of the worst kind. The little kids were crying. The mother was upset. The dad, his entire dadhood at stake, was livid, and crazy, and hurt. The mom tried to calm him down as they had to empty out all their bags, and were searched, and were made to miss their plane.

Bogart kinda smiled at this scene. Kinda.

162

Bogart went right through customs. He usually was stopped. Not this time. He's the kinda guy that should be stopped. Well not really. He just looked like the kinda guy that should be stopped. Actually maybe that "normal lookin'" family were smugglers.

The other mother of the dog Bijou was stopped. She was stopped because she was "the prettiest girl in the world." The man behind the counter wouldn't let her leave his counter. The man behind the counter wouldn't let her leave his counter because she was "the prettiest girl in the world."

"You know you are the prettiest girl in the world," he said.

This is where this story has gotten this phrase.

The other mother of the dog Bijou grimaced. But couldn't. But couldn't grimace. But did kinda. She wanted to go through. She wanted to go through customs.

He talked to her. The custom's guy. To the other mother of the dog Bijou. He asked her questions. He asked her personal questions. He asked her personal questions about personal things. What she did. What she had done. What she wanted to had done. It turned out somehow he knew someone. It turned out somehow he knew someone that knew someone that knew someone that knew her.

"Really?" She said not very sincerely.

Wit returned to the loft and to Bijou. In a way he was a father of Bijou. During the days of Bernice and Wit, because they were kinda stable, because they were stable, with a place 'n all, Bijou had stayed with them. Mainly with them. So he felt Bijou was him too, was his too. He returned to the loft with his girlfriend. This was the girl that he told Bernice about, the girl that he "left her for." It sounds silly but Bijou never liked this girl. That's what Bernice said and I think it's true. She would come over to the loft to have her picture taken. She was a model. I am sorry that this is so obvious. I'm not that sorry. I sorta like obvious. Obviously.

She would come over and Wit would take her picture and Bijou would bark at her.

This time Wit and her came to the loft and put their bags down. They seemed to have a lot of bags. They seemed to have a lot of bags that needed to be put down. Wit and Bernice were sharing visitation rights to the loft, and I guess sorta to Bijou too. Wit was hopin' that the other mother of the dog Bijou might be at the loft. He'd heard she was coming in for a bit. But when he got there she had already gone.

Hurt is an interesting word that we use for a lot of things. A lot of things meaning I guess both physical pain and, uh, the other kind. We get hurt. People hurt us. And that hurt . . . You know whatever. It feels bad. Blah, blah, blah.

It hurt. It began to hurt before it hurt. It began to hurt when he called Japan a lot. When Wit called Japan a lot. They didn't really have a lot of money. They didn't really, Bernice and Wit. What with the loft and everything. I mean she made some money teaching. And he was workin'. Trying. Making his pictures. But he called Japan a lot. "She" was in Japan. Why are you callin' Japan a lot, Bernice asked. He didn't really have any answer.

The loft was bought and then Wit left. They bought the loft and then he told her. They bought the loft. He told her. Two weeks or somethinc. Maybe sooner. Two weeks after they bought the loft. Two weeks after they had done everything. Two weeks after they had done everything to make sure everything was right. I mean with the loft 'n all. He hold her. He told her. You can almost understand. You can. It's so hard. I mean what you feel, and, um, what is right and all that. Sometimes you just can't. You know. You can't do things in the right order.

|| A kindof self-hatred always boomed around inside of Bogart. It was a kindof whiny self-hatred, a self-hatred that wouldn't even allow itself to be noble, but had to have the word "whiny" before it. HE had to put "whiny" before it. It was a manipulative self-hatred. It was a manipulative self-hatred 'cause it didn't exist. It still though, that thing up there, you know with an "h." It still <u>h</u>urt though.

Though? Like we're dough. Kneaded by our own needs. We can

need to kneed ourselfs out of our hurts. Though. Like we tried. Like we're tired. Like we tried. Like we tried not to feel hurt. But we just do, though.

There can sometimes be some beautiful things in a collision. Two powerful things. Bang. Bump. Sorry for the corniness. How manipulative. That "sorry." It still hurts, though. A collision. ||

The right a-bove is kinda somea whatwuz goen on in Bogart's brain the time he was losing the plot in Montreal. Now he's back in New York.

Back in New York, Bogart was insulting a woman from Montreal. An older woman. How funny sounding. I've said that before. But she was older. Bogart was older. Not older than her. But older. Victor was older. Victor was older than Bogart and the woman from Montreal.

Bogart didn't know he was insulting the woman from Montreal. He never knew. He wasn't trying. If you're not trying, can you be insulting?

The woman was the friend of the mother of Bernice (one of the mothers of the dog Bijou). Bogart lived at the Cabweights-Hoog Hotel, NYC. Victor worked there. The other mother of the dog Bijou also lived there. The woman was visiting along with Bernice the other mother of the dog Bijou there. Doreen Snow who's not in this story fucked there once, almost, at the Cabweights-Hoog Hotel. On the fire escape which Bogart would always call "the balcony."

166

Doreen almost fucked there, outside, out there, but she was nervous about (it). Yeah even her. She would get nervous. She was out there and she was like, sheesuz, there are people out here, there are people, there are, there are, and he (it doesn't really matter who he was, nobody you know), and he said, oh no, oh no, there's nobody there, really, baby, there's nobody there, and then she said, oh yes, oh yes, there is, there is, there is somebody there, I can feel it, I can tell it, oh yes, c'mon, c'mon, there is there is, we've got to go in, we've got to go in.

They went in, and then they heard from down on the street this:

"Hey, c'mon. Don't go in. C'mon. It was just gettin' good."

Bogart was insulting a woman from Montreal. Victor was making love to her. Bogart didn't know he was insulting the woman from Montreal. Victor didn't know he was making love to her.

Bogart lived at the Cabweights-Hoog Hotel. Victor worked there. Ivy worked there (and as a chef in a restaurant!) and Slope worked there too. The place was managed by Knot and Deer. The other mother of the dog Bijou lived there, and worked there too. Her boyfriend lived there too. Here's how they met. The other mother of the dog Bijou and her boyfriend, Charles.

HOW THE OTHER MOTHER OF THE DOG BIJOU MET HER BOYFRIEND CHARLES

He looked zactly like and sounded zactly like this guy. He looked zactly like and sounded zactly like this guy that was in a movie. This was a movie whut was a kinda hit at the moment. Ya know there was hype 'bout it. It was called "benchpressing" (all lower-case). It was 'bout some lads. Some lads in the U.K. They would steal some public benches and burn 'em 'n stuff. 'N stuff. They spoke in impenetrable brogue.

"Bepollen pollster donna karana check da meat looker."

"Ya Aunti delinquent sha fart in ah cold slaw."

'Cause he looked zactly like and sounded zactly like this guy, this guy in a movie, and 'cause he was checking into the Cabweights-Hoog Hotel, and not, well, 'nother hotel, Bogart watching him, watching him check in, and listening, and listening to the way he spoke (impenetrable brogue), and noticing, noticing that he looked zactly like the guy in the movie, "bench-pressing," was sure then, absolutely sure, that he couldn't be. He couldn't be the guy in the movie "benchpressing."

"Nah, he's not the guy." He told Deer, one of the managers of the Cabweights-Hoog.

Deer checked the credits on a pirate video of the film. Yeah, he was the guy.

168

But Bogart didn't know that. Later, with Bernice, and the other mother of the dog Bijou, Bogart went out. Bernice was visiting the other mother of the dog Bijou in NYC. Going out often includes lubrication and self-or-other-medication of some sort. Always includes. Bogart, Bernice and the other mother of the dog Bijou were well-roasted by the time they got to the place where soon the other mother of the dog Bijou and Charles, her future boyfriend, would meet.

When they got to the place where the other mother of the dog Bijou and Charles, her future boyfriend, would meet, they saw the guy from the movie "benchpressing" about to leave.

"Hey, you, what's going on, guy who looks like the guy and sounds like the guy but isn't the guy that's in that movie, "benchpressing." How ya doing?" Bogart slushingly said.

"Not very good actually." The guy said in a not impenetrable brogue, not impenetrable at all. "They won't let us in. No I.D."

"Oh," Bogart said. "C'mon."

He got them in and on the way up in the elevator, a very big elevator (they didn't take the first elevator, someone was just throwing up in it, when the doors opened, like a curtain opening up on someone jackin' off, actually that's a very good idea for the first scene of a play) — really a club really shouldn't have elevators (a club, that's where they were, the place where the other mother of the dog Bijou and Charles, her future boyfriend, would meet), 'cept that was one of the features of this one, it was high up (thus, the elevators) — on the way up, amid, amongst, asea with (thus I guess the throwing up in the other elevator) lotsa reved-upers reved-up for a party, Bogart started making mention of the fact that his newfound friend, 'n hotel dezinen, looked so much like the guy in the movie, "benchpressing," but wasn't.

"Can you believe it?" Bogart said slushingly.

"It is him," the other mother of the dog Bijou mouthed the words and pointed with her finger into her palm at him 'cause Deer had told her earlier it was him.

When the bill came for the first drinks the group of them ordered — somehow the group had got bigger and bigger, including some big fellah who was head of a big private detective agency — it was quite considerably, yes quite, bloated. Large.

"Wow," said Bogart for, of course, they had given the bill to him.

But he didn't have time to ponder it that long or the lack of cash in his pocket to cover it, 'cause it was swooped, yes swooped, up from him. The guy from the movie "benchpressing," had taken the check.

"You can't do that," Bogart said.

"Oh yes I can."

"My god, YOU ARE THE GUY FROM THE MOVIE "benchpressing"!"

Across the room, a little later, on the dance floor, not on the floor, sitting near it, on a divan, yes a divan, the other mother of the dog Bijou first saw Charles, her future boyfriend. Charles saw <u>her</u> too. Bernice also saw him. That night they all went back to the hotel, a group, including Charles, but not including the big fellah who was the head of a big private detective agency.

Bogart was insulting a woman from Montreal. Victor was making love to her. Bogart didn't know he was insulting the woman from Montreal. Victor didn't know he was making love to her.

She was an older woman with big breasts. She was a beautiful older woman. She was a beautiful older woman from Montreal. Bogart thought he was having um, banter with her. And in a way he was. But it was scary. It was scary for her. Victor liked her. Victor thought she liked Bogart. Liked his ways. She liked Victor's ways. Victor was gentle. She went upstairs. To her hotel room. In the Cabweights-Hoog. She was a friend of Bernice's mom, visiting NYC with Bernice.

The other mother of the dog Bijou came downstairs. She had been upstairs.

She had been upstairs seeing if everything was alright with the friend of her friend's mom. She came downstairs. She told Victor. Go upstairs. She asked about you. Go upstairs and visit.

Victor went upstairs. Victor went upstairs and visited.

Bogart and the other mother of the dog Bijou were alone, uh, together.

"Where is he?" Bogart asked. "Where is he?"

"I don't know. Whatever. We weren't gonna hook up tonight."

"Why isn't he here?"

Bogart was talking about Charles, the other mother of the dog Bijou's future boyfriend. Something had happened yesterday. Something had happened yesterday that he (Bogart) and I guess also he (Charles) had had a hand in. And I guess she did too, had a hand in. It went like this:

The other mother of the dog Bijou first saw Charles, her future boyfriend, at a club. Charles saw <u>her</u> too. Bernice also saw him. That night they all went back to the hotel, a group, from the club, including Charles, but not including the big fellah who was the head of a big private detective agency who had hung with them earlier.

Charles was a man but a boy. Meaning: he had faith in his boyness and so that

172

made him a man. He was gentle, was like a whisper on a loud day, that you could still hear. He was wearing good stuff. His pants, grey-blue (more blue than grey), stiff, almost like the bottom half of a uniform, his shirt was orange with the words ACME SAFE CO. on it in a grey-green (more green than grey).

He saw her. And she saw him. And they liked each other.

"That's the prettiest girl in the world," he mumbled almost out-loud.

Bernice was wearing a giant hat. A giant hat she had walked off with, jus' cooly walked out of, and then very giggly, ran out of, a big-time hat fashion show with. She was taking pictures of the show on spec for a Montreal mag that had slightly nude women and fashion 'n stuff. She was wearing a big hat. And somehow the big hat somehow became the way they all started talkin'. They all meaning, Bernice, and the other mother of the dog Bijou.

"That's a big hat."

"Yes."

That night in a group of thousands, divide that by a lot, but you know what I mean, in a room at the Cabweights-Hoog Hotel in NYC, a group got together and two people got together. The group was all the group that had been at the club, but yeah not the, well you remember. They bought wine in paper cups from the bar downstairs and smoked some weed. Bernice fell asleep. Fast.

The next day or so Bernice told Bogart about Charles. About this connection they had. About how "she had wings."

Bogart wanted to say:

"You're insane. You were asleep. It's him and the other mother of the dog Bijou. You know that as well as I."

He ended up saying:

 "You're insane. You were asleep. It's him and the other mother of the dog Bijou. You know that as well as I."

Charles kinda hung 'round for a couple of days in various people's rooms. Jus' sorta hangin' 'round comin' and going. Bernice was making a big play. A big play. Remember Wit? Wit had made her fell, feel, like "she had wings."

Remember Wit:

But, and this is where it gets confusing, the other mother of the dog Bijou could tell that Bernice liked Wit. So she didn't. She didn't. She let Bernice have him. Did she?

"Bernice likes Wit. I'm not even going to talk to him," the other mother of the dog Bijou told Bogart after some drama at some little bar where Bernice broke (yes, "broke") into tears and Bogart had to put her (yes, "put her") into a cab.

"That's ridiculous," Bogart said back, melodramatically adding to the melodrama (sorta).

Bogart decided he was gonna "help out.".

One night in the hall of the hotel, on the same floor as Bogart's room, the other mother of the dog Bijou was sittin' strangely on the thinning hall carpet looking at a giant cardboard kid's cartoon map of the world. He had seen her lookin' at it before, almost, kinda, yeah, obsessively. She was lookin' at it again, and, uh, well, yeah, obsessively. She had a problem. She had a problem wit' it. The problem was it was wrong. It was wrong. Its geography or maybe more the size of certain of its geography was wrong, out of proportion.

"Does it make sense?" The other mother of the dog Bijou said to Bogart coming up to her, showing him the big cardboard kid's map.

Bogart had no idea what she was talkin' 'bout.

Charles came out then. From another room. And sat. In his relaxed way. Bogart liked that 'bout him. His presence. O.k. Things are o.k. He, Bogart, looked at the two of them not really. Not really looked, more mentally. He realized there was no way really for them to be alone. Bernice was stayin' with her. He jus' 'round, here and there, but trying to get closer to her. He said, that is Bogart, said:

"C'mon."

They went to Bogart's room and they drank some vodka he'd had. Maybe even Charles had had it. It wasn't really Bogart's drink (how quaint: "Bogart's drink."). He sat, Bogart again, on his couch. It usta be Victor's at Victor's house. The couch. Victor had given it to Bogart for his room. Charles and the other mother of the dog Bijou sat on the bed. Sat up. 'Gainst some pillows. Then Bogart left. All of a sudden left.

"Bye," he, Bogart, said not giving them a chance to say anything. "I'll be gone all night."

He went to his friend's house, Braces X. She was the leader (yes, "leader") of a rock band. The rock band was called, ha, ha, ha (no not "ha, ha, ha"), Braces X. They were friends. It was the middle of the night (whatever, you know pretty damn f-ing late). It was fine. She was having something going on too. By the way, her best friend was Doreen Snow, who is not a character is this story.

Braces was having something going on too. Her cool boyfriend had been arrested in his upstate New York small town for possesssion of marijauana. He'd been ratted on a by a friend's neighbor's kid who also had his own mother arrested. It was very weird. Braces was upset.

"Oooh." Bogart said when she told him.

Bernice lost Bijou. In New York City. Right after Charles and the other mother of the dog Bijou got together, still visiting in NYC, she took Bijou out. Sometimes Bijou walked but most of the time she kept Bijou in a handbag ("a handbag?!"). Her head peeked out. Later on she almost lied 'bout what happened by saying that someone stole the handbag, ripped it right off her, like they do, you know, in New York. But she didn't lie. She told the truth. She had put the bag down. And then forgot it. And walked off.

A couple blocks and she remembered. Running back to the corner where she had put the bag down, she found the bag, but not Bijou. Bijou was gone. She didn't know what to do. She got very scared.

"Bijou!" "Bijou!" "Bijou!"

She said a bunch of french words, it was Bijou's language and Bernice had come from a real pro-French Quebec family, too. But nothing worked. No Bijou. She walked around the immediate area. No Bijou. She asked people.

"Bijou. A little dog. Have you seen her? She's the prettiest dog in the world."

This is where this story has gotten this phrase.

She finally called the hotel. The other mother of the dog Bijou and Charles ran out to meet her to help her to find Bijou.

"Bijou!"

"Bijou!"

"Bijou!"

Bernice was crying. She had desperate wound-up activity nuances. She didn't know what to do. She didn't know what she did. She didn't understand. How could she do it? But she did understand one thing. She did understand one thing that she couldn't tell to the other mother of the dog Bijou and to Charles.

She had been mad at Bijou. Before she lost her. She had looked into the bag and into Bijou's bright eyes and had hissed.

Bogart had come back to the hotel and heard the news and also ran out to help in the search. He'd seen 'nuff movies to know she was probably in an alley somewhere. The only thing, a born New Yorker, he couldn't really remember if he'd seen, been on one, or even really knew what an alley looked like.

They each took an area to look in. Charles went one way. The other mother of the dog Bijou another. Bogart still another. And Bernice. Bernice another too.

But Bernice didn't look. She just stopped. She wanted to. She couldn't. She leaned up against a bus stop enclosure with a sign which every so often changed its ad very mechanically rolling up a different "star" from a TV news program. This feeling she had. She thought when.

She had lost the fucking plot. It was blue. She was blue. The water was a link. A kind of flat,
engulfing lever. By falling into the splash she could reverse everything that had happened.
Make it all go away. She had left the loft with nothing. No keys. No money. No cards. No
jacket. It was cold. It was cold in Montreal. She left because she had to. She had to because
she had to. She just left. Walked to the water.

A friend went looking for her. Found her. Called out after her. She ran. He lost her. She hid
in a construction site. Then slept in a park. She ate city-park fruit off a tree, and wondered
if it would hurt her in some way. She was dry, the lips, the tongue, the mouth. All dry. She
didn't drink. She didn't eat. She left because her mother told her. Her mother told her her
father was sick. Her mother told her her father was sick and they were getting a divorce.
Her mother told her her father was sick and they were getting a divorce and it was all
because of her. It was all because of her because of the problems with the loft. The loft was
bought and then Wit left.

She was having an awful conversation. A horrible conversation. She was
having an awful conversation with herself. A horrible conversation with
herself. She was almost too afraid to continue to live.

Wit had left. It wasn't just that he left. She didn't even know what she
thought of him really. It was so strange. This conversation with herself. The
cold, cold wind. She was talkin' to herself and she was listening to herself
and it was horrible. She knew something. She wouldn't miss Wit really.
That was what was so scary. It was just that. It was just that.

She remembered when Jewelle first brought Bijou home. Found her. Rescued her. Took her home. She was so pretty. She was so pretty Bijou. She was so pretty Jewelle. Jewelle and her became mothers of Bijou, but it was always Jewelle's dog. She knew it. She wanted it. She wanted Bijou to be hers. It was. It was the same with. It was the same with Wit. Wit always loved Jewelle. She knew it. But she had won, right. She had finally beaten. Jewelle. She had gotten. Wit. Wit had been hers. Hers. And now. Now he was gone. The one time she had beaten, finally beaten, beaten her, beaten Jewelle.

Bernice looked down.

She spit into the water, and the water barely noticed.

Knot threw hard a cold floppy slice of pizza at the greeny tint of tv screen

HOTEL STORIES

"Tom, you're fucked."

Bill Bill Bill Bill, a man with four first names, and the stern, atrocious mien of the neanderthal conservative, was calling it like he saw it. Which always, and in his case "always" was what he always stood for, required seeing it in a way that completely benefited him and only him. The fact that he swore, this was cable television, or some kindof cable television that allowed him to do such, shocked no one in so much as it seemed completely right. In other words, whatever he said, always, yes always, seemed to be saying to someone or something that they or it were fucked.

Knot threw hard a cold floppy slice of pizza at the greeny tint of tv screen Bill Bill Bill Bill was bullying from and then went on the search for the remote control. There was a movie on he was sure of it. And it was better than this. Whatever this was. When he turned the tv on, plugging the power switch (with the word "power" very rubbed off) with his meaty thumb, this Bill Bill Bill Bill thing had come on. Deer who was working before him, during the day on Saturday at the Cabweights-Hoog Hotel, watched things like this. Like the news. Knot liked sports and movies. Slope, another hotel worker, liked shows on how to fix up stuff. Victor, also working at the hotel, liked late-night talk shows. Deer was gay by the way. Which by the way has nothing to do with anything. ("All gay people like to watch news and current events." Huh?)

Knot could not find the remote control.

The office of the Cabweights-Hoog Hotel was like someplace upsidedown that was rightsideup. There was lots of little things in it. Little things that seemed to have sorta fallen from somewhere but sorta landed o.k. Like a bunch of tiny living porcelain cats were dumped ceremoniously from a big box and they all managed to right themselves as they fell and when they landed formed very distinguished poses of tiny marble. The things were all kinds of things. And the walls were also walled with all kinds of things. It was corny of plenty. It was shaken and stirred. It was a mess. It was beautiful.

Knot could not find the remote control.

"Damn. Fuck. Shit. Damn . . . Fuck Shit. Damn."

When people are pissed off originality goes out the window. Not a very original thing to say and not a very original way to put it. Knot was always, uh huh, always, pretty pissed off when he started his week on his Saturday evening shift. There was lots to do, for him to do, for him to get done. Things extraneous (extra-anus) to the running of a hotel as it's running. As in stuff he had to do when guests weren't bothering him with stuff he had to do. He picked Saturday night for this because Saturday night was sortof a quiet night. Sortof.

184

This time, coming in, not finding the remote control, having Bill Bill Bill Bill's bullshit on, and then finding out about the guest in a coma, it was a little much.

"Damn. Fuck. Shit. Damn . . . Fuck Shit. Damn. Are you sure? How could you tell?"

The how could you tell was telling. The guest in a coma was the most boring man ever.

The most boring man ever was the most boring man ever. How else can I say this. Hmmm? Let me see. Um. Uh. Well. Jeez. Gawd. Ugh. Snore. Zzzzzzzzzzzzzzzzzzzzzzzzzzzzzzzzzz! It's just. Oh god. He's so dull. Even talkin' 'bout him. I get. Ugh. Ah. Well. You see. Z z z z z z z z z z z z z z z z z z z z z z z z z z z z z z z ! A g a i n . Zzzzzzzzzzzzzzzzzzzzzzzzzzzzzzzzz!

Wait. Oops. I'm awake. What was I saying. O.k. this is it. He lived at the Cabweights-Hoog Hotel occasionally. Come to visit every so. Often. The staff dreaded his visits. This staff. Full of life. This staff. Lovers of stuff, for all their kinda pretend showy grumpy grouchiness. This staff. Even this staff. Dreaded. Him.

"He's so dull. He's so dull. He's so dull. He's so dull. He's so dull." They'd say. He had this presence. This presence that was such a. Absence. Not the kind of absence where you miss their presence. Where you wish they were here.

185

But the kinda absence that meant when he actually was here you could feel feel feel that he wasn't. He made you feel it. He made you feel that even when he was right in front of you somehow he wasn't. It was so annoying. This visible invisibility. He took up space. So much space. With his disappearing.

And. And. AND. When you walked right into him. Walked right over him. Walked right through him. He always would be angry. Like hey, hey, hey (quietly of course, in his not there but there way) what are you doing, huh, didn't you see me huh?, why are you walkin' right into, over, through me. HUH? But, oh, oops, I ah, didn't see you, ah, did I? (But you felt him, ohboy-oboyboboyo, you did. Oh.)

Bogart particularly felt him. Bogart, a sorta permanent guest at the hotel, a storyteller, who has since evaporated from the hotel's view by falling in love with some very long legs and the brains attached to them, got along with the most boring man ever about as awfully as it is possible to get along with somebody. He hated him. He bristled like a hairbrush at every interpersonal intrusion of the vague and distinct interpersonal intrusion of the most boring man ever. It was like oil and water. 'Cept imagine if oil and water were not words, but things, oil and water, and imagine what they were like together, the totally separate and adverse goo.

J.J.J., the young English kid painter of cartoons on walls, who had stayed at the hotel, while painting cartoons on walls (the hotel was decorated in this way, by visiting, itinerant artists) told this terrific story of how completely

186

unplanned, Bogart, and the most boring man ever had ended up at the same art event and how the oil and water mix became highly flammable. It went like this.

J.J.J. had had a friend who had had a friend who had had a friend who was an artist who had planned an art event. He was going to get a bunch of artists together and they were going to work in this large abandoned space and they were going to work in the large abandoned space for at least three days straight with none of them, none of them, going to sleep. If you went to sleep, it was this simple, then you couldn't work any more on the project. It was a combination art happening and depression style marathon dance or whatever those things were called where couples danced until they dropped. There was even talk of the artists wearing numbers in the way that the couples supposedly did at those depression dances. They didn't though, the artists. They didn't wear numbers. They did however show up to do it. To paint and paint, draw and draw, sculpt and sculpt until sleep took them over and put them away.

J.J.J. went, and in the way that New York City often works, Bogart had also been invited, but by somebody else. The artists had been asking their friends to come by and do kinda like shifts of hanging out to help keep everybod, the artists, awake. Bogart was a good choice for this, 'cause on occasion, he could be kinda entertaining. When J.J.J. and Bogart showed up guess who also was there? The most boring man ever.

Whether to fight or switch. Switch is the wrong word here. What I mean is whether to fight or not fight. Like whether to fight or switch — off. Ispose Bogart could've just ignored the most boring man ever, but he took his duties quite seriously, his duties to keep the artists awake, and well, um, the most boring man ever, was definitely about to jeopardize the whole mission. The most boring man ever was telling a story.

As one artist after another began to get really really really sleepy, the most boring man ever's story kept goin' on and on and on. It had something to do with the manufacture of a new kindof brick. He was in the building trade. Maybe it could have been interesting in someone else's mouth, the manufacture of a new kindof brick, but the most boring man ever was turning it into a solid square hardness of dullness. It was especially irritating to Bogart, in that the storytelling was so bad, that he couldn't follow it, and that the not following it wasn't even for some literary purpose, but just because the story had to be made as dull as possible. One artist did fall asleep. The first one to go. Dozed. Woke up and had to leave the space immediately.

Bogart butted in.

"Where is this going? Where is this fucking going? It's boring. It's boring. Boring. Boring. Boring. I don't understand it. Where is the story?!"

Bogart didn't say that. But something. Like it. Maybe just a glare. Implied. It. More than that. The most boring man ever understood. The most boring man ever got very hurt. And cut his story long (it had already gone on too long to accurately describe it as being cut short). Did Bogart do the right thing?

188

Knot had heard this story and had laughed when he heard it but he wasn't thinking 'bout it now. What a pain in the ass. The most boring man ever in a coma. He felt that overwhelming sense of responsibility that can be so, um, overwhelming. Again. AGAIN. Again. Now something else to take care of. Emergency had been called, and they were in the room right now, dealing with him, trying, I guess, Knot thought, to wake him up.

"Good Luck." Knot sarcastically mouthed.

He remembered when the writer Art Beach had disappeared after staying at the hotel for a good six months and there had been all these people looking for him. And like he was supposed to know. Like Knot was s'possed to know where he'd gone. Or when Ruggles of Redhook, the strange NYC fixture who had even appeared in a few movies playing cab drivers, and deranged hot dog vendors, had come to the hotel after his apartment building had been blown up in a badly-done drug raid, when a stray bullet in a boiler had set off an explosion and at the hotel he became too fat to get out of his room, and they had to saw the door and the surrounding frame a little larger so they could get him out and throw him out.

Knot chuckled/giggled as he remembered. Ruggles had been recording his memoirs into a tiny, high-tech, transcriber, and he'd left it, and the tapes, for a few days, while he was paying a visit to a famous NYC hospital. Or as Ruggles said, on the tapes, 'cause of course the staff played them:

"I was born in that hospital. I'm sure as hell not going to die there."

The "Ruggles Tapes" as they were called became nightly amusement for the Cabweights-Hoog folks. Every other comment or so by Ruggles in his life story was punctuated by a phrase that soon was heard up and down the stairs of the hotel. The phrase:

"Actually. NOT very exciting."

Ruggles on a sudden inflammation of his testes.

"My balls became the size of coconuts. Actually. NOT very exciting."

Ruggles on visiting a fat prevention center (fat farm).

"She was so fat. The only way you could find her pussy was to roll her in flour and look for the wet spot. Actually. NOT very exciting."

Ruggles on accidentally drinking his own urine sample.

"I thought somebody had brought me a whiskey neat. Actually. NOT very exciting."

When Knot had first heard that the most boring man ever was in a coma what do you think were his first words out of a somewhat downturned mouth?

"Actually. NOT very exciting."

One of the Emergency guys came down from the most boring man's ever room with some good news. They'd found the remote control to the office tv set in his room.

"He had it. What the hell did he want with it?" Knot asked.

That was another thing that was getting on his nerves. The amount of things that were just getting up and walking out of the office. Shit. The phone would always go. They had a cheap cordless phone and they were always finding it down near the litter box for the tiny dog, Bijou, that was staying with Jewelle, an artist who was living and working in the hotel. How it got there nobody knew, but Knot suspected Bijou. Could never catch her at it. Knot wanted to train one of the video cameras they had installed after they were robbed once by someone "they" (the hotel) usta know and so sorta let the whole thing drop, on the litter box to see what was happening. But he never got around to it. It was just another project on the list of projects.

"We saw a bat too." The Emergency guy said. "It was a little strange seeing a bat. At the top of the landing."

"Shit. Jewelle is feeding that bat again," Knot thought.

Slope was responsible for the cordless phone's walkin' down the hall. He'd pick it up and leave it near Bijou's box 'cause he couldn't stand answering it every so often. All the hotel staff had their own way of dealing with the constant pestering questions of future guests. Once somebody had called Slope reserving a room and then he had told her about the thing that she would have to call back at a certain time to confirm the reservation and she had told him that she couldn't 'cause she'd be traveling and wouldn't be near a phone.

"Not near a phone. Oh. S'cuse me. What you'll be in the jungle or something?" He said mockingly.

Yeah it was true. She was going to be doing some work in the rain forests.

Knot used the remote control and the tv changed from Bill Bill Bill Bill to NY Mets Baseball.

"Ya gotta believe" Knot shouted at the screen, in a way stating his age.

Winkler came up to the office to help with the laundry. Winkler was a kid whose mom had lived in the hotel a while back now, a way while back, the hotel had changed since then, what with all the rooms being painted by artists and such. C.B. ("Radio") B.C. was the last real resident guy from that period.

"We were all winos," he'd tell ya. "All of us were winos."

Radio stopped being a wino, stopped drinking. No one stopped him. He just did it. He'd seen some people die of it. He didn't want to die that way.

Probity, was his friend, he'd died 'bout four years ago. They would sit in the lobby, the small hall space outside the office, and bullshit. They'd argue 'n stuff too.

Knot missed Probity too.

"He'd get that guy outta that coma pretty fast," Knot's head nodded with this thought.

The phone had stopped ringing. He had muted the tv set 'cause there was a commercial on. There was nobody 'round. He leaned back, Knot did, in the old office furniture that served as office furniture, the one he was in, you could lean back really extra far in, 'cause it was so old and stretched out and almost broken, and he breathed in and then out a long languorous but loud sigh.

"Ahhhhhhhhhhhhhhhhhhhhhhhhhhhhhhhhhhhhhherumughahhhhhhhhhh."

"Sorry. Excuse. But I want to inquire . . . "

Knot almost fell, but righted himself with cool dexterity (Knot was not the kinda guy to fall by leaning too far back in an old office chair) and looked at the guest from Germany.

"Yes. Can I help you?"

"We would like to make another reservation?"

"Yes. For when?"

"New Years Eve, 1999."

"I can't do that right now. Call me nearer to it. Ok."

(The guests left.)

"Damn. Fuck. Shit. Damn."

Then this sweeping strange sounding creature with the eyes foreground and everything else just slightly traced in the dark interior night 'round it bashed into a hanging plant in the office and hard-turned and souped right outta dere.

Jewelle came running in.

"Did you. Ah. Did you? I, ah, where. Um. Did you . . ."

"It flew back out."

194

"Thanks. Um. Bye."

Charles came into the office a few seconds later, slowly, casually, up to Knot.

"Have you seen Jewelle?"

Charles was Jewelle's boyfriend. He had also been Ruggles' valet for a short while.

> || "Jewelle, is that Brian fellow 'round? I have some shirts I need taken to the laundry. Coughed up blood the other night on one of them. A white one too. NOT very exciting." ||

"She was just in here. She was chasing . . ."

"The bat. The bat again. Oh."

Charles went out, still casually, but a little quicker.

Knot caught the game again on tv outta the 'ol corner of the eye.

"Shit!"

A Met was caught stealing.

"oreg. ooh." mars, a man from japan, with two bottles of a dutch beer, one ineach hand, was expressing something about the play on tv, lookin' thru the cloudy plexiglass that fronted the hotel office separating it from the lobby.

"Mars! You sunuvagun. YOU SUNUVAGUN!" Knot extravagantly hailed him.

"oh. oh. ohhhhhh." mars said.

he walked up to the knotty pine desk (fake knotty pine desk) that knot had his oversized new zealand workboots and bright cherry red socks resting on and placed one of the bottles of beer with a slight, very slight, flourish in front of the hotel's manager.

"beer?"

"You know I don't drink. C'mon. Mars! Mars! You sunuvagun. YOU SUNUVAGUN!"

mars looked crestfallen.

"ooh. oreg. oh."

A Met hit a high fly ball to center but not high 'nuff or fly 'nuff, and it was caught.

196

Knot looked at Mars' arms, he was wearing a short-sleeved t-shirt with the words, "short-sleeved t-shirt", on it. Mars' arms were scratched. Mars had been feedin' Slope's cat while Slope was on vacation. Slope, the most successful lazy person in the history of the world (accordin' to J.J.J.), was in the Bahamas. Slope's cat was a killer. Every day when Mars would go over to feed it, the cat would scratch Mars. Knot knew this 'cause Mars liked to keep careful records of stuff.

"nine scratches, first four days." mars had a chart he made and he would show it.

"six. six. <u>six</u> condoms." he might say after he cleaned a room (he'd help out 'round the hotel occassionally), after a short stay.

a "Short Stay": three hours for $30

one day he came down from a room with a massive dildo. it was the morning. he was helping clean. this was not a short stay.

"oreg. ooh."

Deer who was on "doodie" took the dildo and waved it 'round and 'round in the hotel lobby.

"Look at this. Look at this!!!. Oooh. Oooh. I betcha someone was having fun.

Oooh. Oooh. I betcha someone was having fun. What room, Mars. Huh, what room?"

"oreg. ooh. fourteen-b. ooh."

"14B. 14B. Lookat the dildo left in 14B!!!"

A very hot sorta pale color took over a young couple leaving their bags in the office to pick up later. They left.

"oreg. ooh. fourteen-b. ooh." mars said.

Deer's mouth opened in a very piercing silent "oh."

mars finished his beer, and then the beer, he had originally put in front of Knot.

"Mars! You sunuvagun. YOU SUNUVAGUN!" Knot said.

C.B. ("Radio") B.C. stuck his head in the office.

"HEAT. HEAT. HEAT. HEAT."

C.B. ("Radio") B.C. took his head outta the office.

"I'm turning the heat up o.k. Radio, I'm turning the heat up." Knot yelled after him.

198

"ooh. oreg. ooh."

mars went to help winkler with the laundry.

Some guests with a reservation hadn't come yet, this late on a Saturday, they were already over two hours late, and Knot had one other room free. He checked the computer. (The computer was a clipboard with yellow-ruled paper and little colored white and pink cards stuck with tape on the papers held with that imposing giant metal clip attached to the board.) Yup. Two rooms open. One reservation late. He took out a very chemically smelly bold blue magic marker and made three signs, very bold, very very bold, with underlines and exclamations, **NO ROOMS !!!!**. He carefully locked the safe. (The safe was a closet with a giant padlock). Then locked the office and walked down the stairs past murals J.J.J. had done of giant lions driving around in a clown car, looking at clowns in natural habitats in the "wild", and taped the **NO ROOMS !!!!** signs all over the front door.

Back in the office, just barely, the bell rang and Knot looked in the monitor and talked into the intercom.

"Yup."

"Ya gotta any rooms for the night?"

"(Damn. Fuck. Shit. Damn.) No. NO ROOMS."

"A short stay. Please. Two - Three hours only."

Knot looked hard into the tv monitor. His one reservation still hadn't shown. And plus he had another room free, anyway. Hmmm. Er, o.k. He buzzed the door.

No response.

He buzzed the door again.

"Hey, hey, hey. I'm buzzing the door. Press the door."

Three people came up the stairs. A man. A woman. A young girl. The woman and young girl had their heads covered with scarves. Knot recognized them. The young girl would always wait for the couple, doing her homework, in the lobby. They usually didn't come at this time, but, ah well.

He gave them the keys, and the girl waited.

Coming down the stairs were four tall stoop-shoulder leather-clad and black 'n white makeup wearing vampires. Their eyes bloodshot. On purpose. Some kinda stuff they put in their eyes. They seemed very old. Very tired. Like the going-out thing was gettin' a little hard.

"The going-out thing is gettin' a little hard," Knot mumbled.

200

He turned back to the tv and watched the Mets win.

Then the most amazin' racket came headed towards the lobby from upstairs, like someone in full armor was carefully but bumpily moving down the floors (4 of 'em) of the Cabweights-Hoog.

A humorous and happy look again (almost peaceful, a kindof peaceful) instilled itself on Knot's outlook. This. This is what he likes. Things. Things as they are. Were. Things as they should be. Things as they will be. The same. But not the same. The same only in that something that wasn't the same has become the same. The normalcy of the strange. Like a belch from a screen goddess.

Knot belched, and as the guest in full armor carefully but bumpily moved his way past the office, Knot gave him a wave.

The guest in full armor slowly, very slowly, lifted his clanking arm, and reciprocated.

Slowly down the last staircase, slowly, slowly, loudly, to the street, the guest in full armor slowly, slowly, loudly, passed Knot's "reservations" finally making their late Saturday appearance. They looked a little startled/stunned at the guest in full armor.

"That wa s . . . ? (Oh never mind)." The "reservations" said.

One of the "reservations" went back down the stairs out the front door to the waiting cab waiting with their bags in it and told the cab (the driver, told the driver) to keep waiting.

"Here take a look at this room," Knot was saying. "It's my last one."

He made sure (he almost did it) not to give the "reservations" the room where he had sent the "short stays."

The last room left was the Pickle room. Embalmed pickles were hanging from the ceiling and attached to the walls, walls in the main painted green.

Other rooms in the hotel (which you remember were all decorated by visiting artists trading New York City free rent for their sweet equity) included:

The Diaper room, where you slept in a cradle.

The Drawing Board room, lined entirely with chalk boards and fitted with allotta chalk and erasers.

The Bachelor Pad, where James Bond music blared when you opened the door, the bed was a see-through waterbed with olives floating through it, the ceiling was mirrored, and the bathroom wallpaper was made with cutouts from old magazines with names like Swank and Swoon.

and the

Hotel Room room, with a framed picture of ducks, a plastic mint taped to the headboard of a sorta brass bed, a phone with a red LCD above it that added up exorbitant amounts to your bill every time you tried to use it (it didn't do that really), a television (the only television in the hotel), and a "do not disturb" sign permanently affixed to the outside of its door.

The "reservation" came down from looking at the Pickle room.

"Thank you very much."

"It's alright then?" Knot said.

"No."

The "reservations" took off in their cab.

"Damn. Fuck. Shit. Damn . . . Fuck Shit. Damn."

It wasn't about the "reservations" leaving. That was o.k. Fine. Hotel wasn't for them. It was that he'd forgotten to turn up the heat.

C.B. ("Radio") B.C. stuck his head in the office.

"HEAT. HEAT. HEAT. HEAT."

C.B. ("Radio") B.C. took his head outta the office.

"I'm turning the heat up o.k. Radio, I'm turning the heat up." Knot yelled after him.

mars made an appearance. And Winkler. The laundry was done.

"Mars! You sunuvagun. YOU SUNUVAGUN!" Knot extravagantly hailed him. "Winkler. WINkler! WINKLER!!" he added.

Jewelle and Charles came in. Jewelle carrying a strange-sounding almost purring creature wrapped up in a bright purple hotel towel.

"The . . . bat?" Knot asked.

"No. Silly. Bijou!'

Bijou barked.

Ivy called. She was going to take over Knot's shift soon. She wanted to see if he wanted anything from outside.

"Coffee. Please."

The "short stays" came from upstairs, and the young girl put away her homework, and went out with them.

mars and Winkler went to clean up the room.

The Emergency guys (and gal) with lotsa equipment left.

"He's fine." They said about the most boring man ever. "It wasn't a coma."

There was all sorts of junk in the garbage area in front of the building, off to the side of the steps. Like a three-legged table. A small old broken refrigerator, all browned like it had been cooked.

THE PHILOSOPHY OF EVERYDAY LIFE

Douche (don't ask!) was lookin' at the kid he and his crew were gonna fuck up good. The kid had pants as wide as tents and a fading neon red hairdo. In a few years, Douche thought, the kid was gonna be wearing a french cut shirt, and a silk tie, but he'd still have the same acne. Private school kid snot, Douche knew. This was easy and FUN. Yo, now. Eyes crossed the small time zones of the club and like as fast as china breakin' a swarm of scared-but-brave-in-groups kids 'n semi-adults mobbed the suburban roustabout and took everything he had. He was left practically naked (or impractically naked) with his stomach kicked and a bruise in his body that quickly swelled to the purple of an unripe mango (I have no idea what the color of an unripe mango is).

In editing, in the movies, there are different types of cuts. You know, to get you to think that it's all happening right. Someone leaves a room, and the camera picks them up from the other side, um, leaving the room. But you don't know it. You don't know that the perspective, the angle, has changed. You just blink, or don't blink, and it all makes sense. With two people there are two cuts. I have that now. Two cuts with two people. One is on the floor. One leaving with his posse in tow ("posse in tow" is being used with a slight wink). Wink. Slight.

I'm now going to flip a coin to see who we follow first (which of the two cuts). Heads, the suburban kid on the floor. Tails, Douche. Here goes.

It's tails. But I'm ignoring that. I want to write about the suburban kid.

When he was 8 his soccer coach stuck his finger up the crack of his ass. When he told his mother about it, she told him not to tell anybody about it. But she stopped him playing soccer. He was bored. He was bored a lot and when he told his mother she told him to find something to do. She was very busy. She and his dad had divorced when he was around 5. His dad was a drunk period. A drunk period, is that anything like a high exclamation point? Yeah, it is. He never saw him, sometimes. When he did, he stunk. His dad did. Stunk to low hell. Like he didn't wash right, plus the booze. He became pretty tall pretty fast but that made him pretty gangly pretty fast. He got into music. He'd go into New York (he lived in New Jersey) to clubs alone when he was 16. They were clubs that wanted teenagers. He felt welcome, sortof. He could blend in. He wore pants as wide as tents. And neon red hair. He didn't have a tattoo. He didn't have jewelry stuck in him in. He didn't have friends.

The first time he took Ecstasy it wasn't Ecstasy. It wasn't aspirin. But it was something like aspirin. He didn't know that it wasn't aspirin. He found out later that it was some kinda breath mint that had some kinda pattern on it that could pass. Actually he never found out. But he did know that it wasn't real. When he did one that was real.

A girl had given him the real one. He gave her $25. She'd said, "here" and that's it. He took it. She walked off. It was funny. He didn't trust her. Was it real? It was real. He fell in love with the girl that had given him the "e." She had a gaunt face (what is a gaunt face?) and hollow eye sockets (ditto, hollow eye sockets). She had platform shoes that were like shoes with these big platforms on them. She had a kinda stammer. He remembered her, the way she spoke.

He had just seen, talked to her, looked into her, and she was already a memory. She was a chess board in his mind. And each part of her became a square on the board. Each part of her that he knew. He knew all parts of her. Each part seemed to be another chess board. Each of these new chess boards led onto new chess boards. She was someone that he had known forever and could know forever. All he wanted was. All he wanted was. All he wanted was. All he wanted was what he wanted. All of it. All of her.

The room of the club seemed darker now, darkened now. But with outlines of the figures in a brash cold lone light bulb blur. The figures. Figure this. Figure 1. The total weight in tons of the total weight. He felt the club's room tilt. Like it actually titled. He felt excited. He felt happy. And, um, happy. He felt, oh, like, um, well, it was just, ooh, he, he wanted to, he wanted to be, he wanted to be wit' someone. Somehow.

He saw her again. She "beckoned" him. He thought she "beckoned" him. She was talkin' with her hands to her friends, that's all. But he came over, and looked, up and down kinda, all goofy. She looked at him:

"What.?"

"Um, yeah, you know, uh, thanks."

"Fuck off."

He walked away. Did she say "fuck off," she couldn't have said "fuck off," why would she say "fuck off," why would she do that, I mean say that 'n shit, "fuck off," huh, what did he do, yeah, why did she say "fuck off." ?????

He got so sad. He got so goddamn sad. His heart became some kinda weird waterfall. It sprayed this water out, through him. But it didn't come out through him. He came on all bloated. A sack of ocean. He felt this pounding. This thundering. The thing about to explode. He was going to. Burst.

He took a piss.

The place you take pisses was the club's bathroom which was like all club's bathrooms a club's bathroom. An inferno with stopped-up plumbing, a depth so deep into the core of degraded space, that the term space isn't good. There is no space. No light. No toilet paper.

Pissing into the yellow piss blocked up in the urinal before him, and into gum, sandwiches, tin foil, butts, n' broken glass, the suburban kid thought woozily 'bout this time he'd got caught pissing just a few blocks from this club 'gainst what he thought was a dark deserted thing (wall).

"Hey, motherfucker, don't fucking piss here."

"Oh yeah, oh yeah, oh yeah," he'd said to the suddenly opened window, shutting off without even really going, and hurriedly zippering.

But here he could piss, in the club's bathroom, some of it getting on his loafey brown brushed suede slipper-sorta shoes.

Brenda Kill Starr, "Kill" to her friends (she added the "Kill" but it was her baby boomer parents that had called her Brenda, with their last name Starr, thinkin' that was cute), the girl that had sold the suburban dweeb the "e", was getting the fuck outta the club 'cause she had seen Douche.

(this is another cut by the way)
"Yo, Kill. You seen him?"

"Yeah. Yeah. I seen him."

Douche was no fuckin' good. Worse than no fuckin' good. Double-secret no fuckin' good. His crew was the Droppin's, 'cause they did what wuz called drop-in crimes, quick sudden on-foot maneuvers, fucking total allout invasions, quick drive-by's, 'cept New York stylie, everythinc on the ground, person-to-person, not a vehicle thing. They wuz bad fuckin' news. Worse than bad fuckin' news. Double-secret bad fuckin' news. They were fucking crackin' up the young dance scene. Selling fake shit. Bustin' up other dealers. Stealing. General fuckin' mayhem.

"Ahem . . . Kill! Mary's here wit' his broomstick."

"Yeah. Yeah. Yeah. Yeah."

The young kid dealers were passing the news. They did not want to be the next wrecked by Mary. "Mary" was what they called Douche and his gang.

She'd done o.k that night. She'd sold a few. Some weed. She was gettin' out now. She didn't need no aggravation. She stepped out thru the exit doors and a guy in makeup held up a stamp to see if she wanted to come back in.

Douche felt the place clear out, not clear out, but clear out of the people that knew who he was. Basically, the dealers, and a couple, you know, right-on kids. In the know. He felt his presence felt. He didn't know what to feel. That is the problem with a feeling. It is never a feeling. There are many feelings that make up a feeling. And all those feelings are different. And they make a mess. When described as "a" feeling.

Douche talked 'bout his feelings a lot. You can do that when you have some power. You'll notice that. When you have some power you can talk 'bout your feelings. When you don't have some power you get smacked. "Shut up," someone says to you when you talk 'bout your feelings.

Douche could do it. Douche could. In the record store (yeah, they had vinyl records n' shit, you know sorta "ski" clothes and shit, bicycle riding, that kinda stuff, rollerblading, skateboarding, blah, blah, blah, a record store etc., magazines) where he kinda hung wit his team, wit his "a" team, not everyone in his thing could be dere, you had to work up to it, Douche would talk 'bout his feelings. You know what I'm feeling, he would say. No quotation marks. It doesn't need quotation marks 'cause it was more than conversations. It was statements. Statements from the deeps of his soul. You know what I'm feeling, he would say. You know what I'm saying, he would feel. I feel. That's it.

He didn't know what to feel 'bout feeling his presence felt. I mean one way, it was good. It was all good, ya know. I mean he was bad. They thought he was bad. They were leaving. They were gettin' out. That was good. On the other, ya know, in another, it was bad. They were leaving. They were gettin' out. They were on to him.

His beeper went off for like the eighth thousandth time in like the last eight minutes but he still ignored it. It was good to ignore it. He didn't really want to carry it 'cause he didn't really use it. He didn't let it beep that's for fucking sure. Your beeper should not fucking beep. It vibrated against the top of his underwear band. He liked to use the cell phone anyway better.

He needed somethinc. He needed somethinc bad. It wasn't anything in particular. It was almost like that was it (what?). Yeah, like that was it. That it wasn't that he needed anything in particular, it was that he needed somethinc to need. If he could find this something, even if he had to make it up, even if he had to just invent it. You know manufacture in himself the want. Then,

213

then, he could fulfill. Fulfill it. Fill it. He was searching for what he was searching for.

(two cuts come together and then apart to become two cuts again (pretentious, moi?))

His marks were exiting. One was entering. The stoned/high bumbling dweeb, the tall rich kid, was coming outta da bathroom. He liked his odds, Douche did, he liked the weakness of the kid, he liked fucking up kids dat were fucked up. He liked fucking up good. Kids that were fucked up good.

"Good. Good." Douche felt.

(another cut, oops, here goes)

Kill made her way in the cold down fifth ave. It was a really weird part of fifth ave. This weird part of fifth ave. that was really weird. It was cold. She made her way in the cold. Kill had a gaunt face and hollow eye sockets. She had platform shoes. She walked. deliberately. And here's some other ways she walked:

consciously, expressly, intentionally, voluntarily, willfully, calculatedly, cautiously, considered, premeditated, and studied

she was a tough shell of girl. she was fierce. she was like a giant peanut shell walkin' down that big ave. Mr. Peanut without the peanut. Ms. Peanut.

214

she was walkin' deliberately,

This one guy decided he was gonna rape her. He was slinkin' in a doorway. Yup, yup, he was. He was slinkin' in a doorway of an electronics store. You know where they're always having goin' outta business sales. Where everything is marked up 8 million percent. Where you can buy four year old gear (which in "gear years" is like a thousand years old) for twice the prices of new stuff, 'specially if you're a tourist. PSCAM. GREAT SCAM. PASCAL. PASQUE. HUH?

He was slinkin' in a doorway and he pushed out and pushed into her, pushed her, pushed her into the doorway. Metal shiny in the not-strong lighted night of the city sky hangin o'er an empty part. She had her keychain in her hand. It had pepper spray on it. She pushed it into his face and pushed it on. He screamed. Held his eyes. She pushed away. She pushed away from him. Didn't even bother runnin'. Just left him. Knew he wouldn't follow. He didn't.

She raised her hand. A yellow thing stopped. She opened the door (duh?). Got in (double duh?). She was breathin'. She knew it hard. A lot.

"O.k. You o.k."

Cab driver. She hated them.

"Just drive." She said. "Just drive."

Passengers. He hated them.

"Where." He said. "Where?"
(I'm cutting, (yeah, yeah, yeah, 'nuff 'already), o.k. I'm not)

"I want to go where I want to go." She said.

"Mumble. Mumble. Mumble." He said.

He drove down that weird part of fifth ave., that very weird part of fifth ave. They were silent. It don't need me to comment on the weirdness. The weirdness of the sometimes close proximity (like what other kind?) of people who aren't close. A cab I s'ppose is not that close. There's that thing in the middle. That thing.

Just keep driving. He knew that's what she wanted. So he did it. He also didn't mind so much. He also didn't mind so much that he was ripping her off. That his meter was fixed to bounce up an extra quarter mile every three quarters of a mile in price. He liked ripping her off.

She was thinking in the back about the subway. She was completely blankin' on what had just happened to her. She was thinkin' 'bout the subway. The subway was ridiculous recently. Totally, fucking ridiculous. The crowds were like all the time. You were totally fucking treated like a fuckin' nothing. Banged tight into a crate and then jolted back and forth into the packedness. She couldn't fucking stand it. It was humiliating.

She was trying to get by. A girl trying to get by. In that weird space. In that weird space 'tween high school and whatever. She had her diploma. She finished high school. She was pretty fuckin' smart. O.k. her grades weren't fucking good. 'Cause she didn't fuckin' study. That's all. But she didn't know what she wanted to do now. She didn't even know why she fuckin' had to know. She wanted to goof down a 'lil bit. Ya know. Take it the fuck easy. She was makin' her money. She was living on her own. O.k. she was living with three (sometimes six) other girls. In Williamsburg, Brooklyn. But payin' her own way. It was so difficult. With the fucking trains. Being so crowded 'n shit. The way it made her feel. Bad.

"Alright here!"

It seemed like it wasn't right, the fare, but she didn't fucking care. She was tired. She was so fucking tired. Fuckin' Douche. The fuckin' guy that fuckin' attacked her. This fucking asshole driving this fucking cab. Fuckin' men were fuckin' assholes. Shit. Even fuckin' earlier, she had gone to the fuckin' movies. She liked goin' to fuckin' movies in the day. She could do that with the way she worked. Ya know. Perks. So yeah, movies during the day. They were empty, during the day, she liked that, the movies, with no fucking people. But this fucking guy, the fucking manager, got into a fucking fight with her, 'cause she wanted to stay and watch the fuckin' film at the beginning again, 'cause she missed it, the beginning, and he was like no, ya gotta pay again. The fuckin' jerk. There was no one there. What the fuck was that?

The bar she was going to meet a friend in was designed to look like the inside of an ocean liner. Not that her generation had any idea what the inside of an ocean liner looked like. All this constant xeroxing of xeroxing, things passing down to her, from things passing down to her, was building up on her brain like gold waxy buildup. Not like she had any idea what gold waxy buildup was.

She was tooted on board deck (ushered into the bar) and sat down in a booth in front of fake portals. A guy with a weird haircut. A really weird guy with really weird hair and a big glaring half-smile came up to her. It hurt. It was painful. It hurt. It was painful. To see him. He had slept with one of her roommates. He was horrible. Awful. Disgusting. I mean he was o.k. Nice ya know. But god. But god. Ecch! Ecch!

She got rid of him. She liked doing things like that. She just liked the way it sound-ed. She got rid of him. Then it really. Then it really began to get on her nerves.

She worked in clubs, bars, that kinda stuff. You know bartender. Waitress. Coat check girl. It was always these dweebs. Like the guy that ran, actually owned, this place. His hair. Lookit his hair. It was shaved sortof. Like maybe he was bald. Sortof. And it was died sortof. He looked like a skunk. He looked like a skunk with a bad haircut.

It was always these dweebs. They couldn't meet girls so they dressed up as somebody else. You know they got some of the accountant buddies (that's unfair to accountants, Kill thought to herself as she was thinking to herself) and they put money together and the money was put together and that was it. Money, bad taste, and boom.

Funny, tho she kinda liked the ship look. But she knew it wasn't his idea. Although he did tell her once long and boringly that it was his "execution."

"I can't believe Kelley slept with him. Ecch!"

B. came in then with this boy. This boy. This boy was sorta BOY.

They slided. Uh, huh. Slided into the booth. That was always fun doing it. B.'s clear vinyl raincoat stuck strangely on the slide and squeaked.

"Hey, mouse."

"Hey, drug-dealin' slut."

The two girls kissed long, long, long, on the lips, lotsa tongue. Long, long, lover's kiss. Lotsa tongue. They looked. Sorta did. Not actually. They didn't look at him. At BOY. But they knew he was lookin' at them. Sorta. Pretending not to. They knew he was smiling. He was. Smiling.

They didn't like girls. Ya know LIKE girls. Like 'nuff to kiss long, long, long, lover's kisses, lotsa tongue. They did things like that, with each other, long, long, lover's kisses, lotsa tongue, 'cause they did.

B. stopped kissing Kill and then started kissing BOY. Long, long (but not so long as she had kissed Kill) lover's kiss, lotsa, ya know.

Then B.'s boyfriend, or some guy whatever that she was "dating," arrived.

"Hey."

"Hey."

"Hey."

"Hey."

"Hey." He said again.

B. had stopped kissing BOY before he'd come. So everything was o.k.. O.k.. O.k.?

"Everything O.k.," B. looked at him.

He mumbled back.

"Show some awakeness. G - O - D !" She yelled.

Her boyfriend, or some guy whatever that she was "dating," was doing that boy (lowercase) thing, that she had often talked over, discussed, gone into, with Kill. They get depressed. They get down. They mumble. They sleep for days.

BOY had gotten up and allowed B.'s boyfriend or guy that she was "dating" whatever to slide (yup slide) next to her in the booth in front of the fake portals. BOY came up 'round the other side to slide (yup, slide) next to Kill.

They kissed meaning B. and the guy she was "dating" but it was more a peck thing than the smooching that was going on jus' earlier.

But the minute B. stopped kissing the guy, she started kissing Kill again, just a quick sorta sloppy kiss. BOY smiled, again. And so did the guy, but, a smile, a smile that wasn't really exactly a smile. The smile was there. On his face 'n all. But he didn't mean it. Or all of it. It was an unhappy smile.

Then Kill looked at BOY next to her and she planted a big one on his lips and looked straight in his eyes. BOY smiled, again. Kill noticed he had a cold sore to the far right on his upper lip.

Drinks came. Black and White Russians. B. had ordered them. White Russians for the girls. Black Russians for the boys. The guy had wanted a different drink but B. had ignored him.

"Drink up stereotypes," she yelled.

They got drunk. It was good. Their bones became moist. The ones in their heads and their bodies. B. and Kill got up and played headless ghost. B. pulled her mac up over her face and buttoned it. Kill stuck her head through B.'s arms and talked for her. It was funny. BOY and the guy laughed.

BOY 'n Kill were gettin' along. They were laughing. As a team. A laugher. A couple o' laughers. The guy kinda treated them like they were boyfriend and girlfriend. And he was like boyfriend and girlfriend with B. Like they were double datin' or somethinc. This annoyed B.

"He's so cute," B. said to Kill 'bout BOY.

"What'd you say. No whispering." BOY said.

"I said you're not very attractive," B. said.

Later as seat places were changed in the booth, B., now to the side of BOY, said to BOY, in a stage (but very real) whisper:

"You're very attractive. Stay around. Tonight. Stay around."

BOY got up and made a phonecall. B. kissed the guy, a peck again sorta. B. reached over long, she was sittin' one away from Kill (she hadn't moved closer when BOY got up), and kissed Kill, a most enveloping kiss. BOY came back. Kill sliding (yes, sliding) outta the booth, BOY sliding (yes, sliding) into the booth between Kill and B. The guy was on the other side of B. where he had been all the night, nearest the door, although the door was as far away from their booth as you could get in the not very big ship's cabin bar they were in.

Then B. kissed BOY.

"What. What. What?" The guy said.

B. kissed BOY kissed long, long, long, on the lips, lotsa tongue. Long, long, lover's kiss. Lotsa tongue. They looked. Sorta did. Not actually. They didn't look at the guy. But they knew he was lookin' at them.

B. stopped kissing BOY and then Kill reached over long, and kissed B. Long, long lover's kiss, lotsa, ya know.

Then Kill stopped, looked at BOY next to her, and she planted a big one on his lips looking straight in his eyes. BOY smiled, again. Kill noticed again he had a cold sore to the far right on his upper lip.

"What. What. What?" The guy said.

"What. What. What? What. What. What?" The guy said.

"What. What. What? What. What. What? What. What. What?" The guy said.

"What. What. What? What. What. What? What. What. What? What. What. What? IN THE FUCK ARE YOU DOING." The guy said.

"FREAKS. FREAKS. FREAKS. FUCK YOU. FREAKS. WHAT THE FUCK ARE YOU? WHAT THE FUCK ARE YOU DOING." The guy said.

B.'s neck bent along with her head, all in one motion, not jerky, like a crumpling but smoother, and she cried, soft sobs.

BOY put his arm around her.

"WHAT DA FUCK. WHAT DA FUCK. DON'T YOU FUCKING TOUCH HER. DON'T YOU FUCKING TOUCH HER!"

He hit BOY's arm and BOY withdrew it to his own body.

Kill was like whatever.

"Let's go," she said to BOY and they got up and B. got up and followed. And the guy got up and followed. AND THE GUY GOT UP AND FOLLOWED.

A bouncer, with bouncer intuition, stepped in his way (that's what they do you know), and let BOY, B. and Kill leave.

Outside, near Tompkin's Square Park, New York City was green 'cause New

York City was dark. So much of the colors of New York City are the colors of darkness. We have greys, greens, and browns in our blues, reds, and yellows. (What the hell am I talkin' 'bout?). B. went across the street, leaving Kill and BOY, and went into a deli. She bought a flat square of cake. And ate it in one ateitness. She wanted to sober.

Up.

Down. Down. Down. Kill was sinkin' to her knees. But she wasn't. Internally she was sinkin' to her knees. She was standin' straight up. BOY was whoozy. Ozzy. Whooshey. Whatsit.

They joined B. in the deli.

"We gotta get condoms," B. said mouth full of cake.

BOY smiled. The cold sore more noticeable in the bright deli store.

BOY saw his brand of condoms and bought them. Kill bought cigarettes.

B. bought some potato chips.

They walked together. Interlocked arms. sillyilly. they also walked:

foolishly, irrationally, nonsensically, senselessly, giddily, mindlessly, shallowly, absurdly, asininely, pointlessly and ridiculously they were having fun.

Kill felt jealous. B. felt jealous. BOY liked Kill more than he liked B. This confused him. He wanted to fuck Kill and B. together. This was all happening back at B.'s place. B. sunk to her knees. B. cryed. B. cryed. B. cried:

"Who do you like better? Who do you like better? Decide. Decide. You like her better. You do. You do."

BOY didn't know what to say and so (duh) didn't say anything ('cause he didn't know what to say).

Kill got very tired.

Kill was like whatever.

Kill left. She heard B.'s voice:

"See that's what happens. You come onto two girls."

Kill felt sober now. She wasn't happy 'bout it. She almost made a big pretentious statement. Like, oh I can't even repeat it, 'cause she's forgotten it. But it came into her head for a sec. Some big summing up thing. Some statement. 'Bout when drunk wantin' to be sober, and sober wantin' to be drunk.

She walked by a video store that was done up to look somewhat like a little movie theatre. On the fake marquee was the film "Accident" by Joseph Losey. Accident. The word stuck. And suddenly she noticed somethinc she hadn't noticed before. Maybe noticed is the wrong word. Maybe she saw. Saw. Saw saw. Accidentally. Accident. An accident.

A guy on a bike, seemed like a guy delivering some food, went over the front of a big dark blue car, and flipped in the air, both him and the bike, lookin' like they were doing gymnastic jumps.

She'd never seen an accident before. I mean seen one. They probably happened 'round her all the time.

Was it real. Did she feel. Should she feel?

She realized somethinc in seeing. She realized that she wasn't feelin'. The guy that jumped her. Everything that had happened. The shit with B. 'n BOY. It made her. It made her. It made her. She didn't have the word. (The word is numb.)

She got on the subway to go home. It was late. It was almost early. On the subway a man was tellin' everybody to be happy. He had a cup out for change. Be happy. He said. Be happy.

She was takin' the L train to Brooklyn. To Billyburg. "L" for love, B. would say. It usta to be the double L train. "LL" for double love, B. would say.

B. could fall in love, or at least seemed to, a lot, Kill thought bitterly.

Here's some foreshadowing. Some foreshadowing following. Some fore-shadowing coming. Foreshadowing alert. Foreshadowing. Next stop fore-shadowing.

The announcements on the subway loudspeakers were again muffled and muffled.

foreshadow: to present an indication or a suggestion of beforehand; presage

She had a lot of money in her apartment. It's where she kept her money. In her apartment. Cash. From the stuff that she sold. The drugs that she sold. In her apartment. She kept the money. There.

The money.

The door at the end of the subway car she was in, the door you opened and walked through to get to the next car (they seemed to be locked most of the time now, Kill thought) opened with that special boulder rolling down and breaking a shack at the bottom of a mountain sound and another man, like the "Be Happy" man, another "bum", came into her car. He walked up to her and standin' holdin' on a pole, his head framed by an ad for "feed the starv-ing children before it's too late", looked at her, looked at her, looked at her, and said:

228

"I wanna kill someone like you."

He kept standing there and Kill was like, she was like, um, she was, she was uh, she was (still, still, coldly still).

The "Be Happy" man, more in the classic hobo tradition, came over to the "I wanna kill someone" bum and said:

"Hey, hey, hey, you don't want to do that. Oh, no, no. Be happy. Be happy."

(Advice, he's giving him advice, Kill's mind stiff still like everything else 'bout her pondered this almost strangely, humorously.)

Then the "Be Happy" hobo announced to the train and the subway riders who were desperately trying to avoid any involvement in any of this:

"I have TB. Can anybody help me. Please. Please. Be happy. Be happy."

The train got to Williamsburg. Kill got up and got out. So did all the riders.

Kill was near zombie-like now, really. Her neck hurt. She tried to crack it as she walked home, and she looked odd, her neck circling, and her head following. It happened. Crack. A woman walkin' a dog looked, shivered. The dog didn't seem to care.

Kill stopped in at a fruit stand just opening with the morning light. She bought a couple of purple plums, almost like three-dimensional bruises, and put them on the counter. The woman with bleached hair behind the counter snarled at her. But took her money. But didn't say anything. Kill didn't say anything either. It was like that in that store, but she went in there anyway. They didn't want her there. Wasn't like them.

The woman's bleached hair made her think of the morning when she was in the laundromat. The woman that worked there was wearing a surgical mask 'cause of the bleach. It wasn't workin'. Or it was too late or somethinc. She'd shown Kill her face under the mask, all red, and her throat too, she croaked, her throat had gotten fucked.

Kill bit into one of the plums. It was squishy and not good. She dropped it. Two cops walked past her.

"Gotta new pair of Timberlands."

"How much dey cost ya?"

"Nuthinc. Ya know."

"Nuthinc?"

"Yeah. Ya know. They brought this drug dealer down by da house. Ya know he lost his shoes down lockdown, so ya know dey fit pretty good."

230

One of her roommates went out wit' a cop. Not exactly a cop. He wanted to be one. His pops was one, and two of his uncles. He was in rookie school or somethinc, what ever the fuck that was. It was really weird considering what Kill did. The girl was like 25, much older than her. Also older than him. He masturbated a lot. She kept jelly 'round, lubricant 'n stuff. 'Cause he was makin' his dick so raw. She'd leave it at his house. He still lived with his parents. She'd leave it in his room. And tell him, "ya know look, when I'm not there, and you do it, make sure you use the jelly, o.k., so you don't hurt yourself."

She was such a crazy chick. Why was she going wit a cop? Her last boyfriend had his dick pierced. She used to laugh about it. She said it was hard for him. He used to get it caught on stuff. There was this thing they'd read that they'd laugh 'bout, her n' Kill, about this couple that supposedly got stuck together cause she had an I.U.D. and his dick was pierced. And they had to go to the hospital wit' a blanket over them, and the doctor had to take 'em apart.

"Urban myth," they joked but it was a good story, like gerbils up the butt and that kinda shit.

She got to her apartment building. There was all sorts of junk in the garbage area in front of the building, off to the side of the steps. Like a three-legged table. A small old broken refrigerator, all browned like it had been cooked. Piles and piles of newspapers and magazines for the recycling. Bags of cans. Oh yeah it was recycling night.

She looked at the restaurant across the street. It didn't open yet. She hated that fuckin' restaurant. $18 for like a meal. It was bullshit to have that out here in Billyburg. It was the kinda place that got packed for brunch.

"Brunch." Kill said out loud disgustedly.

"Shit." She also said disgustedly and loudly. more Loudly. LOUDLY. "Shit. Shit. Shit."

She couldn't get her key to fuckin' work. She could never get her key to f-ing work. Damn it. Damn it. Damn it.

"Hey." She yelled out. Loudly.

"Hey." She yelled out. LOUDLY.

"Shut up." Someone yelled from 'nother window.

"You shut up." Kill yelled back.

"What. IsthatyouKill?" Her roommate, the one that was going wit' the future cop, peeked a nightgown wearing, bed-headed, figure outta their top floor window sleepily. And then threw her a key, in a sock (there was no buzzer), knowing what the problem was, 'cause it happened so much.

Her roommate's key worked and Kill made her way slowly up the stairs.

In the apartment, her roommate, a nightgown wearing, bead-headed, figure, and her boyfriend, in jeans 'n open dress shirt, were sittin' at the kitchen table.

Her boyfriend was playing with his gun.

It was still in its holster attached to a belt, but he was sorta fingering it, holding it, moving it around slightly in his hands. Like he was about maybe to put it on. Put the belt on. But didn't. He seemed like he was getting dressed.

"Bob's leaving." Her roommate said.

"Whatever." Kill said.

Kill sat down at the table. Her nerves were nervy. She felt something. And it was so weird. All night, she was. What was that word? (The word is numb). All night she was like that. She couldn't get the juices in her. She couldn't get them to. What was that word? (The word is flow.)

All night. And now.

The morning was bright. Brighter than it ever seemed. It almost hurt her. The light. She wanted to sink. Become part of the floor. A tile on the floor. (Their kitchen floor did not have tiles). It was. It was. (And now. Now she felt. And the feeling wasn't 'bout what had happened earlier.) It was 'bout what was happening now. She felt funny. Something in the room. Something was wrong. The way her roommate and her boyfriend were being. The way he was he was he was what is the word (the word is finger-ing). The way he was fingering his gun.

Why the brain is a constant center of decentering. Why it goes off on its lit-tle goesoffness. Why it likes to spiral. You know it's that ol' expression, "anybody's guess." But it does. The creepey crawlies creepin' n' crawlin' inside Kill. The ones now. NOW. Not from any buildup, but from commu-nication currently communicating itself to herself (the way he was finger-ing his gun). These creepey crawlies suddenly gave way or maybe started or attached themselves or went fishing for and dredged up, that's what I'm try-ing to say, dredged up, memories.

Ah, memories. Remember them. We remember them, just like they are remembering something. There is never a first memory. It is always a remembrance of a memory. A thing past. Nothing ever happens. It is only remembered. Nothing is ever remembered. It is only a memory of a remem-brance. To know is to pass by what you are knowing (once again, preten-tious, moi?).

She used to live in Long Island. In a house. At the end of a drive. It was a big house, on land that two houses could have been built on. Her father built the house. He ran a contemporary furniture store. Not, you know, sales, lay-away on sofa sets (soundin' a lil' snobby, huh), no, new, cool, Italian, dare I

234

say it, mod, stuff. He would take lots of trips to Europe, her dad did. He collected etchings. To this day she still didn't really know what an etching was. She also hated navy blue. This has nothing to do with anything. 'Cept that she would say, the fact that she hated navy blue, was 'cause of her mom's 70s way of dressing.

Then he lost his money. His best friend had been his partner, and somehow, his best friend had somehow cheated him. He lost his best friend. He lost his house. His business. Lost.

He got divorced. But that was happening anyway. A sort of parallel disaster.

She hated that word, Kill did. She hated the word, "disaster." He would always say it. To this day, her dad did. She couldn't stand it. "Oh, it's such a disaster." "Oh, no a disaster." "Yup, a disaster."

He got remarried. Moved to Alaska. Kill went to high school there. Until she left early, though she graduated, to come to New York, where her mom was. When she left her step-mom apologized to her saying she, "wished she'd been better."

Kill "wished she'd been better" too.

She remembered being happy. She remembered the memories of being happy. Of Long Island. Of the big house. Of her dad collecting etchings.

Before his "disaster." Before he remarried. Before he moved to Alaska. Before he moved her into a home where she was hated and tormented. And the only thing she could do was leave, come to New York City. Be in this apartment. With lots of cash hidden in a sock drawer. And a soon-to-be-cop fingering his gun.

In lotsa literature people snap back outta things. Where they're remembering. And then they're brought back. To earth. Like where were they. They were on earth. They were jus' dreamin or thinking or, in this case, remembering.

Kill snapped back.

It's not really right to describe it that way. It's not really what she did. But more. But more. But more what happened. It makes you feel what happened. The "snapped" part. The "back" part. It makes you feel what happened and . . . what's about to happen.

"Hey." Her roommate's boyfriend said.

"What." Kill said.

"I hear you deal drugs." He said.

"Whatever." She said.

"Make a lot of money" He said.

"What?" She said.

He raised the gun and the hole at the front of the pistol looked at her.

"I want the money."

"BOB!" Her roommate yelled.

"Shut up. I want the money."

He got up. Took one quick step. In one quick motion. He'd hit her. Hard. And. She. Fell. Put her hands behind her back on the floor hard. Pushed her face into the floor. Hard. And he produced handcuffs. And cuffed her. And the gun went to her head.

"Where."

There is no reason to write what I'm about to write. It's so obvious. So I won't.

(two cuts come together and then apart to become two cuts again)

His marks were exiting. One was entering. The stoned/high bumbling dweeb, the tall rich kid, was coming outta da bathroom. He liked his odds,

237

Douche did, he liked the weakness of the kid, he liked fucking up kids dat were fucked up. He liked fucking up good. Kids that were fucked up good.

"Good. Good." Douche felt.

The suburban kid stumbled outta da bathroom into the big room of the club.

Eyes crossed the small time zones of the club and like as fast as china breakin' a swarm of scared-but-brave-in-groups kids 'n semi-adults mobbed the suburban roustabout and took everything he had. He was left practically naked (or impractically naked) with his stomach kicked and a bruise in his body that quickly swelled to the purple of an unripe mango (I have no idea what the color of an unripe mango is).

He looked at me like I was some kinda slut, trying to seduce his prissy boyfriend into orgies and disco.

COMING IN

The first word in the diary was "fuck."

Deer looked at the word a long long time. A long long time ago he might not have looked at someone else's diary. Actually, he would have. But he would have felt more compunction (izat the word?). Alright, he still felt compunction. But he eagerly (howbout "eagerly", is that the word I mean?) read (red!) ahead.

Fuck!

Fuck. Fuck. Fuck. Fuck. Fuck. Fuck. Fuck.

The next seven words in the diary were also "fuck."

Deer had the diary 'cause he worked in a hotel. Sometimes people left things behind. In their rooms. And those things were thrown out, taken, or stored someplace. The diary was in a pile waiting for a final determination as to its future. He picked it up. He saw the word. (The word was "fuck".) He read.

Today is like every other day. Because I can't. I can't. I can't.

The phone rang (or beeped or buzzed or burped or growled or groaned or throttled the neck of a turkey, whatever the sound that phones make now).

Deer waited then said something into it.

"Hello, Cabweights-Hoog . . ."

(space for other person to talk)

"No. No. No." Deer said. "No. No. No. I'm sorry."

("No I'm not," he said after the call ended.)

He wanted to get back to his page-turner, the diary. But then life like it always does overtakes with galloping speed the donkey of literature (what, Mike?). He was busy. He had to do stuff. Not hotel stuff. Personal stuff. He had a dinner party to arrange.

Boris was a guest at the hotel, had been a guest, was still a guest, oh whatever. He wore bowties and gold socks. He dressed like a dandy but an erudite dandy, a professor dandy, a horticulturist without the horticulture. But with culture. Line drawings. Symphonies. Lamps. He was nice too.

Deer and Boris got along.

The dinner party Deer had to arrange was for Boris and Boris' boyfriend. Boris' boyfriend was also erudite. In fact he was the reason for Boris' eruditeness (erudition, I know, I know, I have afterall a lot of eruditeness myself.) He was not nice though. He was scary.

242

I'm gonna be pretty obvious 'bout this, "tell" ya know not do that other thing, but Boris felt like really free when he was away from his boyfriend. Which he was when he was staying at the Cabweights-Hoog Hotel.

That night, (it's a great phrase, "that night, comma", so storybook, so, well in my writing it doesn't really make sense, what night?, where are we? etc.). That night, Deer wasn't sure. Deer wasn't sure if he should take the diary home with him, when he was um, going home. He was going home now. Leaving the hotel. It was Saturday. Knot, a fellow hotel manager, had shown up to take over. It was night. He had a week. He had a week to make this dinner party. He was nervous about it. It's only 'cause "nervous about it" is such awfully overused stuff that I'm using it. It's tinniness makes you feel the "nervous about it" vibe.

Deer was nervous about it. But that wasn't the only it. I mean about the diary too. He was gonna go out anyway tonight probably. Or maybe stay in and watch a movie. But the thing is, the thing is, he really wanted to read. He wanted to read the diary. But the thing is, the thing is, wasit? wasit? wasit right? Wasit right to read someone else's dairy.

Deer was from the midwest.

Sometimes he would try to get really sarcastic, really, really, oh yeah, really sarcastic with hotel guests. Deer could be really funny. Sometimes. When they were acting like assholes, or not acting like, just being like. When they were being like this (assholes) sometimes he ya know wanted to let them have it verbally whatever, but he always stopped himself.

Deer was from the midwest.

Was it right to read this diary. He sat down. Which people do when they are working out complex problems of morality. He stood up which people do after they have worked out complex problems of morality.

He sat down again.

The hotel workers had lockers where they could keep stuff (yeah like what else would a locker be for, dummy?). They put stickers on their own lockers. And cards. And funny stuff. Their lockers were their own. Deer opened his locker with the wee key. And put the diary there. Under a folded rust sweater.

If he had kept reading he would have read this:

Today. A day. I'm here. I was here yesterday. I'm here today. I talked to Florida today. She's my Aunt. My Aunt Florida. It's ridiculous. She lives in Florida too. Nah, just kiddin'. I'm not kiddin'. She asked me about my love life. When was I going to meet a nice woman. Settle down. I told her. I mean I didn't tell her. She means well. I'm not that wild. That's the thing, though. I told her, Aunt Flo, I said, I'm not that wild. You know Aunt Flo it's not like I'm not trying to settle down. It's just that.

Dear Diary, Dear Dear Diary.

Fuck. Fuck. Fuck. Fuck. Fuck. Fuck. Fuck.

There are some things. It's so amazing. There are some things that are so amazing. Like why can't I. I can't I. Why can't I?

Today is like every other day. Because I can't. I can't. I can't.

Home, Deer watched a porno movie. (Should I so specifically link a gay man, (Deer was gay by the way. Which by the way has nothing to do with any-thing) (NOT!), to a sex act? Look jus' cause someone is identified with their sexuality doesn't mean they don't have a RIGHT to their sexuality. Straight men, gay men, the smell of the bendy cheap black plastic jello mold holder for video tapes, and glossy, way way glossy, cardboard dipped in gloss, in way way gloss, — is a turn-on (I love that phrase "turn-on")).

Deer was thinking of turning in (I hate that phrase "turning in"). He was tired. Tiredness is weird. Sometimes you're tired and you can't sleep. Sometimes you're really energetic and you crash.

Dear was tired and turned in.

Boris, at the Cabweights-Hoog, a hotel decorated by many artists, in the "White Room" (with Black Curtains — a joke). The room was painted white, all white. And it always had a paint brush and white paint in it and guests were encouraged to touch it up.

Boris liked that. He liked to touch it up. A little here. A little there. He did it in his suits and ties. Painted a little here, a little there, in his suits and ties. That he always wore. Impeccably. That was his boyfriend's word. Impeccably dressed. Is how he should always be.

Boris did not jerk off to video tapes. He was shocked. Shocked. SHOCKED. When Deer played it out in the open. Out in the open open. Right there. In the office. On the office TV. A video. "BALLS ON FIRE!"

"Ouch," Boris had said when Deer showed him the box.

Boris and Deer would talk a lot 'bout musical comedies. (Should I so specifically link gay men, to discussions of musical comedies? Look jus' cause someone is identified with their discussions 'bout musical comedies doesn't mean they don't have a RIGHT to their discussions of musical comedies.)

"Hello, Auntie Mame."

"Hello Liza with a 'g'."

Boris' boyfriend, still at home, did not like musical comedies. And especially did not like certain stereotypes. Certain ones. Like the liking of musical comedies. I can see his point. About stereotypes. I like musical comedies, by the way.

You might be wondering what "still at home" means. You might have wondered back when I said Boris was living at the Cabweights-Hoog. Why was Boris living in the Cabweights-Hoog. How was he "away" from his boyfriend? (Remember, when I was talking about Boris being "free" <u>away</u> from his boyfriend.)

Boris was <u>away</u> from his boyfriend, because he had travelled to New York to find a job and to find an apartment because his boyfriend had found a job already and was moving to New York in September. His boyfriend was an academic.

They were from the midwest. Not really. But that's where Boris' boyfriend taught at a prestigious college, and Boris worked as an architect in a pretty good firm albeit (whodat? it be al!) a midwestern one. It was that really cold place they lived in, that begins with an "M."

Back at the hotel at the beginning of the week, the week that was to bring his dinner party at the end of it, Deer was excited. In his locker. In his locker. In his locker. Well you know what was in his locker. He took it out. And as he did he had this dreamy feeling that it was wrapped, lo shrouded, in a red felt vestment (once 'gain, is this the word I mean?). But it wasn't. It wasn't even leather or anything. Or even fake leather. It was just a book. Almost a notebook. That this guest left. That this guest had written in and left. That this guest had written in every day and left. That this guest had written in every day and told a very deep secret and left.

He hadn't come to the secret yet. But Deer knew. He knew that if he read on in that diary. That something was going to be told. How he knew? How does anybody knew. They do.

It was very romantic. She had blue eyes. They stood straight up in her face. She stood straight up. Stiff. Erect. A little almost awkward. She had a boyfriend. But that didn't take much away from it. He was back in the midwest somewhere while she was here looking for a job. She was an architect. She was very smart. She knew a lot. She was ... what is that word ... that word is ... she was erudite.

I could love him. She was smart like I said. But not brainy. Not boring brainy. And there was something. There was something about her. She was nervous kinda. She knew things but she didn't bang them over over your head with them. With the things she knew.

She was very good-looking. She was. She was cute. She was well-proportioned and um, those eyes, those blue eyes.

Oh I can't talk about it. Oh why. What's the point. These same endless useless crushes. She has a boyfriend. Right and besides. Besides, you know there's.

I can't. I can't. I can't.

I don't want to any more. Go on.

"Go on!"

Deer reading the diary whispered it. Whispered it loud.

He wanted to flip ahead. He wanted to go to the end. He knew somehow. In the way that I mentioned. The way he knew. He knew that it was in chrono- logical order. I mean in order. That it was all in order. That it would break that way. That it would build. And at the end. He would find out. He want- ed to. Deer did. He wanted to find out.

I met her at the hotel where I'm staying. It's a crazy place. She's staying here. It's a crazy place. One of the managers is really crazy. I don't know if I like him. He stares at the people as they walk up stairs. Well, the men. The boys. He makes comments. I heard one of them once. And he's crazy. That's all. Flamboyant. Oh not really. Out there. At least a little. Sometimes he can be kind of nice and reserved. I had a nice conversation with him once. We talked about dogs. He likes cats. They have a dog here at the hotel, Bijou, very small, very, I don't know I don't have a word for her, the dog, it fits, she fits, in the hotel.

"He talked 'bout me," Deer said again loudly to himself in that way you know what I mean that way you do when you talk loudly — to yourself.

"What are you doing," Slope, who worked with Deer at the hotel said.

"Nothing." Deer said.

"Not that I care." Slope said.

Deer again stopped. Reading. The diary. He had another thing to do. He had to make a list. A list of things to do. Things to do. 'Cause . . . is this boring, IS THIS BORING?, this is life, LIFE, LIFE!. What is life, life, life? What is life?

Life:

for the party

1. get chairs.
(Chairs, chairs, chairs, (thinking patterns of Deer's thinking), I don't have enough chairs. I have to get chairs. That's why 1. is "get chairs".)

Boris was talkin' to his boyfriend on the phone. He was in the lobby of the hotel. He was standing up. He was wearing a green three button suit and a red with hard to see thick black stripes sortof fuzzy tie. His shoes were wing-tips. Real ones. They said "wing-tips" to you. If of course they could speak. Which, ah, well maybe Boris' shoes did speak. They said "wing-tips."

"Fine. Of course. Yes. Everything. And Dandy. AND DANDY. Yes. Yes. I miss you. I miss you. I do. I do. Oh you know. With Deer. Yes. Last night. Uh, huh. It was exciting. Oh of course it's not your thing. I know that. Yes it's not Mozart. No. But. What. Well. Yes, it's not even West Side Story. Yes, of course. But. Yes. Yes. I see what you mean. Well anyway. It took some stress away. What. Oh. The job. Well I'm going back for a third . . . uh, huh, it looks promising, we shall see, we shall see see."

Deer could hear (he wasn't deaf for christ's sake) Boris on the phone. An

250

anger, yes an anger, rose, yes rose, with all its' thorns through his body lacerating his insides 'till it hit his tongue. Then stopped. Hot. Cold. Warm.

Deer was from the midwest.

He smiled, for some strange reason. His anger stopping at his tongue produced this (this would be the strange reason).

"What are you smiling for," Slope asked.

And continued:

"Not that I care."

Boris was scared.

Boris was scared of this dinner party. Deer, his friend at the hotel, had invited him and his boyfriend to dinner. His boyfriend was coming to visit Boris. He was only going to stay a week. (He was not going to stay at the Cabweights-Hoog.) He had arranged with friends for him and Boris to stay for a week. It was supposedly a great apartment. A loft. In (duh!) Soho (ho, ho). They were going to be alone there. His friends were going on vacations. They didn't even have any cats or anything. Or any plants or anything. There was nothing for them to do. Just live. It was perfect. A good situation.

Boris didn't want to do it. He didn't want to leave the hotel. But he understood. He was thinking of keeping his room, and his stuff. But it didn't make sense. Financially, blah, blah, blah, or otherwise.

Deer did the invitation immediately. Immediately Deer said.
"Hey, why don't you and your boyfriend, come to dinner, the first Saturday he arrives."

"Sure." Boris said brightly.

Yes, or in this case "Sure," is a funny word.

You say Yes, or in this case "Sure," and you want to take it back. Retract it.

Uh, uh, could I say, uh, uh, could I say, NO, instead. Please.

Boris felt that way. That way, that over, ever, present, not a present at all, a gift not-right, worry that what you've just said yes to, you should have said. . .

"No." Boris' boyfriend said on the phone. "I don't want to do it. I'm sure he's a very interesting person. But really. The time will be short."

"I said yes," Boris said much more timidly than the strongly sounding words imply. "We have to go."

Deer had dread 'bout this whole thing too. But sometimes he also had 'nother thing. Joy. A joy. A joy to the void. He liked Boris. He honestly did. And his brain, his mind, his soul, whatever, had like all peep's have, all humane beans, a certain marked way of beaning. A way that he did things, and nobody else did. And his way was to think different things at different times and not have those different things at different times meet up and cause conflicts.

Deer could tell Boris' boyfriend was an asshole and he wouldn't get along with him, but he also wanted to have dinner with Boris. When he thought about Boris' boyfriend he felt dread. When he thought about Boris he felt joy.

It has come to my own attention.

Can I really write this way. A strange parody of a diary. Not a diary. A distancing ... but even that would be better. I am close. Close to some beating heart. Is it mine. My beating heart.

It has come to our attention. Can you believe they wrote that to him? Can you believe it. I read it in the paper today. His school sent him that letter. The religions college he graduated from. That letter that said he was, he was, and he should, he should ... R E P E N T!

Deer had skipped ahead in the diary. He understood. He knew what the initials WWJD meant. They meant "what would Jesus do?" He couldn't tell if the writer of the diary was religious. But Deer had been. He had believed but the belief was all fussed up in the not believing. In the not believing about himself. The not wanting to believe about himself. It was hard. But it was easy. It was easy and free. He was. Easy and Free. He didn't know if everybody else knew it. About themselves. The things, the things of life, that are easy, like who you are, are so much more easier, when you weren't sure.

It seems easy for other people. They do it. They say things. I can't. I can't say it to myself. That's the thing. I can't even think it. That's even more of a thing. To myself. How can I be so separated. How can I be so separated from me?

Deer went back to earlier entries.

Went to the Empire State Building today. It was fun. A lot. The weather was beautiful. You could see a lot. I didn't know that. I had my first New York hog dog. On the street. I know it's silly. But it was somehow fun. Have a hot dog, visit the big building. It's really big. Really. You go up and up and you lose your stomach. And then you break out, like, you look out, over this big city. You can see. You can see. You can see everything.

I saw her again today. In the lobby. She was talking to her boyfriend. She seemed agitated. I waited around a little bit. I wanted to make her feel better. But she didn't get off the phone.

for the party

1. get chairs.
2. Foie Gras
3. CDs
4. Booze!!!!!!!

On the day of his party Deer got up early. It was Saturday, and Saturday, as everybod knows, is a sleep-late day. No hangover, Deer didn't need his Dr. Pepper (his hangover cure), he had gone to bed early the night before. All in all he felt refreshed. His eyes wide, he bounded to coffee maker, and then to toast, fruit, and cereal with non-fat milk. He picked up his vacuum cleaner. A small portable thing, inotherwords puny, and without any grumbling, attempted to force it to pick up shit from his floor. He was smiling. He could feel his cheeks pinned up into the grin. He was excited. His heart and the blood to his heart pumpin'. He was playin a new radio station that had just started up playin thumpin' disco n' little soul. He kept on cleaning his house. Gettin' it clean.

The phone rang (or beeped or buzzed or burped or growled or groaned or throttled the neck of a turkey) and he avoided it. Space, flat and zipped-up quiet, was all he heard as whoever called hung up on his answering machine. He was in the bathroom. Washing. Getting at the base of the toilet, collections of mottled hairlings.

He was filling his head. He was in a rush. He was filling his head. He was in a rush. He was filling his head. He was in a rush. He was filling his head. He was in a rush. He was filling his head. He was in a rush. He was filling his head. He was in a rush. He was filling his head. He was in a rush. He was filling his head. He was in a rush. He was filling his head. He was in a rush. He was filling his head. He was in a rush. He was filling his head. He was in a rush.

Then he sat down. This time it was not a moral dilemma. He got tired.

When you're tired the kindof entertainment you choose is the kindof entertainment you want when you're tired. He had the diary at home. And it had a sorta thing around it. Ya know the light was on it, the light was on it and the light was full of dust, so there was this dusty light on it, a sort of slightly attention-gettin' glow on it, like somethinc, ya know, somethinc, was pointin' at it. But that was just it. When you're tired the kindof entertainment you choose is the kindof entertainment you want when you're tired. And the kindof entertainment you want when you're tired does not have somethinc pointin' to it.

Deer grabbed at a magazine that was on the top of a pile of magazines that he was going to tie up and put downstairs to be recycled.

The magazine had very big type and lotsa pictures. It was fun being a movie star except when it wasn't. He read about rumours of this star or that star being gay. It made him feel bad somehow. Something about it. Or maybe he was already feeling bad. It was the opposite of his morning hyper-alterness.

He stopped even reading after a while. Even though there wasn't really much to read. He just turned the pages. Slowly feeling the way the pages felt. Between his fingers. As he pushed them over each other. He then did something, and the word that describes this something has lost all meaning, but I'll use it anyway. He sighed.

He woke up an hour later. O.k. not a hour. Some weird amount of time like forty-eight minutes or fifty-three minutes or even fifty-seven minutes, somethinc like that. He woke up, and you know that, that typical thing, 'bout where you are, when you wake up. Like, where am I? Yikes. You know. Deer didn't have that. He knew exactly where he was. He was in his apartment and he was cleaning up for this dinner party. And he'd been asleep. 'Cause he got tired.

"Ya know what," he said. And he did say it, again aloud. "Fuck it."

On his table among a bunch of mess, although a neat sorta mess, a mess in the process of being tidying, the tidying might even have caused the mess, was the diary he had found at his job at the hotel that a guest had left, and that he was reading. The light was shining on it giving it a glow. He picked it up and sat down. And read.

The words will come. I write them down. This is somehow assuring. There is no separation. There is no separation between the words I write and me. I write them so they are me. And they are me so I write them. It's obvious what I want to say. And I will say it. It is perfect. I am perfect.

I am

There were no more words in the book. That was the last entry.

Deer continued his preparation for the party.

After the party, a few days after, Deer started makin' notes in a kinda jour-nal, alright let's put it this way he started keepin' a diary. The first entry was the description of his party. This is what he wrote:

Oh my god. Oh my god. Oh my god. All I can start from is the middle. Can you believe it? There was this one point. This one point when I was lying stomach down on my bed, lying among the coats of Boris and that asshole, total asshole, that he's seeing, while they were still in my living room, and hysterically trying to breath to stop myself from throwing up. But I don't know if I was liquor-sick or company-sick. I mean my god what an asshole. He looked at my apartment like he was looking at a ship that had just docked with plague. And he used that word too. The plague. The gay plague. That's what he called it. I can't believe what he said. If we weren't so promiscuous he said, then there maybe wouldn't be this gay plague. And he looked at me. He looked at me like I was some kinda slut, trying to seduce his prissy boyfriend into orgies and disco.

(Which of course I am.)

No, of course not. BORIS IS NOT MY TYPE. No way!! Of course, I love him. I adore him. He's dear to me. But not for sex. No. No. No. Anyway, I did not know what to do. I did not know what to do. I mean I cannot not be polite. It's like some gene. They were guests. Even HE was a guest. Although I can't believe that I ever let that thing in my house. He was practically dusting with his finger. Checking for dust. And he always had this grimace on, like,

he   was   going   eeeeeeeeeuuuuuuuuuuuu-
uwwwwwwwwwwwwwwwwwwwww!

Well, I mean he didn't like me that was obvious. Which I sortof took as a
compliment. Do you think I've been through every thing I've been through
in my life, come from where I'm come from, so that occassionally, occassionally, I can feel o.k. about myself, feel that I'm not like, fucking Jesus up the
ass everytime I fuck a boy. (Maybe I am. Oooh. Why is that makin' me
tingly.) Anwyay that I can feel o.k. about myself, and now this asshole is
going to look down on me. Look down.

You know what. You know what I think. I think he was jealous. That's
what I was thinking. I was lookin' at his cashmere coat. My stomach and
head dipping and swerving and I was thinking he's jealous, and I should
throw up now, I should throw up on his coat. But then I thought, no that
wouldn't be nice. What's wrong with me. It's that polite gene.

I feel solid for a couple of seconds, so I go back in the room. They're sitting in
my sofa very unrelaxed both of them, and I'm like sum' coffee? and they're
like, well he's like, but Boris was like whatever he wants, so basically they
were both like, we gotta go. And I was like, yeah, you do. (O.k. only in my
head.)

What I said out loud was:

I hope to see you both again sometime soon.

They shared lots of stuff, but they never shared a lover.

FRIENDS?

"Fuck men!"

"Yeah!"

The two friends said. This was before. Way before what would later happen. Which of course it had to be if it was before. What would later happen would be a big fight (made up of many fights) and they wouldn't be friends anymore. But not now. Now, Braces X and Doreen Snow were the best of best. Friends.

"Do you remember your first blow job?"

"Yeah, pee."

Doreen Snow was beautiful with big tits. Girls with big tits are crazy. We all know this (when anyone writes anything like "we all know this," we all know that we all don't know this, 'cept in this case). They are crazy 'cause they have this thing that is very desirable (big tits). Very desirable isn't really right. There is another word needed: "obviously," like, obviously very desirable. By adding obvious to anything you get something obvious. Meaning that essentially, that, um, uh, well, you see, um, it's just that, this is it. There is a difference 'tween very desirable and <u>obviously</u> very desirable. It is a big difference. It is all the difference in the world.

Doreen Snow was very desirable but not because she was obviously very desirable. This was a confusion for her. And for many big-titted gals (how come big-titted girls are always gals?). I love sneaking an expression like big-titted gals into literature. That's why girls with big tits are crazy. (Not because I love sneaking an expression like big-titted gals into literature, but because of the other thing, before that.) That other thing being this:

Doreen Snow was very desirable but not because she was obviously very desirable. This was a confusion for her. But even things that are a confusion for a person, can lead to an external working out of this confusion, that is not very confusing. Confusing? The only problem is when the person herself thinks, oh this is so confusing, and worries that her external working out, as unconfusing as it may be, is confusing, 'cause its source is confusion. Not true. Bad metaphor coming:

Where a river starts is confusion. A river is not confusing. Ah, jeez, I have no idea what I'm talking 'bout (the river thing I mean.)

If you think 'bout how language first began (and reading my writing has gotta make you think something like that, like, why, why, did they have to invent it), you begin to realize that it wasn't like someone had a thought first and then spoke to express the thought, but they actually spoke first and then that became a thought.

How is this important. It is. It is. Very. Very. How is this relevant. Um . . .

Many people called Doreen Snow a slut. Sometimes to her face. Sometimes not to her face. She had a very pretty face, by the way, did I mention that? You'd think with such a pretty face you'd want to say stuff to it. Maybe if the stuff you're saying is so ugly then you don't. Whatever.

Doreen Snow complained 'bout "serial monogamy." She was right. It was hypocritical. To go from one person to the next but each time being so dedicated. I mean it's o.k. Just don't go lookin' down yer noses at someone who is fielding the play, if you know what I'm saying. (Nudge, nudge, wink, wink.)

She was a juggler, Doreen Snow. Apples, oranges, scissors. Just kiddin'. What I mean is she would see (look there they go, I *see* them!) a couple people at a time. Sometimes there would be for example: rich businessman ("too fixated on my tits, kinda infantile"), neighbor ("nothing to talk 'bout with, but good because more time for body-rockin' sex"), musician ("not a drummer, never a drummer"), professor ("likes to be spanked"), writer ("I would clean for days before she came, I really enjoyed that, makin' sure everything was spotless, you could eat the floor"), ex-boyfriend ("ah, so, so, ah, hmmmm, sigh, ah well, his teeth weren't great."), you get the idea.

Or do you. What is the idea. Why does the idea always come first. Like our own private cloud. Hangin' over us. Even if we run.

It's so hard to talk 'bout a woman who has sex with a bunch of people, because it just means what it means regardless of what it really means.

Braces X discovered sex (LOOK, SEX!) with the **Carnies**. Typing "Carnies" is really makin' me crack up. You know guys that would help put on the carnival when it came into her town. They had this great smell and dusty chic. And looked at you like a razor cutting flesh. There was no stoppin' em, no denying 'em, and hell you didn't want to. Yee Haa!

Later on she went to an Ivy League college. She missed the Carnies.

Braces X and Doreen Snow had different types. Different tastes in other people. Always helpful.

In a friendship.

The ship of friends docked, and the two friends, with that supreme power of friendship, ascended onto the land. What I'm saying is that the girls were goin' out!

There is nothinc like it girls goin' out, 'cept maybe boys goin' out. Goin' out. It's just so damn fuckin' good. The excitement is like being beaten on your head by your head. You can't wait. But you can. And you do. You tease yourself. You take your time. You hurry up. You take other people's time. You hurry them up. You get going. You forget somethinc. You go back. You back out. You stay in. You go back out.

Weed makin' you sleepy and shaggy and slowey and stoopid and smart.

264

Beer making you bubble 'n belch. Cocaine makin' you a space rickshaw rider, giddy-up theory of strings, changed to theory of lines. Shrooms makin' you giggle within your organs, 'cept you only have one now, you're one big head. You're saving stuff for later. Pills. Speed. X. More snort. More booze.

Cigarettes.

Your friends just yell on the street. Youse career like outta control ice-capaders. Youse hail cabs and none stop. Your friends just yell on the street.

There is nothinc like it girls goin' out. Girls in this time. In this time I'm writing about. Before. When it all is your adulthood just begun. When it all is your sexiness. Your total absolute sexiness. When it all is your love. And your love doesn't have an object. Just the one big one. The vast one. The one. The world.

You're in the bathroom and the boy you're with doesn't know how to snort cocaine from a key. And you show him. And you take some. And you give him more. And that's what you do. You show him. And you give him more. And you like that. That he can't do it and you can. And you also don't like it. But you want to kiss him. But you also want to kiss that guy that was dancing. That was so idiotic in a way. Cause he was so preeney, preeney. The way he danced. But still it was sexy. And you're sexy. And you just wanna. Oh. No. No. He blew some coke onto the floor. Oups. Lets get outta here.

And you're back outta here. And you go up to Braces, and she's talkin' to sum boy who you know she thinks is cute, and who you don't, and you hope don't think you're cute, 'cause you know well sometimes, but he likes Braces, and that's cool, and they go off to smoke some weed, and you go off to the arms of an old guy, must be like 33, who hugs you 'cause he says he knows you and you don't know and you don't care, but Braces cares and she comes over just to see who this guy is, and she stares at him, and the signal is passed, and you pass away from him, into a night made for the two of you and who you decide on and who decides on you and not for outsiders.

And this goes on and stays and remains and stays and goes on and remains. As things change, which things like to do so much that the expression "things change" never changes. It too means so much in its meaningless way. Take it from me, things don't change.

Things learn.

And as things learn there are differences. As they got older they remained friends. This was still before. This was before. Way before what would later happen. Which of course it had to be if it was before.

They had jobs but they were still close.

One night they talked on the phone all night like teenagers.

One night they organized a sleep-away at a hotel with pool.

266

They formed an organization.

They did a zine together.

They recorded music together.

They got serious jobs at the same place although at slightly different times.

What would later happen would be a big fight (made up of many fights) and they wouldn't be friends anymore. But not now. Now, Braces X and Doreen Snow were the best of best. Friends.

"Do you remember your first blow job?"

"Yeah, pee."

They could talk about blow jobs and pee and pay the rent.

They shared lots of stuff, but they never shared a lover.

If a lover of one of them came on to the other one, this lover was booed and hissed. Did not make it into the ballpark. Forget about first base.

Doreen Snow was very desirable but not because she was obviously very desirable. Yeah, she did have big tits. Yeah. Yeah. Yeah. (There was a theory passed around by a respected journalist that knew her that television watching reduces the size of women's breasts. When he met a woman with large breasts he would ask if she had watched a lot of television as a kid. Doreen Snow actually grew up in a house without a TV!, he liked to repeat.) But even if she had small tits. The smallest tits imaginable. Tits so small, they were really holes in her upper body, she would still be very desirable. O.k. if she were a freak with holes in her upper body she might not be that desirable. Her desirability was just sexy. And there's nothinc "just" about it. You could feel yourself taking your own temperature when you saw her.

The external working out that we talked 'bout earlier. The one that Doreen indulged in was this. Since the problem was that she was desirable and obviously very desirable, and it was a difficult distinction to make, she decided not to make it. She would just be desirable. And there was nothinc "just" 'bout it.

It was what she was. It was what she did. It was how she lived. It was her.

Her friend Braces was different. Her friend Braces had a life as a musician. It was what she was. It was what she did. It was how she lived. It was her.

Now there was lots of pretense on both sides (thank, God!).

Doreen liked to pretend that she also was interested in other things besides her desirability (and in some ways she was, of course this added to her desirability) and Braces liked to pretend that she was interested in her own desirability and not always music (which of course sortof she was, although her music was one of the things that made her desirable).

Society.

Society in its usual criminal mixed-message mugging (for the camera?) wants everyone to be desirable, tells everybod they should be, and then also disparages the desirable. Be attractive. Don't rely on your looks.

Huh?

So some of this pretense was needed for both of 'em. A defense. A defense 'gainst things they needed a defense 'gainst. But friendship is so odd in its friendliness. Sometimes people just become friends. And there's nothinc "just" 'bout it. And somehow certain things, labels or whatever (I'm a gum-smackin' teenager, I'm a gum-smacking teenager!), don't matter. You like each other, and you know, whatever, it's like, um, you like each other.

You call each other up.

You hang out.

You have jobs but stay close.

You talk on the phone all night like teenagers.

You organize a sleep-away at a hotel with pool.

You form an organization.

You do a zine together.

You record music together.

You get serious jobs at the same place although at slightly different times.

You can talk about blow jobs and pee and pay the rent.

You share lots of stuff, but you never share a lover.

If a lover of one of you comes on to the other one, this lover is booed and hissed. Does not make it into the ballpark. Forget about first base.

This didn't happen once.

The booing and hissing.

Once.

Doreen was rich (from rich folk, well you know, shrinks, both her parents, BOTH, were psychiatrists.) Braces wasn't (not poor, Muddle Class.) When they seemed to both notice that men would seem to complain a lot that women got sad a lot, they came up together with a response which they used: "Better sad than stupid." Doreen liked to kiss the feet of her lovers. Braces liked to fuck in cars. (I'm providing a quick rush of details, I'm continuing). They tried to fight the stereotypes of women, not to be pushed around into them. But it wasn't always easy. It was very often hard. Sex-negative. About aging and women. Explosive. Biological crock. They came up with a phrase, "the hetero-homo." He didn't like to sleep with women and he didn't like to sleep with men, and he wasn't asexual. Or, "Jack-offs of no trade."

John Wayne.

They had a friend who was a hetero-homo. He only liked lesbians. Which made it difficult to have sex. They also both liked and peripherally knew a rock musician who was gay and only liked straight men. Which made it difficult to have sex. He was homo-hetero.

That was this one thing they had in common. This one thing. This one thing that was kinda airplane glue all about and around the vague toy stealth bomber that is the mysteries of friendship. They both liked sex. They both had sex.

Braces X and Doreen Snow had different types. Different tastes in other people. Always helpful.

In a friendship.

Doreen Snow fucked once, almost, at the Cabweights-Hoog Hotel. On the fire escape which the person she almost fucked would always call "the balcony." Doreen almost fucked there, outside, out there, but she was nervous about (it). Yeah even her. She would get nervous. She was out there and she was like, sheesuz, there are people out here, there are people, there are, there are, and he (it doesn't really matter who he was, nobody you know, uh it was Bogart), and Bogart said, oh no, oh no, there's nobody there, really, baby, there's nobody there, and then she said, oh yes, oh yes, there is, there is, there is somebody there, I can feel it, I can tell it, oh yes, c'mon, c'mon, there is there is, we've got to go in, we've got to go in.

They went in, and then they heard from down on the street this:

"Hey, c'mon. Don't go in. C'mon. It was just gettin' good."

Bogart, a sorta permanent guest at the hotel, a storyteller, who has since evaporated from the hotel's view by falling in love with some very long legs and the brains attached to them, and whose less ridiculous name, "real name," was Devin Milrod was a hetero-hetero.

One night Bogart helping out two friends that needed to get togther (he set 'em up in his room at the Cabweights-Hoog Hotel) needed another place to stay so he went to his friend's house, Braces X. She was the leader (yes, "leader") of a rock band. The rock band was called, ha, ha, ha (no not "ha, ha, ha"), Braces X. They were friends. It was the middle of the night (whatever, you know pretty damn f-ing late). It was fine. She was having something going on too. By the way, her best friend was Doreen Snow, which of course you already know 'cause she's a character is this story.

Braces was having something going on too. Her cool boyfriend had been arrested in his upstate New York small town for possession of marijuana. He'd been ratted on a by a friend's neighbor's kid who also had his own mother arrested. It was very weird. Braces was upset.

"Oooh." Bogart said when she told him.

She also told him she was a little upset, well more than, with her friend Doreen. Doreen didn't really sympathize with it really, well, with what her boyfriend was going through. First Doreen had stopped drinkin' 'n stuff you know a while back, drugs etc. She was you know that thing, double "A," and I'm not talkin' 'bout the Automobile Association (or Automobile Club of America) or whatever it's called (I guess that's triple A isn't it). Anyway you know what I'm talkin' 'bout. So the drug bust thing didn't really sit that cool. Plus, she didn't really like Brace's boyfriend. Didn't think he was right for Braces.

Braces was a little pissed 'bout this. Her reaction. She was tellin' Bogart this. She also wanted to ask Bogart sumthinc else. Doreen had let it slip, just let it out, that she had, Doreen had, done, done a little with Bogart at the Cabweights-Hoog Hotel. Braces wanted to ask Bogart 'bout it but she didn't.

A few weeks later Braces X and Doreen Snow stopped talkin' to each other for good.

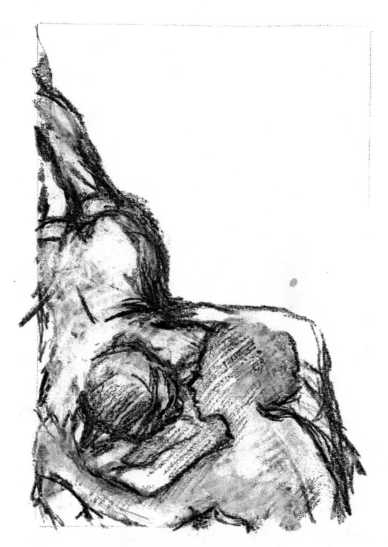

And all I want to hear from you is yes.

A BEAUTIFUL WOMAN IS A MEDLEY (ANNOYING TITLE STORY)

Mars picked up Bogart's limp hand and put a cigarette in it, and then with a too-high flame from a plastic lighter burned the tobacco stick's tip. Bogart sort of inhaled but it was a strange movement. The only one of a crumpled body and the kindof motion that something crumpled makes: not on purpose, just a continuation of the crumpling.

Mars needed things to be right, around him. Things in their order, in their place. If his taste in order was somewhat of a cliche, it still had moments where the flower arrangement of an obvious bouquet produced disquieting results.

Once on TV, a commercial with ballplayers wearing the right-colored hats but the insignia of their team missing (probably not part of the sponsorship), bothered Mars so much that he had to point it out to everybody by actually touching the TV, making a circle around an absent logo.

"oh. oh. ohhhhhh." mars said.

Mars' arranging was takin' place in the lobby of the Cabweights-Hoog Hotel, NYC. The lobby had been recently redesigned, there's probably a better word than "redesigned" but so what, redesigned by Jewelle, the mother of the dog Bijou, one of the animals of the hotel, and her boyfriend Charles.

They had made it look like an Austrian ski resort. No one really knew why?

"strudel?" mars passed the fake desert cake sculpture to a guest just checking in to the hotel.

The hotel was decorated in this way, by visiting, itinerant artists. Mars, a man from Japan, had done a room, a bathroom, and made it look like the inside of a mathematics textbook. Charles, who could learn things, you know things, just stuff, very easily, learned advanced trigonometry, or at least Mars' version of advanced trigonometry, from Mars' bathroom.

Mars now worked at the hotel, along with Winkler. Winkler was in the lobby sitting in a chair across from the crumpling Bogart. Bogart, a sorta permanent guest at the hotel, a storyteller, almost evaporated from the hotel's view by falling in love with some very long legs and the brains attached to them, but something had gone wrong. Winkler was a kid whose mom had lived in the hotel a while back now, a way while back, the hotel had changed since then, what with all the rooms being painted by artists and such. C.B. ("Radio") B.C. was the last real resident guy from that period. "Radio" would have probably been sittin' in the lobby too 'cept he wasn't in the hotel. He was in the hospital. Suddenly Winkler sighed.

"I'm sighing," Winkler sighed. "I'm sighing."

Khaki, who cleaned the rooms, and was extraordinarily protective of the way the colors, or lets say multi-colors, of oddly matched sheets and pillow cases, were placed in a room (he placed them beautifully, so that's why he was extraordinarily protective) looked at the sighing Winkler and said:

"You thinking too much. Don't think. Make you feel bad. Relax. Relax."

This made Bogart start, or stop, or somethinc.

"I'm not a kid." Winkler said. Speaking. To the narrator of the story. "I'm not a kid."

Bogart had had a manicure earlier in the day, well it was almost night, late afternoon. The woman holding his fingers and scraping with her tools felt his tight hands fully.

"Too much thinking," she said.

A man came up the stairs of the hotel. "A man" is the best way to describe him. He wasn't exactly a hotel guest (this hotel, I mean) type.

"Dr. G.O. Best, yes, you know me, fine. Is Slope around?"

Slope was around, but hiding in the back of the hotel office. Slope "the most successful lazy person in the history of the world,"* was married to Franklin who ran one of Dr. Best's restaurants for him. Dr. Best was drop-

*Jesse James Joyce (J.J.J.), a young kid English painter of cartoons on walls

ping something off for Slope to take with him when he got off his work at the hotel, because he was gonna see Franklin before Dr. Best would. Slope was married to her afterall. She'd taken off a little time to visit her father who was sick in Connecticut, and Slope was to join her there. Slope did not want to speak to Dr. Best.

"I ate at your restaurant last week. It was beautiful." Victor said, taking a package of papers from Dr. Best, conscious of the crouching Slope in the back room mouthing the words "no, no, no" while waving his palms.

Victor worked at the hotel along with Slope. Ivy worked there too. The place was managed by Knot and Deer.

Ivy had just had a baby, Rosellini.

"Are those new pictures of Rosellini?" Victor asked after Dr. Best had left about some new snapshots Ivy had taped to the inside of the office's window onto the lobby. "They're beautiful."

"No those are pictures of Ivy holding somebody else's baby that she just decided to tape up for no good reason." Slope replied coming out of his hiding sarcastically.

"They're beautiful," Victor said 'bout the pictures.

"You know can you believe it," Slope said. "Here, it's ridiculous, she's takin' some time off, a little time off, her father's sick, wow, god, no, she can't even, he's gotta bring her work to do."

Slope sat down, something he was very good at, in his special comfy chair. It wasn't really his, I mean everyone in the office sat in it, but when he sat in it he made it special. He gave this silly piece of sorta old (in years), kinda modern (in design), at least it was modern when it was first produced, office furniture a grandeur. When he sat in it it became the "Chair of Refutation."

"You know I'm thinkin' of painting again," Knot said. "You know bring my watercolors go up on the roof. That kind of thing."

"You know what could use some painting," Slope said in the Chair of Refutation. "That bathroom Mars did. Paint over all those sums."

The office of the Cabweights-Hoog Hotel was like someplace upsidedown that was rightsideup. There was lots of little things in it. Little things that seemed to have sorta fallen from somewhere but sorta landed o.k. Like a bunch of tiny living porcelain cats were dumped ceremoniously from a big box and they all managed to right themselves as they fell and when they landed formed very distinguished poses of tiny marble. The things were all kinds of things. And the walls were also walled with all kinds of things. It was corny of plenty. It was shaken and stirred. It was a mess. It was . . .

"oreg. ooh." mars came into the office.

"Oh, oh, oh," Slope said in the Chair of Refutation. "What do you want. What do you need. What are you here for? Oh, why. Why. Why are you here."

"He works here," Knot said and then shouted, "Mars! You sunuvagun. YOU SUNUVAGUN!"

mars was holding a rubber duck with a condom pulled over its head.

"Is that a rubber duck with a condom pulled over its head," Knot said.

But he knew the answer. Every week a "short stay" (a "Short Stay": three hours for $30) couple would come and someone would sneak up after they left and before Mars went to clean and sneak something strange into the room.

"too much, this time too much," mars said holding the rubber duck with a condom pulled over its head.

"Mars! YOU SUNUVAGUN!" Knot yelled.

Victor had stopped smokin' so lit up a cigarette to begin again.

> Down the drowning lane, the footpath awash with castoff from the
> overrunning sewers, a figure of an old man, that is bent over and
> walking with a cane, not making any attempt to shield himself

against the onrushing torrent from the heavens and yet not seeming to be getting wet or being pushed back or hampered in any way by the extreme winds, made his course through the puddles and melting, soggy earth, towards the shapeless blotch forming in contrast to the almost solid pattern of total chaos of the howling storm in the sky, his house.

At the door it did not even occur to him that he had not seen this carved sliver of tough tree with the brightly dull brass knocker in fifty years. He just knew that he had to open the door and go inside and he knew it would not be locked. The door, wet and warped and the hinges in need of oil, still opened cleanly, easily slipping from its frame, without much effort from the old man, and he looked through before stepping in and over its arch, a golden, sizzling light cascading to all the corners and blanketing the walls with a thick fabric of vibrating warmth from the roaring fireplace, engulfing his view. There, he saw, sitting in a simple chair, but ornate in the power of its symbol, the figure of an old man, himself, telling a story. It was called The Return of the Storyteller *and it began this way:*

Down the drowning lane, the footpath awash with castoff from the overrunning sewers, a figure of an old man, that is bent over and walking with a cane, not

Two beautiful girls leading with their mid-driffs, lugging sexily luggage up the hard worn stairs of the Cabweights-Hoog, clonked down in the lobby.

Winkler looked up. Bogart did not. Their eyes were red and their smiles were big.

"Hi."

"Hello."

They said.

"Hello. Hi." Victor said back.

People like to fuck in hotels.

People like to fuck in hotels because a hotel is not a home. Home is where the heart is, but it is not where the fucking is. Babies come from homes and hospitals (which are like homes, which are not in any way like homes, but are like homes, like) and babies come from fucking. But fucking does not take place at home.

mars came out of the office holding a rubber duck with a condom pulled over its head.

The girls looked at him and giggled.

Victor lit up another cigarette.

Bijou started yipping at Victor's legs.

Winkler sighed.

Bogart moaned (a quiet small one).

The phone rang and rang.

The fan on the lobby ceiling banged slightly 'gainst a fake wood (made of plaster painted brown) beam that was hangin' too low.

A light bulb fireplace sizzled with analog tape static.

A newspaper photo of the great actor Sir Alec Guinness pinned to the lobby bulletin board loosed itself from one of its pins and slung to the left.

The phone stopped ringing.

The phone started to ring again.

Slope reached for the phone in the office.

The girls sat down on their luggage to fill out cards with their addresses.

Knot through a wadded up piece of wad at the hole of the top of trash.

Victor dragged and blue.

The lights got dimmer than brighter.

Bijou ran around and around Victor's legs.

And then:

Bijou was beeping around the hotel lobby like a computer game blip. She was so fast for such a slow creature. She had the energy and drive of digital code in an analog body. She scampered, scampered, scampered, and got nowhere. Fast. In a slow way. She had bright eyes. "Bright Eyes" is what the character was called in the Planet of the Apes films. The human character, by the apes. I think it was a joke. 'Cause we often call our animals that or think of them that way. Bright Eyes. But what does it mean? What's behind the gleaming glow of an animal's bright eyes?

Behind Bijou's it was obvious. There was something. An intensity of love and an energy of hope. It wasn't just the small thing's large ambitions. It wasn't cuteness. Funnily 'nuff Bijou wasn't cute. Bijou was sexy. And in that way I guess she was cute. Bijou was a star.

She wasn't no lap poodle puppy dog popcorn sized individual kernel of corny cat/dog. She was no cat. She was elegant, coy, dramatic, silly, — by the way nothinc against cats, it's just that she was no dog posing as a cat, she was all dog — wherewasI, she was coy and dramatic and silly and elegant and startlingly erudite and sometimes vulgar, o.k. not vulgar exactly, but just willing to get down. She was a down dog. She was a down dog for such a charismatic beauty.

Charisma. Pawproppelling herself in her upped, hyper fashion she still managed to exude a kind of exacting, striking balance of reserve and gushing lifeness. When she came down stairs it wasn't your usual animal stampede but almost, in the dog equivalent, a soft striding ball gown-wearing staircase descending debutante.

She was underfoot. She did get underfoot. But even in her getting underfoot it was different than getting underfoot. She wanted to be noticed. And you wanted to notice her. She wanted to be involved somehow. Be a part of it. Maybe even be a major part of it. She was, afterall, Bijou.

"The prettiest dog in the world."

"She is so pretty."

The two girls looked at Bijou and giggled. And giggled. And laughed. And stopped laughing. And very seriously finished filling out their cards, checked in, and went to their room.

In the room the luggage they had sexily lugged up the stairs was ignored. One of the girls pulled down her pants, then took down some tights, then removed panties and then reached and untaped a sorta pad that had been wrapped around her. She gave the pad to her friend and pulled her clothes back up. Meanwhile her friend had taken the pad apart, and then took a plastic bag outta the pad. She handed the plastic bag back to her friend who opened the plastic bag and took out the jus' a lil' moist, almost dry, not that green, but not that grey, clump 'o lil' bush. Their pot.

A new pack of cigs was released from its plastic. A slightly rumpled pack of rolling papers was produced.

Um. The joints were ready. They were big. I mean you could look at them and you could figure out. They were big. Of course they were cut. They cut them in Europe with tobacco, which I don't know they just do. But there still was a lot of fuckin' shit. And they were like, well they weren't perfect. I mean I've seen joints that were made like, like that were factory made, you know they almost came in colorful boxes with a surgeon general's warning. But these did have filters, they do that in Europe too. They weren't perfect, but they were beautiful. Anyway they lit 'em up. They were, they were, there were so mid-driff. Not the joints, the girls. Ha, ah, ha, eh, hee, hee. They took these, big, big, beautiful, puffs. They shotgunned. They made pipes outta their fists and they shared it with each other. They took their time. They loved to smoke.

Knot, who along with Deer managed the Cabweights-Hoog, had a moment of silence.

288

It was rare. In his life. His life. was. Noisy. He'd been going threw something recently, that was, well, somethinc. It seemed, it was, or maybe it jus' seemed that the littlest things, like stuff, he couldn't get done. Like this if he asked for a cup of coffee at a deli. They'd give him tea. Or if Winkler went out to get him a ginger ale, "in the can please, not one of those big plastic bottles," Winkler would come back with a big plastic bottle and say:

"Here, I got you one of those big plastic bottles."

Knot liked coffee. He liked alota coffee. He liked coffee a lot. His energy could sometimes mutate 'round the drug and produce a nervyness that along with a sorta peaceful disposition created a nervy peacefulness.

"Damn. Fuck. Shit. Damn . . . Fuck Shit. Damn."

When people are pissed off originality goes out the window. Not a very original thing to say and not a very original way to put it. Knot was always, uh huh, always, pretty pissed off when he started his week on his Saturday evening shift. There was lots to do, for him to do, for him to get done. Things extraneous (extra-anus) to the running of a hotel as it's running. As in stuff he had to do when guests weren't bothering him with stuff he had to do. He picked Saturday night for this because Saturday night was sortof a quiet night. Sortof.

This wasn't Saturday night. This was right smack dab in the middle — I don't like that — This was right in the middle of the week, and right in the middle of his moment of silence. A brief moment. Moments are brief.

"Excuse me, I am in fourth floor, and the shower is locked."

"Is the water running?"

"Pardon."

"Do you hear water running?"

"Ya. And someone singing."

"Someone's in it. Someone else, someone other than YOU, is using the shower."

The doorbell rang. It was a "doorbell" that was what was so funny. It was a doorbell and it sounded like a doorbell.

"Adoorbell."

Knot looked into the b/w small box producing granny (not granny, grainy) shots of those waiting at the door of the hotel.

"Beautiful," Victor added.

"Buzz her in. Slope. Slope. Will you buzz her in."

Victor buzzed her in. Then he lit a cigarette.

Brenda Kill Starr, "Kill" to her friends (she added the "Kill" but it was her baby boomer parents that had called her Brenda, with their last name Starr, thinkin' that was cute), her hair green, and her new tattoo hurting her arm, stood in the lobby. Bijou started yipping at her legs.

"Room." She said.

"Reservations." He said. (He being Knot.)

"About you. Yes."

It was an old joke and he'd heard it before, lots, but he laughed. He being Knot.

After getting her room Kill lay on her bed. It sounds stupid but it's true. When people get into their hotel rooms they basically, well they do, do the same thing. They lay on their bed. She had left the door unlocked. It opened.

She was in a hotel room with a stranger who was familiar. Almost familiar. There are many strangers that can be familiar. Most can. Everyone you knew you once didn't knew. But that's not what I'm talkin' 'bout. That's so obvious. It's stupid. What I'm talkin' 'bout is this. The almost boyfried. I mean boyfriend. The almost girlfriend. you can almost be bored. you can almost be bored with. You can almost be bored with them. How beautiful to be. How beautiful to be bored with. How beautiful to be bored with them.

did she know him it was a strange thought aren't all thoughts strange he had left to take a shower and come back and so she had a second a second she had more than a second good he took long showers did she know him that was her question her question for her for herself you meet someone and you love them maddly passionately all that stuff but was all that stuff did she know him and did he know her and she couldn't even remember and she couldn't even remember what the question was about what the question was about why was it a question what is a question

A man got out of the subway and started to get towards work. Another man looked at him and he looked at him. They talked and went to a nearby hotel that took "short stays."

(a "Short Stay": three hours for $30)

One of the men not that tall but kinda built, and handsome worked in the word processing department of a law firm, and had a friend at work, Palace, and fuck, she was pretty. He thought about how she could get so physical with him. About how she would push up against him. And sit in his lap. And how he'd put his strong arms around her. How he'd squeeze her. How he would sometimes almost kinda grab her. How it kinda made her feel good. Like good. Ya know. Good. Like good. Good. Good, down there. Good down there at the top of her legs, 'round from her ass. She could tell he felt good too sometimes. She knew he had a kid, but that happened a long time ago.

"You have a kid right," the other man said.

"Yeah."

Ivy had just had a baby, Rosellini. She was workin' reduced shifts. She came in jus' for a few hours.

"Ivy, IVy, IVY," Knot yelled at seeing her.

They were both Mets fans (they being Ivy and Knot, Mets being NY METS). Ivy was a big baseball fan. She watched baseball almost, more than almost, like the way it was played, with a slow intensity. A focus, but a focus that didn't require focus, something more organic, an act of active repose. Ivy was a big baseball fan.

"How they're doing."

"Up, UP, UPPPPP," Knot said.

Ivy, liked to get everybody out when she settled into her shift, 'specially 'cause she only came in a few hours — needed to make it hers (actually, they all, the hotel workers, did that). And with a game on, mmmmm!, that was nice.

But Slope had a problem leaving. Knot always had a problem leaving. He would always be "out the door," but not actually out the door, something else would come to his mind to say or do, but that wasn't Slope's leaving problem. Slope's leaving problem wasn't a general leaving problem, but a problem leaving at this moment. At this moment there was something wrong.

"Something's wrong," he mumbled.

Slope was gonna meet his wife Franklin, who ran restaurants for Dr. G.O. Best, in Connecticut. She'd taken off a little time to visit her father who was sick, and Slope was to join her there. The problem was when he called there, she hadn't arrived yet, and he'd done an all-nighter at the hotel, and he'd called once at home in NY and no one picked up and he was sure she left last night but why hadn't she arrived. Why hadn't she arrived yet. Why hadn't she arrived yet. In Connecticut.

"I'll just go," he thought.

Alone. Ivy. At last. Focused on the game. With one out and two men on the Met centerfielder caught a ball and then calmly walked to the stands and handed the ball to a kid.

"THERE'S ONLY TWO OUT. THERE'S ONLY TWO OUTS!" Ivy talked at the screen. "TWO OUTS. TWO OUT!"

But it was too late. The centerfielder had thought that his catch had made the third out. And so he gave the ball away. It was a horrendous mistake. Two runs scored.

"That is what I like 'bout baseball," Ivy thought. "You always see something new."

Victor did not like hospitals. He could not smoke for one. And for two he could not smoke. Also, he felt. Huh? Wha? We all feel. Yeah we all feel. But Victor felt. Like felt. His emotions were smooth, elongated, open. Not the dense weave of the tortured feeler. But the soft cashmere of the compassion- ate. It was strange, but to Victor the hospital was almost

"Beautiful," he whispered, a nurse somewhat like a runway model, but with more exterior padding, silently involved with thoughts, padded by.

"Slippers," Victor thought. "Her shoes are like slippers. Women should walk around in slippers."

He then slipped into a little foyer right outside C.B. ("Radio") B.C.'s private room. A sign on Radio's door said:

MASKS MUST BE WORN ON ENTERING

Victor slipped a mask on and slipped inside.

"What are you an alien," Radio snapped.

Victor almost slipped. Somethinc liquidy on the floor. He balanced.

"Radio."

"What."

"Beautiful. Your room is beautiful."

"What do you mean. What are you stupid. This is a hospital. Nothing's beautiful."

"You have your own room. A private room. That's good."

"Good to die."

"You're not gonna die, Radio."

"Well you are." Radio said. And laughed and laughed. "Ha ha ha ha ha ha ha ha ha ha ha ha."

Victor smiled.

Then another visitor. Deer, one of the managers, with Knot, of the Cabweights-Hoog. Holding his mask to his face, and walkin' round the something liquidy on the floor.

"Another alien," Radio said.

"Shut up you grumpy old man," Deer said. "I'm here to cheer you up. And you are going to be cheered. up."

Deer was from the midwest.

Sometimes he would try to get really sarcastic, really, really, oh yeah, really sarcastic with hotel guests. Deer could be really funny. Sometimes. When they were acting like assholes, or not acting like, just being like. When they were being like this (assholes) sometimes he ya know wanted to let them have it verbally whatever, but he always stopped himself.

Deer was from the midwest. So he felt bad this had just come out of his mouth:

"Shut up you grumpy old man," Deer said. "I'm here to cheer you up. And you are going to be cheered. up."

So, Deer added,

"Radio, Radio, here look what I brought you."

"Flowers. What do I want with flowers. Now we got to get a vase. We have to get a vase."

"There's one right here."

"Yeah, o.k., put 'em in. O.k. Good. Good. And move 'em closer. Yeah. Over here. Good."

Victor started to fuck with the TV.

"Don't fuck with the TV. What are you doing." Radio said.

Victor always thought it would make a good story. Or a good part of a story. He thought this you know when he was working at night at the Cabweights-Hoog a couple of hours after Radio died. He thought it would make a good story that this thing happened. Well this thing happened. Just a couple hours. A couple hours after. About, ooh, yeah, uh, right, about, jus' 'bout midnight, all the lights in the hotel brightened quickly and then darkened slowly to black.

"Radio." Victor said.

Of course the lights were always going off every now and then, more than that, in the Cabweights-Hoog. It was an old building and the electric stuff was old.

"That is what I like 'bout baseball," Ivy thought. "You always see something new."

The Mets won even tho their centerfielder had done somethinc ridiculous, and she turned the TV off. She missed her baby. It was not a thought. This missing. She wasn't aware of it but she was painfully aware of it. She did not want to be here. She wanted to be with her baby. She never thought about her husband this way. This is the wrong way to put this. It's not that she never thought about her husband this way. It's that she never thought about her husband in this way. It was a different thought, a different way, to think about the two of them. She loved her husband. She missed her baby. She felt sometimes that her husband felt it. That her husband felt that she didn't miss him. No that's wrong. It's not that she didn't miss her husband. It's just that she missed her baby. Her 'n her husband hadn't had sex in almost a month. He sort of talked 'bout it. But he was so sweet. Suddenly, she missed her husband.

"I miss my baby she thought."

It was not a thought.

The carride to Connecticut for Slope was Gross. Gross, capital "G" Gross, which is even grosser, than jus' plain 'ol "gross." Capital "G" Gross is when the grossness is an emotional gross, or should I say Grossness. An emotion-al Grossness. We take out our emotional grossness on our machines. Frankly, they deserve it. Maybe "take out" is not right (plus it's makin' me hungry). We express ourselves, what ourselves are expressing, through our machines. Slope was driving with an emotional Grossness. He's a good driver for what it's worth. What is it worth?

Slope was Canadian. From the English speakin' part, thus the expression, "Canadian." Well he wasn't Canadian. He was American (United States of) now. He'd moved south (is it?) in North America. He'd married Franklin in what they joked was a "green card marriage." Slope and Franklin had to do their green card shit. Their green card shit, although I'm not sure of the details exactly, had to do, at least as far as they told me, with someone in a bureaucracy (and I'm trying not to use this expression in a bad way, like not using it as an expression, but as identification) meeting with them and making sure they were in love. That they weren't faking it. That they were really married. That they . . . etc., etc., etc. What a job! Franklin always said that all anybody would have to do in order to believe they were really married would be to see the two of them in their mini-van, Slope driving, Franklin navigating, and uh, you can guess the rest.

In case you can't

"We're supposed to turn here. We're supposed to turn here! We're supposed to turn here!!"

Slope turned there, very quickly 'cause he had to.

He knew this way pretty easily, but his mind. His mind was. Was. Wasn't.

"People come and people go," Slope thought. He had no idea what he meant.

"I'm going." Slope continued. And went faster.

In a restaurant Doreen Snow who I've decided is a character in this story was telling Bogart what she thought about when she used her Sunbeam. Her "Sunbeam" was a joke between them. As in,

"Why do I need a man, when I've got my Sunbeam."

She was in Austria jus' traveling and had some "pussy problem" (her words) ["I've had that problem," Bogart joked stupidly], and so went to the local gyno. Married, hot, the white coat the whole thing, there was an immediate thing thing 'tween the luscious (Bogart's word) Doreen and the Doc. The first visit was uneventful (some other person's words). But then she had to go back. He had to examine her more closely (again someone else's words). She got on her hands and knees on the table and kinda looking over back over sorta she could see he was hard. Nothing happened. It ended there. But not for her and her sunbeam.

"Wow." Bogart said.

What else could he say.

They were at a party for two returning returnee's. Two returning returnee's that had been part of a group and had left and were back jus' for a lil' visit and then they would go again (duh, that's the def of a lil' visit) but then their coming reformed the group. Gawd that was a complicated explanation of something very simple. Maybe I should have spent my life writing instruction manuals (maybe I have, huh, you're right, definitely huh?).

It was a big group, mixed up, and various variousness. Some people worked here or there, some people knew people from people that worked here or there or from some people that knew people.

By the way the returnee's were returning separately. They were not together they jus' happened to be returning at the same time.

Victor noticed a fat woman sitting down in the restaurant and he told Piper, one of the returnee's, this story in a drunken whisper (which has a sorta loudness to it).

"I was in love with her eyes. They were beautiful. Her eyes. When she started taking off her clothes. I looked at her. She was so fat. I realized there was no way I could do it. No way I could get hard. I tried. She tried. That was the worst. The way she tried. She got on me, bounced up and down. Tried so hard. I was so soft. It was terrible."

Then with dramatic effect (please register dramatic effect),

"I have broken so many hearts."

Jesse James Joyce (J.J.J.), a young kid English painter of cartoons on walls, the other returnee, began talkin' to Doreen after he sorta kinda well I guess did essentially overhear Doreen discussing her sunbeam. He told her this story of this girl he'd met at a bar the night before.

"She talked, you know, like, it was totally American." (This from a guy who when he was in a club and the D.J. asked is "Brooklyn in the house" thought he was in heaven.)

The other time he talked 'bout a girl talkin' totally American was when he talked 'bout meeting this girl who said she was the daughter of the head of the Greek mafia, and who claimed she sat in on their meetings. But that's 'nother story.

"She talked, you know, like, it was totally American." J.J.J. continued 'bout the girl he'd met at a bar the night before. "She'd say, 'DUDE' this, or 'DUDE' that, she'd say things like 'Dude, Dude, you're English Dude, you ARE English Dude.' We left the bar and we go to get something to eat but she said the place we went was too bright, 'Dude, Dude, that is bright, that is bright Dude, that IS bright Dude.' So instead she had to get rolling papers, so she did, to roll a joint. I don't smoke, so we sat on a stoop and she smoked the joint, and she said 'Dude, Dude, that is so fucked up, that is SO fucked up, Dude,' that I didn't smoke, and she said 'Dude, you must be an alcoholic, right Dude, you are a fucking alcoholic, you are SO fucked up, Dude,' and then I said do you think you could maybe be a little nice to me and she said

'Dude, Dude, DUDE, you wanna me to be nice, you wanna me to be nice, nice, NICE, DUDE, see that guy over there,' pointing to someone passing the stoop 'I betcha he's nice, I betcha he's so nice, I betcha he's so nice he'd want you to fuck him up the ASS, Dude, the ASS, DUDE.'"

The group left the restaurant and for a second (okay a couple of seconds, longer even) the two returnees were alone inside the doorway of the restaurant next to a pay phone. They'd been here before. They'd had a "date". You should always put "date" in quotes (why, why?, I dunno, you just should, should!!). It wasn't really a date (oh, that's why). It wasn't really a date because oh, one thing, Piper was married and J.J.J. wasn't. To her.

Piper had two "beautiful" (Victor's word, but it was true) kids since she knew J.J.J. They'd come on this visit, but they were being looked after by friends. J.J.J., cliche or no, a young kid English painter of cartoons on walls, had begun to become ("begun to become" sounds ugly) a famous artist.

"You didn't talk to me," Piper said. "Too busy rapping to Doreen Snow."

"Now don't be jealous," J.J.J. said.

"Who the fuck da ya think you are J.J.J.?" Piper said in her way.

Outside, the restaurant, as the group dispersed but didn't, you know what I mean, Deer was also rapping to Doreen, but in this case it wasn't rappin'.

Deer had been religious.

Deer had been. He had believed but the belief was all fussed up in the not believing. In the not believing about himself. The not wanting to believe about himself. It was hard. But it was easy. It was easy and free. He was. Easy and Free. He didn't know if everybody else knew it. About themselves. The things, the things of life, that are easy, like who you are, are so much more easier, when you weren't sure.

"So yeah," he was saying to Doreen, maybe he was kinda rappin', Doreen Snow was beautiful with big tits. Girls with big tits are crazy. We all know this (when anyone writes anything like "we all know this," we all know that we all don't know this, 'cept in this case). They are crazy 'cause they have this thing that is very desirable (big tits). Very desirable isn't really right. There is another word needed: "obviously," like, obviously very desirable. By adding obvious to anything you get something obvious. Meaning that essentially, that, um, uh, well, you see, um, it's just that, this is it. There is a difference 'tween very desirable and <u>obviously</u> very desirable. It is a big difference. It is all the difference in the world.

Doreen Snow was very desirable but not because she was obviously very desirable.

Nah, he wasn't rappin'.

"So yeah," he was saying to Doreen, "the guilt was terrible, but the thing was this kid Tommy who was also in my bible class, we'd go out to this back shed and we would screw around, but he would come so fast, and then <u>his</u> guilt would start, but I'd still be hard, and ready and he'd already be all guilty."

The group dispersed. Almost.

"Hey, where's Slope? Why wasn't he here?"

"Slope is on his way to Connecticut to see Franklin." Victor answered lighting up a cigarette glad that no one had asked him where someone else was.

. . . and she couldn't even remember and she couldn't even remember what the question was about what the question was about why was it a question what is a question

Ah, memories. Remember them. We remember them, just like they are remembering something. There is never a first memory. It is always a remembrance of a memory. A thing past. Nothing ever happens. It is only remembered. Nothing is ever remembered. It is only a memory of a remembrance. To know is to pass by what you are knowing (once again, pretentious, moi?).

She used to live in Long Island. In a house. At the end of a drive. It was a big house, on land that two houses could have been built on. Her father built the house. He ran a contemporary furniture store. Not, you know, sales, layaway on sofa sets (soundin' a lil' snobby, huh), no, new, cool, Italian, dare I say it, mod, stuff. He would take lots of trips to Europe, her dad did. He collected etchings. To this day she still didn't really know what an etching was. She also hated navy blue. This has nothing to do with anything. 'Cept that she would say, the fact that she hated navy blue, was 'cause of her mom's 70s way of dressing.

Then he lost his money. His best friend had been his partner, and somehow, his best friend had somehow cheated him. He lost his best friend. He lost his house. His business. Lost.

He got divorced. But that was happening anyway. A sort of parallel disaster.

"Hey, Baby," the unlocked door (yes, slightly ajar, very slightly ajar, that's how it remained unlocked) of Kill's — Kill in her underwear (yes, in her underwear, not ‹skimpy›, but not really not not ‹skimpy›) — room in the Cabweights-Hoog opened. "Gawd, that shower is a disaster."

She hated that word, Kill did. She hated the word, "disaster." He would always say it. To this day, her dad did. She couldn't stand it. "Oh, it's such a disaster." "Oh, no a disaster." "Yup, a disaster."

He got remarried. Moved to Alaska. Kill went to high school there. Until she left early, though she graduated, to come to New York, where her mom was. When she left her step-mom apologized to her saying she, "wished she'd been better."

Kill "wished she'd been better" too.

She remembered being happy. She remembered the memories of being happy. Of Long Island. Of the big house. Of her dad collecting etchings.

Before his "disaster." Before he remarried. Before he moved to Alaska. Before he moved her into a home where she was hated and tormented. And the only thing she could do was leave, come to New York City.

"Baby. Are you o.k. Honey. Sweetheart. What's wrong."

"What's bad 'bout the shower?!"

He didn't answer. He looked at her. Understood. The way eyes work. Wet. With his towel still 'round him. He moved to her. Close to her. On the bed. Whispering.

I make you breathe. This is totally different than leaving you breathless. You do not exist before I touch you. Before I touch you are fire in a bowl of water. You are the desert frozen. You wait as you have always waited. Waited with all the impatience that eventually leads to patience. I will take that patience. Make you squirm. Need. Want. Bring you backwards towards the inability to sit still. Bring you down. All you have gained. All you thought you have achieved. From your losses. All that. Gone. You do not gain from losses. You know that what you are is lost. You know that you will find yourself again. Find yourself again in the word no. Not your word no. My word no. Your no is against your nature. Against your desire. My no makes you. My no says no. NO. You do not decide. You do not think. Yes it is your will. Yes it is your will more than you've ever felt it. Yes. It is your decision. Yes it is your yes. Your yes and my no.

No you are not yours. You are mine. You have decided this and now that you have decided this you have no more decisions to make. If you think you are about to decide. You are wrong. No. If you are about to make a choice. No. It is not your choice. If you want to do something you cannot just do it. You have to ask first. And unless I want to do it. It will be no. No. You will learn to only ask for things I want to do. Otherwise, it will be no. No matter how you plead, no matter how you beg, no matter how sweet and nice you ask (and you better do these things anyway) if you do not ask for something I want, the answer will be no. NO.

And all I want to hear from you is yes. Everything I require, everything I request, everything I demand, always from you yes, simply yes. You thought you would never say that word again. You thought that was the word that got you in trouble. But it was not that word that got you in trouble. We must reconfigure you. We must reconnect you. Unconfuse you. Your desire is not a problem. Your desire is you. You will always say yes to me. Always. Because you cannot do otherwise. Because you do not want to do otherwise. Because you must. Because you lust. That is what my control gives you. That is what my no gives you. It gives you you. My no is to the lies. My no is to the fraud-ulent that floats without the dirty ground squishing between the toes. Without the grass tickling your ass. Without my hot skin heating yours.

Now you breathe. Now you see. Now you feel. Now you know the no. The power that will not let you die from lack of breath. The power that takes you tight. The power that makes you mine. Mine. To do what I want with. To have in any way I need. And to watch you and to delight in you and the way you give. Completely. Fully. Wholly. Give. To me. Here.

Yes. Here. Please don't say no. Please I know the no. I don't want you to say no. Please. Please I am asking. I am asking so humbly. Please. Please I am asking only what you want me to do. Only that. Please I am only asking what you desire. Please let me do what you desire. Please let me do for you. Please let me serve. Please let me say yes to you. Please I know you can say no. I know. If you do I will listen of course. I will obey. Of course. You are the one that can say no. And I am the one that can only say yes. Yes. With all my breath. Yes.

No. Don't say no. Please. No.

The carride to Connecticut for Slope was Gross. Gross, capital "G" Gross, which is even grosser, than jus' plain 'ol "gross." Capital "G" Gross is when the grossness is an emotional gross, or should I say Grossness. An emotional Grossness. We take out our emotional grossness on our machines. Frankly, they deserve it. Maybe "take out" is not right (plus it's makin' me hungry). We express ourselves, what ourselves are expressing, through our machines. Slope was driving with an emotional Grossness. He's a good driver for what it's worth. What is it worth?

Not much really. 'Cause the truth is. THE TRUTH IS! What is the truth? The truth is this: he might not have been a very good driver. (You don't know what the truth is do you? Yes, I do.) His wife, Franklin, didn't think he was a good driver. He drove with a kind of jerky aggressiveness that kindof that kindof made her think he was jerky and aggressive. Did he really drive that way? Probably. Was he a jerk and aggressive. Sometimes. Was he a man yes. Was she a woman. Yes. Were they people too. What the hell are you talkin' about. Were they individuals I mean beyond their thing, their bio-thing, their gender. A car, in this case a mini-van might be a time capsule, a fish-bowl, an experimental chamber (what the hell are you talkin' 'bout? maybe, you're right now, maybe I don't know) that takes gender and makes it bigger than the people, the individuals they are. There are other places, other ways of interacting, where the opposite is true.

Where the opposite is true is a line of poetry. Yes.

On the way back from Connecticut (I always have to think very hard when I spell Connecticut. Stop interrupting. O.k. I will, the book's 'bout over.) after a strange, strained 'couple of days the couple, Franklin 'n Slope, were not even arguing. Not 'cause they were happy. 'Cause they were tired. Mean hard looks looked mean and hard on their faces. And the outside like the outside often does reflected their inner moods. The vagueness of dusk, the yellowish high-way lamping not yet the illuminating harshness that contrasts with the real night, was ghostly and ghastly: painting pastel beige eerie reflections of the side-show of white 'n green signs across their eyes. They didn't look at each other. They didn't look ahead either. Their minds could be described as blank.

311

'Cept they were seething.

Slope had to stop. Suddenly, quickly, suddenly, he pulled off onto a side of a road which was dark. They started to kiss.

The Cabweights-Hoog hotel did not have phones in rooms, they had buzzers. When they wanted someone to pay the rent or to come to the phone or whatever the buzzers were buzzed. Slope was buzzing one of the buzzers. He was trying to get Bogart down, 'cause he had a story to tell.

"Bogart's in another room, I think," Victor said.

Slope buzzed the other room. Hard. Bogart came running down wearing only a towel. Victor and Slope laughed.

"What. What. What?" Bogart said. "Slope! What happened. How are you 'n Franklin."

Slope said, "We fucked."

Berlin, Buenos Aires, Sydney, New York

Printed in the United States
102855LV00002B/112-126/A

9 781599 370118